THE FOX'S CURSE

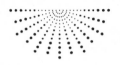

SARAH PAINTER

Siskin
Press

For my lovely readers

CHAPTER ONE

Lydia Crow picked her way along the half-finished rails in the abandoned underground tunnel, her torch beam wavering on the curved walls and catching the occasional movement as something skittered in the darkness. Her companion was a station worker called Faisal who she had persuaded to help her with a flip of her gold coin and a little bit of Crow Family whammy. He was chatting happily, completely at home in the dusty and strangely warm subterranean world. 'This bit never got completed,' he was saying, 'it's never been used at all, but up ahead we'll have a treat.'

Lydia was decked in a hard hat and a high vis jacket, matching Faisal's. Although his jacket fitted him properly and Lydia's hat kept slipping. Her forehead was sweaty and sore from the rub of heavy plastic and she ached to take it off, but Faisal had become so agitated the last time she had tried that she had worried he would snap out of her hold and demand to know exactly what the hell she thought she was playing at.

Which would be tricky to explain. Lydia had agreed to do a job for Paul Fox, although agreed was too strong a word. Had been blackmailed into accepting the case, would be more accurate. Whatever the semantics of that little arrangement, she was now chasing a rumour deep in the disused tunnels around Euston Station. Explaining to Faisal why he should show her around first, not just call the police in, would involve describing her ability to sense the powers of the four magical families in London. The families which most people thought of as bedtime stories.

'Here we go,' Faisal said, as the tunnel curved to the right. After the bend it opened to a wider space with a raised area on one side. 'This would have been a platform, if this had ever been finished,' Faisal explained, hoisting himself up. He turned and held out a hand for Lydia, helping her up. 'Through here.' An arched passage in the wall led to a hall which was eerily familiar. It was lit and Lydia switched off her torch, blinking in the sudden brightness. The electric glow illuminated the white and blue tiles on the walls, the classic styling of the underground that Lydia was used to power-walking past, Oyster card in hand. These tiles were in various stages of decay, grey brick showing through where the tiles had fallen away or been nicked as souvenirs. 'Cool, right?' Faisal was visibly excited, he pointed to a ripped film poster for Psycho. 'This was in use up to 1961 then it was closed off.'

'Why is this bit lit?'

'They run the occasional tour,' Faisal said. 'But mainly it's for maintenance access.' He shot a crooked smile at Lydia. 'Gotta make sure the place isn't caving in.'

Suddenly Lydia was glad of her hard hat. 'Can we go further?'

'Sure,' Faisal said. 'Is there something in particular you want to see?'

Nothing, Lydia thought. She wanted to see absolutely nothing suspicious, nothing dangerous and nothing tragic. If she could check out the tunnels and then report to Paul Fox that there was nothing untoward, she would be done. She had agreed to this one job and if it ended abruptly and easily, there was nothing he could do about it. Foxes were tricky, everyone knew that, but she knew that Paul would abide by the word of their agreement. He wasn't stupid enough to renege on a deal made with a Crow.

Faisal was frowning, as if something had just occurred to him. 'What was it you needed again? Is this a project? Or a...' He visibly struggled to think. 'Who are you, again?'

Lydia produced her gold coin, spinning it high into the air and watching Faisal's eyes as his gaze followed it. He watched the coin rotating impossibly slowly in the air between them and his eyes glazed a little. Satisfied that he had calmed down again, Lydia pocketed her coin and asked Faisal something innocuous about the lighting system to distract him while they continued on their subterranean ramble.

Faisal relaxed back into tour guide mode. 'The

3

station was built on farmland first, but then they expanded a few years later. This was back in the nineteenth century, Victorian times, innit?'

Lydia nodded encouragingly. As long as Faisal was chatting, he was happy.

'Expanded into a graveyard of a church. St James's. Loads of bodies had to be moved, got reburied elsewhere, but loads weren't...' He paused, waggling his eyebrows in a suggestive manner. 'Imagine that.'

They passed a wide expanse of grey brick, an old exit which had been bricked up when another tunnel had been closed, the layout changed in the name of redevelopment and progress. Further on, and Lydia felt something. A flicker at the back of her mind. She stopped and then backed up slowly until she was right in front of an expanse of tiles. Thick cables ran overhead and the light remained steady. There was nothing to see, nothing to differentiate this bit of wall from any other part. There it was again. A bright flash of red fur. The taste of earth and blood in the back of her throat. Fox.

'What's behind this wall?'

Faisal frowned. 'Nothing.' He looked left and right as if orientating himself. 'Ventilation tunnel, maybe.'

'Can we get into it?'

Faisal nodded. 'Down here,' he led the way through another tunnel and then another, while Lydia tried not to freak out about how thoroughly lost she was. If Faisal did a runner, she could be wandering around this warren for days before she found her way back out.

'Through here,' Faisal opened a service door and at once they were in a dark circular tunnel, with a narrow flat path running down the centre and walls made of metal girders. Bare light bulbs in metal cages hung from the roof, a little too far apart to light the tunnel adequately. Lydia coughed from the dust in the air and then realised that it wasn't just dust, it was the earth taste, getting stronger by the second. She took a few steps, trying to feel for the place that she had sensed Fox. At once it was there, hitting her full force with the scent of rich black soil, blood and bone, fur and claw. She saw a low red body moving through trees, a white-tipped tail and then, suddenly so close she must have been nose-to-nose with the creature, a pair of yellow eyes.

Stumbling back, Lydia put out a hand to steady herself. The cold iron touch of the wall was enough to bring her back to herself and to her surroundings. She wasn't in a woodland or underneath the ground, safe in a den. She was in a cold metal tunnel. Underground, yes, but trapped in an industrial landscape which hurt her paws. Lydia shook her head slightly, trying to clear it. Hurt her *feet*. Not paws. Not red fur and tail, but black wings and sharp beak. She wanted to hold her coin and, instantly, she felt it in her right hand. Closing her fingers around its comforting shape, she felt her senses clear.

Faisal was frowning in concern. 'You all right?'

'Fine,' Lydia said. She moved a little further down the tunnel, using her torch to supplement the scarce lighting. The tunnel was arching upward as if skirting over a small hill and the incline meant that Lydia couldn't see more than a metre or two ahead. She had control of her senses, again, and was aware of the strong scent of Fox without becoming overwhelmed by it. She squeezed her coin to make sure she stayed rooted in her own body, her own mind. The scent was getting stronger, though. And it came with a warning. 'There's something up there,' Lydia said. 'You might not want to see it.'

Faisal smiled quickly as if she were joking, then stopped when she realised she wasn't. 'What do you mean?'

'I don't know,' Lydia said. 'Just that it might be best if I take a peek first.'

'I don't know about that,' Faisal said, and she caught him looking sharply at her, other questions forming behind his lips. Awkward questions.

'Whatever you want.' Lydia forced a shrug. It only took a few steps to reveal the thing she had dreaded finding. She heard Faisal swear, his panicked fumbling for his walkie talkie. Mobile phones didn't work down here, so the engineers all used two-way radios.

Lydia walked up to the body. It was a young man, sitting with his back against the curved side of the tunnel, his head slumped forward and his chin almost touching his chest. His jeans-clad legs were stretched out in front and there was a faint odour of rot beneath the layers of Fox that Lydia could detect. He was definitely dead. There was that unnatural stillness and the unmistakable emptiness of the space which Lydia remembered from her previous experience. The person had left and Lydia was certain she was looking at a soul-case and nothing more. Thinking about DCI Fleet and the procedure he loved so much, she crouched down and touched the man's neck, feeling for a pulse in the base of his throat. He was cold as iron to touch. And, as she already suspected, definitely a member of the Fox family. Main bloodline, she would guess, judging from the strength of the Fox vibe.

Faisal was gabbling into his radio. Lydia thought about calming him down. She could use some of her Crow mojo to smooth his panic, but she wanted to concentrate. The dead man had long dark-brown hair, greasy looking and hanging over his face in ropes. Lydia took out her phone and snapped several pictures. Then she crouched down and used a pencil from her pocket to move the hair enough to get some images of the man's face. He had tanned skin, light hazel eyes and she would guess he was in his early thirties. He had a few acne scars on his forehead and he was in need of a shave. Lydia found she couldn't study his face for long. His eyes were open and staring at nothing and Lydia felt a cold sweat break out on her neck. She let the curtain of hair fall back and studied the way the man was sitting.

'What the hell are you doing?'

She didn't waste time explaining to Faisal or looking at the expression of disgust he was no doubt wearing. More people would arrive any moment, she would be moved away from the scene. She had to find out what she could before that happened. Then she could decide how much of that information to put in her report for Paul Fox.

Snapping on a pair of latex gloves, Lydia steeled herself to feel in the man's jeans pockets. Nothing. No money, wallet, keys, or Oyster card. Not even a used tissue or packet of chewing gum.

7

'You can't do that,' Faisal put a hand on her upper arm, his fingers curling around her bicep.

Lydia looked up at him and then, very definitely, down at his hand.

Faisal let go. He swallowed, his Adam's apple bobbing.

'Help is coming,' she said. 'You should go and meet them.'

'Right,' Faisal said, he backed away a few steps before turning and hurrying away down the passage.

Lydia turned back to the corpse. She was just in time to catch movement. The shock forced her upright, adrenaline pumping. She stared at the man, waiting to see the movement again, her mind stuttering with shock. He was definitely dead. He couldn't have moved. It could be the body settling, some kind of phenomena that occurred naturally. Or, maybe insects or a rodent moving from beneath the man's jacket. Lydia swallowed down a sudden wave of nausea. She was not going to be sick. She was a professional. And a Crow.

A door clanged somewhere, and there were footsteps. Many footsteps, their sound echoing down the narrow chamber of the tunnel. Lydia looked in the direction of the noise and then turned back to the body. A man with long ropes of brown hair and eerily light hazel eyes was standing right in front of her.

CHAPTER TWO

Lydia took an involuntary step backward. She managed not to scream, but a small sound had escaped. Not a squeak, exactly, but uncomfortably close to one.

The man's face twisted in anger and he lurched forward, arms coming up as if to grab Lydia. She threw up her own hands, took a defensive stance. At the same time, her brain was catching up with the evidence of her eyes. The man was slightly translucent. He was not the dead Fox magically brought back to life, but the Fox's shade. His corporeal body was still sitting on the floor, and the ghost was standing inside it, his legs cut off at the ankle where they disappeared into the corpse's lap.

'I'm here to help,' Lydia said.

The ghost opened his mouth, making shapes as if speaking, but no sound came out.

'It's okay,' Lydia said. 'I'm not going to hurt you. Don't be scared.' It wasn't the most rational thing to say, but Lydia was filling air, trying to reassure the ghost, and maybe herself. 'It's okay,' she said again.

The ghost looked at its own outstretched arms, his furious expression falling into blank incomprehension. The floor and body below were visible through his limbs and Lydia tried to imagine how terrifying that must be for the Fox. He was realising that he was dead, and that he was a ghost. She wondered if she could counsel him through it, get him to stick around long enough to be able to communicate. If the dead guy could tell her how he died, this could be the quickest solved case of her career. She wished, suddenly and fervently, that Jason was with her in the tunnel. A literal spirit guide.

The ghost opened his mouth again and looked into Lydia's eyes. They widened as if in recognition and he moved forward, grabbing at her with insubstantial hands. It felt like being touched by icy mist, which quickly formed and grew more solid. Lydia moved away, waving her arms to fight off the ghost. Now, he had his hands around her throat, and was applying pressure. He was becoming more corporeal and stronger with every passing second. Lydia cursed her gift, the way she seemed to power-up those around her, with either magic or life force or whatever energy animated the spirits of the dead. 'Stop it!' She pushed her hands up between his wrists and pushed outward, loosening his grip. Then she tried a good, old-fashioned teacher voice, hoping to break through whatever madness the ghost was experiencing. 'I am not your enemy'. Her words died away on the last word as he gave up on attempted strangling and simply walked into her. Instantly, she was frozen through to her bones. That wasn't the worst thing, though. The worst thing was the sudden and complete sense of despair. A howling wasteland of nothingness and futility. She ought to just lie down. Little sparks of light were going off behind her darkening vision, and her thought processes were stuttering and slowing. Lack of oxygen. She wasn't bothering to breathe. There was no point.

Loud footsteps, voices. Faisal was saying something urgently. Hands on her arms, turning her around and his face swam into view. 'Lydia!'

Light spittle on her skin. Warm patches where his hands were gripping, thawing the ice of her limbs. The Fox ghost was inside her and that was an awful thought. With massive effort, she produced her coin. It didn't appear on the first try. She brought it to her mind's eye. The crow in flight, the way the light caught the golden surfaces, glinting even when there was no light to be seen. Shining even in the darkness.

And then it was there. Resting on her knuckles. She flipped it once, over to the next joint. It was clumsy, but she was warmer. She took a deep breath and felt her oxygen-starved body drink it in. She flipped the coin again, to her little finger, and then back again across the knuckles of her hand.

Something screamed in her mind. It wasn't her. And then it was gone.

WHEN THE GHOST left her body, Lydia didn't see it go anywhere. It didn't float away down the tunnel or beam up to heaven. At least, not as far as she was aware. She had still been feeling light-headed and shaken from the experience of sharing her body with another soul and would be the first to admit that her witness testimony was not the most reliable for the minutes which followed.

Lydia had walked through the busy cafe and up the stairs to her home-and-office above The Fork. Now, she wished she had taken the time to snag a decent coffee from Angel behind the counter. She flipped the switch on the kettle and located a jar of instant. By the time she had a mug of steaming caffeine and was sat on her bed, the duvet pulled up high, and her laptop balanced on her legs, she felt normal again. Still worryingly cold, but able to think clearly.

The underground staff and transport police had asked lots of questions. Lydia had answered everything truthfully, leaving out the ghost part, naturally. And the true reason for her visit. She had told Faisal that she was writing an article, using her Family coin to make sure that he fell in line with her requests. Now, she stuck with that story, even as the officer asking questions raised a sceptical eyebrow. 'Retraining, are you? Change of career?'

Lydia shrugged. 'Got to diversify your income these days. Freelance is precarious, the more strings to my bow...'

'Uh-huh,' the officer said. 'Got a commission for this piece, have you?'

'I'm writing it on spec,' Lydia said. 'Going to sell it once it's done.'

He gave her a long look which had been an article of

its own, one which detailed the various ways in which he did not believe a word Lydia was saying, and then wrote something in his notebook. Fleet had explained the importance of a copper's notebook at great length. Everything went into the notebook. Every detail. But it wasn't just a copper's memory aid, it was vital evidence that they were following procedure, working a case without bias. And, Fleet had explained, it put the wind up interviewees like nothing else. Even in this day and age of multiple CCTV and YouTube and cameras on every phone, there was something about a human being writing down their words with a stubby little pencil that freaked people out. And, unpleasant as it sounded, slightly freaked out was exactly how you wanted every person you questioned. You were more likely to get the truth that way.

Lydia moved her laptop and opened her own notebook. She clicked her mechanical pencil and began writing everything she had seen and felt in the tunnel. After twenty minutes of scrawl, she felt her breathing had finally returned to normal. She looked at the messy handwriting and felt calm. The incident had been contained. Examined. Not explained, as yet, but the first step had been taken.

Her door opened a crack and Jason said, 'knock, knock.'

'I was just going to look for you.' Lydia closed her notebook.

'I don't like the smell in my room,' he said. Lydia had painted over his mathematical workings, after he had covered every inch of his bedroom walls using coloured

Sharpies. It had taken three coats and the odour was lingering despite the window being open twenty-four-seven.

'I know. I'm sorry. How are you finding the exercise books?'

'Not as good,' Jason said. 'I like working big. Can you get me A2 sheets, instead?'

'Sure.' She could order a stack online. Anything to stop him from defacing the decor again. Now that Fleet stayed over semi-regularly, there was a chance he might see the maths-covered walls and she preferred to minimise the number of outright lies she told the man she was sleeping with.

'Something weird happened today,' Lydia said.

'Just the one?'

'Ha. Yes. For once...' She smiled for a beat to acknowledge the joke. Then, 'you know I went to the tunnels at Euston?'

Jason's mouth turned down at the corners. He did not approve of Lydia working a case for Paul Fox. He had a point, but Lydia hadn't been able to see any way out of the situation. Paul Fox knew that she had worked to put Maria Silver in jail for murder. If that bit of information got out to Alejandro Silver, head of the Silver Family, then Lydia's life would be in danger. And the peace which existed between the four magical families in London could be shattered. Crows and Silvers had historically been allies, and if that broke then who knew what the fall out would be?

'What happened?'

'There was a body.'

Jason perked up. 'Murder?'

'I don't know. I couldn't see any obvious injury. He was just sitting there.' Lydia recalled the scene, searching for details. 'It was like he'd just decided to have a rest, leaning up against the wall. He was in one of the ventilation tunnels. They're rarely open to the public, just the occasional tour, and they aren't part of the active underground system. Not since the sixties.'

'Will we get details from the post-mortem?'

Lydia nodded. 'I can ask.' There were advantages to sort-of-kind-of dating a copper.

'Bastard.' Jason folded himself into a lotus position on the end of Lydia's bed. As always, he was wearing the grey eighties suit he had died in. His wedding suit. Poor Jason wasn't only deceased, but he was doomed to forever resemble the lost third member of Wham!

'Who?'

'Paul Fox,' Jason said in a tone which implied it was obvious. 'I bet he knew what was down there. He probably did it. I told you not to take the job.'

'The dead guy was a Fox.' Lydia was a Crow. The daughter of the rightful head of the Crow Family, Henry Crow, although her dad had abdicated his position in order to bring Lydia up away from the Family business. The Families didn't have much of their old powers left but, by rights, Lydia should have been holding a good chunk. Instead, she had always believed that she was a damp squib. Essentially powerless, but with the ability to sense power in others. If she met a Pearl, a Fox, a Silver or a Crow, she knew it instantly. Could taste the flavour of their magic, even when it was faded and old or diluted across the generations. The 'essentially power-less' had turned out to be not exactly true, however. It seemed she powered people up, too. If they had a trace of magic, contact with Lydia seemed to amplify it. At least, that was her working theory. Before she had moved into The Fork, for example, Jason had been an ethereal spirit, unable to touch anything physical, let alone speak to a living soul. Now, he could make a cup of coffee. A bad cup of coffee, but still.

Jason was sucking his teeth, deep in thought. Finally, he said: 'That doesn't mean Paul didn't kill him.'

'I know,' Lydia rubbed her arms.

'Sorry,' Jason made to move away. One of the side-effects to being a ghost was that Jason gave off a chill. Free air-conditioning.

'It's not you,' Lydia said. 'I've been cold since the tunnel.'

Jason was already up, he moved to the chair in the corner of the room which was covered in a pile of Lydia's clothes and grabbed her hoodie.

'Thanks,' Lydia pulled it on and tucked the duvet more tightly around her legs. The chilled feeling was still there. It was like a block of ice was sitting in her stomach, radiating cold. And it contained the memory of that sense of desolation, the futility of existence. Coffee hadn't done the trick, she would try whisky next. 'I met the dead guy's ghost.'

'You what?' Jason sat on the bed, again, closer this time. He vibrated slightly, which gave Lydia a headache to look at. It seemed to happen in times of stress or high emotion. Or when Lydia had been away for any length of time and Jason's grip on his physicality was weakened.

'It appeared. Standing over the body. I tried to talk, but...'

'Bloody hell,' Jason said. 'I wish I had been there.'

'Me, too,' Lydia said. 'It... He...He sort of stood in me.'

'What?'

'I don't know how to explain it without it sounding filthy and weird. His ghost sort of went into me.'

Jason reared back. 'Is it still there?'

Lydia shook her head.

'Well that's something.' Jason looked concerned, which was nice.

'I just feel really cold. Since.'

'No wonder,' Jason said. 'How did he do that, though? Did he look like me?'

Lydia knew what he meant. 'Not as solid. Nowhere near, actually. I could see the wall through him.'

'Did you talk to him? How long had he been there?'

'I tried, but he didn't speak to me. Just hopped on board, so to speak.' Lydia decided not to mention the expression on the ghost's face. It hadn't been restful and she could see that Jason was agitated. He was taking the news personally. Which was understandable, but not helpful.

'Another ghost, though,' he said. 'I've got to go. Maybe I can talk to him.'

There were two problems with this scenario. First, Jason was unable to leave the building. And second, the ghost had disappeared. Lydia had no idea whether it was still there. She went with reason number two.

'You can check,' Jason said, unperturbed. 'You'll be doing your investigation thing, anyway, won't you?'

'I don't know,' Lydia said. 'I did what Paul asked. I went to the tunnel.'

'Yeah, but you found a dead Fox. You don't really think that will be the end of it, do you?'

The ghost had a point.

CHAPTER THREE

Lydia made another coffee, adding a generous splash of whisky, and sat behind her desk. She wrapped her hands around the mug, still trying to get properly warm, and took a moment to survey her domain. It was a funny mix of work and domestic, which was the curse and the benefit of working from home. Not to mention being self-employed in a job with such long and odd hours. There was no separation, the professional bleeding into the personal and their colours swirling together to make an unbreakable pattern.

She clicked to open a document. Some case notes that needed to be written up for a recent client. Business had been steady, which was a relief, and Lydia's finances were looking better than they had in a long time. The main issue remained, though; she needed help. If Jason could leave the building and help her out with surveillance, that would be massively useful.

Looking at client work and thinking about her workload and accounts, added extra weight to the troubled thoughts about the Fox ghost. She rolled her shoulders to ease the tension and allowed herself a moment to anticipate some stress-relief with DCI Fleet. He had texted her earlier to complain about his day being entirely gobbled up by meetings and to say that he was hitting the gym after work. It was cosy. It was nice. It was the kind of message which made it abundantly clear that Fleet considered Lydia his girlfriend. She was in a relationship with the copper and she couldn't keep denying that fact. Of course, she kept to her rules. She still hadn't been to his flat. She hadn't introduced him to her best friend, Emma, or her family. He knew about her Family and the lore surrounding it, but not that she lived with a ghost, powered people up, or any of the pertinent details of her gift for sensing Family power. It was a looming conversation, but one she was happy to put off as long as possible. Fleet had shown himself to be incredibly openminded and supportive, believing in her abilities but not asking a load of questions which, must, Lydia realised now, be killing him. You don't get into detective work without a boat-load of curiosity, after all. She should know.

Her mobile rang and she answered right away. 'What's wrong?'

'Why would something be wrong?' Her mother sounded genuinely bewildered, which was reassuring.

'You never call my mobile. Is Dad okay?'

'He's fine. Sends his love.'

'Okay. Good. That's good.'

'I was planning a trip to town next week and I

wondered if you might be free for lunch?' Her mother sounded slightly breathless and there were traffic sounds in the background. She wasn't calling from the house.

'Of course,' Lydia said. 'Are you okay?'

'Fine!' Her mother's breezy tone wasn't in the slightest bit convincing but Lydia didn't have a chance to press further.

'Got to run, darling.'

LYDIA WENT BACK TO WORK, sipping her spiked drink and focusing on manageable issues and the soothing rhythm of ordering her notes into case files and client reports. Making sense of the world through times and dates, facts and figures.

After another hour, she went to find Jason. He was in the small kitchen, meditatively making a cup of fennel tea. 'I can't stand that stuff,' Lydia said. Emma had bought a selection of herbal teas, saying it would be nice for clients. She had proved to be right, but Lydia was a die-hard coffee fan and still couldn't believe she had become the kind of person who had turmeric teabags under her roof.

'I know,' Jason said. He was pressing the bag against the side of the cup with a spoon, squeezing out every last drop of yellowish water. 'It smells like arse.'

'Good that you can smell things, though, right?' Lydia was trying positivity, hoping to jolly Jason out of his permanent bad mood. It didn't really suit her.

'These days,' Jason said, alluding to the fact that

Lydia had increased his corporeality. 'It's not always a blessing.'

'Not when you're making arse tea, I imagine,' Lydia gestured to the mug of herbal nonsense.

'I think that might need a re-brand.' Jason stopped torturing the teabag and looked at Lydia. 'What's wrong?'

'Nothing. Mum rang to arrange a lunch.'

'And that's bad?'

'Not at all. Just unusual. She doesn't often come into town these days.'

'There's something else?'

'No,' Lydia shook her head. 'Just wanted to warn you that Fleet is coming round in a bit.'

'So I should hide.'

'Sorry.' Lydia didn't know if Fleet apparently catching sight of Jason a few weeks ago had been a one-off or a misunderstanding, but she didn't want to take the chance.

When Fleet arrived, shower-fresh and carrying a bottle of red wine and a pizza box, Lydia closed the lid of her laptop and went to get glasses from the kitchen. It was almost nine and, out in the country, it might have been dark. In Camberwell, the dusk was hidden by light pollution and Lydia hadn't yet closed her curtains. She had been engrossed in work, doing her accounts to avoid thinking about her day.

Fleet had opened the wine and put the bottle on the desk. He took the glasses from Lydia and put them next to the bottle. He had an expression which seemed miles away. 'Long day?' Lydia asked.

He focused on her, then. 'A bit.'

Lydia stepped into his arms, reaching her hands up to his shoulders. Her hand found the back of his neck and then they were kissing. Lydia had become used to Fleet's strange energy. The faint gleam that wasn't Crow or Fox or Silver or Pearl. It wasn't strange to her, anymore, now it just said 'Fleet'. And, as usual, it made every part of her body wake up and vibrate with desire. Fleet walked her backward toward the sofa, still kissing, and then sat down, pulling her onto his lap.

SOMETIME LATER, naked and pleasantly exhausted, Lydia went to the desk and poured the wine. Fleet was watching her from his prone position on the sofa. It was listing slightly, not being sturdy enough for what they had just subjected it to. 'Cold pizza?'

'You need to put some clothes on,' Fleet said. 'Or dinner will be further delayed.'

Lydia passed him a glass of wine and took a sip of her own. The air had cooled and her skin was goose pimpled in the draught from the window. She stretched, feeling the satisfaction in every muscle in her body.

'Lyds, seriously,' Fleet said, starting to rise from the sofa.

'Fine,' Lydia grabbed Fleet's discarded work shirt to use as a dressing gown. Then hunted down her underwear.

Once they were a couple of slices and half a glass of

wine down, sitting in the middle of the ex-living room, current Crow Investigations office and part-time sexy times venue, Fleet turned serious. 'I heard you had a busy day.'

Lydia chewed her mouthful of pizza and swallowed before saying. 'From who?'

'What is it with you and finding dead bodies?'

'It's a gift, I guess,' Lydia said. She regarded him over the rim of her wine glass. 'Do we have an ID, yet?'

'I was hoping you would be able to help with that.'

'I don't know him. I take it he hasn't popped up on the database?'

Fleet shook his head. 'Nothing from facial recognition, yet, or missing persons. DNA will take a bit longer. Lab is stretched as always.'

'I couldn't see an obvious injury and he didn't look old enough for it to be natural causes.'

'Not impossible, though.'

'True,' Lydia regarded him over the rim of her wine glass. 'He was sitting upright, though. And his face was relaxed. Either it was really quick and he didn't have time to react, or someone posed him afterward.'

'Are you going to tell me how you happened to stumble across a body in a disused ventilation tunnel? What were you doing down there?'

'A job,' Lydia said. 'I can't divulge the details of my client. Not unless it's pertinent to an ongoing police investigation.'

'Very funny,' Fleet said. 'Spill.'

Lydia hesitated. 'You're going to think I've lost my mind.'

'That ship sailed long ago.'

'Now who's funny?' Lydia looked at Fleet over the rim of her glass, weighing up whether she could avoid telling him. 'Paul Fox sent me down there. He booked my services.'

'Paul Fox,' Fleet spoke slowly. 'Son of Tristan Fox, head of the Fox Family?'

'Yep.' Lydia chugged some wine.

Fleet no longer looked amused. 'Why would you do that?'

'He knows I put Maria Silver away and is threatening to share that information with Alejandro Silver if I don't do this job for him.'

'Why?'

Lydia shrugged. 'Shits and giggles? The man loves to mess with me.'

'He's bad news,' Fleet said, sounding exactly like Jason. Her flatmate would have been thrilled if he had heard and usually Lydia would expect him to pop up at this point and do an elaborate 'I told you so' dance, but Jason had promised to stay in his room.

'Agreed, but I don't have a choice. Hopefully it will wrap up quickly and I can go back to ignoring him.'

'What's to stop him keeping you on the hook for other stuff?'

The thought had crossed Lydia's mind. 'He won't. That will push me into outright conflict and he can't risk me getting Charlie and Tristan involved. He doesn't want a war.'

'You're sure about that?'

No. 'Of course.' Lydia finished her wine and stood

up to get some more. On her way to the bottle, a thought occurred. 'How did you know I found that body today? Euston isn't your manor.'

'I've got an alert set up in the system. Any mention of Crow and I hear about it.' Seeing her expression, he added, 'no one will think it's about you specifically. Everyone knows Camberwell is home to the Crows and Camberwell is mine, so...'

'Right,' Lydia said, trying to push away her misgivings. She trusted Fleet, but every other copper? That was a different matter. Lydia had been brought up outside of the Family business but she had heard the stories, whispered at weddings and birthday parties, and some from her dad when he'd had a couple of beers and was feeling nostalgic. In every single one, the police were to be avoided. Not only because some of the Crow Family business had questionable legal status, but because they represented an anonymous bureaucracy which struck fear into every wild Crow's heart. The rule-following factory was seen as the polar opposite to the mystical freedom of the Crows. And now Fleet had forged this link, chaining them together in the eyes of the world and, more frighteningly, in the faceless eyes of a police database. It made Lydia want to fly away.

THE NEXT DAY, Lydia steeled herself. She had put off phoning Paul Fox for as long as she could and couldn't delay it any longer. She hated the feeling of being backed into a corner, but that was the situation she was in. And now her 'one little job' for Paul Fox had turned into a murder investigation. What Lydia didn't know was whether Paul would be surprised to learn that the victim was a Fox or not.

He offered to come to her office, but Lydia wanted neutral ground. Somewhere nice and public, just in case Paul decided to shoot the messenger.

Burgess Park was perfect. Halfway between their territories but on Lydia's side of the river so she still felt a home-turf advantage. Filled with families and runners, dog walkers and commuters getting their daily portion of relatively fresh air and green space before heading down into the bowels of the tube system. Lydia arrived half an hour before their meeting and did a quick lap of the park. No Family members of any flavour, and nobody who looked like hired help, either. There was a man with a buzzcut and muscles who made her look twice, but when he turned around she saw that he had a baby in a sling attached to his remarkable chest.

Lydia took her place on the appointed bench, still a couple of minutes early. She was just in time to watch Paul Fox amble through the nearest entrance, his dark hair grown out a little from its usual close crop. He was wearing his habitual fitted black T-shirt and jeans and he still looked alarmingly good in them. At least Lydia could understand why her younger self had fallen under his spell. She comforted herself that, while it had been insanity for a Crow to date a Fox, at least anybody with a pulse would forgive her lapse in judgement.

'Hello, Little Bird,' Paul said, settling a little too close to Lydia on the bench. He stretched one arm out along the back and Lydia had to force herself not to flinch away.

'I don't know what you've got against email,' Lydia said, handing him the envelope which contained a single printed sheet.

Paul didn't dignify that with an answer, which was fair enough. He studied the brief report while Lydia looked everywhere except at him. The familiar Fox tang was there, warm fur and dark earth. Her heart rate had kicked up and it made her want to run barefoot through woodland and to do other, more carnal things, besides. The Fox magic was very animal. In all senses. It was another reason Lydia gave herself a pass for falling in lust with Paul Fox when she had been a hormonal teen. Good thing she was a cool, controlled adult now.

Paul hadn't spoken for a long time so Lydia finally looked his way. He was watching her and for a second she felt the urge to beat wings and fly.

'Where's the rest?'

Lydia made herself look in to his strange light-hazel eyes. They had flecks of yellow which became more apparent in certain lighting. 'You asked me to check the tunnels. I checked the tunnels.'

'You found a dead man.'

Lydia stayed quiet.

'You will find out who the man is and how he died.' He spoke flatly. It was an order, not a suggestion.

'The police will do that,' Lydia said. 'Better than I can. You don't need me.'

'You're being modest,' Paul said. 'I do need you to be

more complete in your reports, though. This,' he waved the paper, 'is an insult.'

'I gave you the facts.'

'Hardly. For example, was he Family? I know that you know.'

'What makes you say that?' Hell Hawk. Did everybody know about her secret gift? Had Uncle Charlie taken out a newspaper ad?

Paul just looked at her.

After a short silence, Lydia gave up. She had no wish to prolong the conversation and she could tell that Paul was confident in his knowledge. 'He was a Fox.'

Paul's jaw tightened.

Lydia felt the urge to apologise. 'I took photos,' she said instead. 'Do you want to see if you recognise him?'

Paul nodded. Lydia swiped through to the clearest picture and angled her phone so that Paul could see.

After a moment, he shook his head.

'You don't know him?' Like Jason, Lydia has assumed that Paul had known exactly what she had been going to find in the tunnel. The Paul Fox she knew never did anything without working all the angles. The Fox Family were known for being tricks and Paul was the son of Tristan Fox, head of the Fox Family. He had learned from the master.

Paul was staring at her, again. He looked as if he were wrestling with something which either meant he was genuinely thinking something through or that he wanted her to believe that he was. Lydia waited. She wasn't going to rush to fill the silence.

Eventually, he said: 'I expected you to find some remains. I didn't know it would be a Fox.'

'Who did you expect?'

Paul shook his head. 'You need to focus on what you did find. I want to know who did this. Keep in touch and tell me everything.'

'I did the job. I'm out. That was the deal.'

'Job isn't finished,' Paul said. 'You know that I can still expose you. What would Alejandro say if he knew you put his daughter in prison? What would he do? I hear your dad isn't doing so well these days, I hear the Crows are weaker than they used to be. How well would your family stand up to an attack from the Silvers?'

Lydia bit down on the urge to tell Paul to shut his mouth. She didn't want to show how much he bothered her, that hearing him mention her father made her skin crawl and her muscles jump. Her body reacted instinctively, though, and she found herself inches from his face. 'Who says we're weak? Give me a name.'

Paul blinked. There was a pause and then he looked away. 'No offence intended.'

Lydia sat back, forcing her fists to unclench. 'Good. I'll work the case for a bit longer. But you'll need to pay. And my rates are bloody high.'

'You think I care about money?'

'I have no idea what you care about,' Lydia said. She stood up, ready to leave. 'And I don't give a damn, either.'

Paul put a hand to his heart. 'You wound me, Little Bird. Why so cruel?'

CHAPTER FOUR

Lydia was more settled in the flat above The Fork. She had stuck up some art prints on the wall of her bedroom with thumb tacks and Fleet had created bookshelves using planks of wood and piles of bricks. That wall was a source of joy and comfort. Whatever else happened in her life, books were a constant. Reliable and distracting. And they kept their secrets.

The living room was a good size and it doubled as her office. The sofa was ugly but comfortable, and the office chair was decent. Lydia had rescued a small beech-effect filing cabinet from a skip and repurposed the top for her booze bottles. Fleet had bought her a green-shaded reading lamp with a heavy brass base, as he put it 'to go with her film noir vibe'. Lydia wondered whether it was him staking his own claim on her environment after Paul Fox had installed a door with 'Crow Investigations' picked out on the frosted glass panel like Sam Spade's detective agency from The Maltese Falcon.

As a whole, the flat was a mix of furniture which had already been in-situ, gifts from Emma, Fleet and her parents, and her small number of personal possessions. Not to mention the resident ghost. And her book collection. All-in-all, the office looked pretty decent these days and Lydia no longer felt embarrassed when clients walked in. She just had to work out a way of handling her client work to maintain money coming in, while also getting enough sleep to stop her from becoming psychotic. She went into the kitchenette off the main room and found a cereal bowl filled with cornflakes and a ghost staring disconsolately at them.

'I forgot,' he said, glancing at Lydia.

'Forgot what?'

'I poured them before I remembered.'

'Ah.' Jason's increasing abilities to affect his world had been a source of great delight, but recently he was visibly frustrated with the limitations of being deceased. It was human nature to always want, of course, but that probably wouldn't be much comfort.

'I don't even like cornflakes that much,' Jason said. He wiped his face as if expecting tears, looking at his dry hand in momentary confusion. 'It just sucks, you know?'

'It does,' Lydia said. She didn't know what else to say, but thankfully Jason turned away from the offending cereal and changed the subject.

'Any news on the other ghost in London? I can't stop thinking about him.'

'There are probably hundreds,' Lydia said, jumping

on the chance to encourage Jason to leave the flat. 'If you got out and about-'

'I might meet a nice girl?' Jason interrupted. 'I don't think so.'

'No news,' Lydia flipped the switch on the kettle and got a mug from the cupboard. 'Police don't have a clue who the guy is and Paul says he doesn't know him, either. Not sure what I can do.'

'You can't leave him alone,' Jason said, his face crumpling. 'He must be frightened. He's only just died and now he's a spirit. It's a lot.'

Lydia patted his arm. 'What was it like for you?'

Jason was vibrating, his outline shimmering in the way it did when he was upset. Lydia was used to it, but it still gave her a headache if she focused on him.

'I don't remember,' he said. 'I've tried to think back, but it's like I was dreaming. Everything is weird and time doesn't make sense. I think I only really became reliably conscious about two years ago. But, as you know, it really came together when you moved in. He's all on his own, you have to find him.'

'I know,' Lydia said. 'I'm stuck with the job until Paul lets me off the hook, really.'

'Not identify him, find him. Speak to him.' Jason snapped his fingers, the noise loud in the small space. 'He could just tell you who he is, too. Case solved.'

LYDIA CALLED Fleet on his mobile, hoping there would be news from the lab. A quick result via a bit of insider police knowledge would be just the ticket. Then she could close this case and, hopefully, finish dealing with Paul. Which would make for a more restful existence. Case in point, Fleet was still stuck on the whole 'working for Paul Fox' issue.

'If your lot could do your job and identify the deceased, I'll have something to give Paul and I won't have to deal with him anymore.'

'Not that you would pass on information pertinent to an ongoing police investigation,' Fleet said, not entirely joking.

'Naturally not,' Lydia said, trying to work out why Fleet was in a weird mood.

'Where did you meet him? Paul?'

'At the park,' Lydia said. 'Why are you so interested in every detail. It's not that big a deal.'

'Anything to do with the Fox Family is a big deal in my book. I know the stories.'

'I know the reality,' Lydia tried to soothe him. 'And it's not that impressive.'

'Well, Aristotle called foxes 'wicked and villainous'.'

'The animals or the Family?'

'The animals, I think, but who knows? It was so long ago. Either way, it's not a great sign.'

'One person's opinion, though. And labelling a whole species like that. That's very old school.' Lydia had been going to say 'bigoted' but she thought better of lecturing Fleet on the realities of discrimination.

'I thought you and Aristotle were of one mind on this issue?'

Lydia shrugged. 'I dunno. I'm trying to keep a more open mind.'

'Open minds are good. Don't jump to conclusions, go where the evidence leads.'

'Exactly,' Lydia said, pleased that Fleet seemed to be coming round on the issue.

'But you can't ignore evidence, either. You've got to take it all into account.'

'Sure,' Lydia said. She couldn't get Paul's expression out of her mind and it kept interrupting her thought processes. He had looked almost lost for a moment, something she had never seen and wouldn't have thought was even possible.

'And taking all the evidence into account on Paul and his relatives, adds up to one obvious conclusion,' Fleet was still talking. 'Lydia?'

'Sorry, yes? I'm listening.'

Fleet blew out a sigh of frustration. 'You can't trust him.'

'You know me,' Lydia said, after a moment. 'I don't trust anybody.'

LYDIA HAD a quick check-in surveillance job to do for a long-term client. On the third Tuesday of every month, she watched a tired-looking middle-aged man meet an equally tired-looking middle-aged woman in a Costa near Kennington Park. The woman always ordered a slice of carrot cake and an earl grey tea, the gent had a plain black coffee. They chatted for an hour or two, sometimes having a second hot drink (hot chocolate for her, mint tea for him) and then shared a brief hug goodbye with a chaste cheek kiss. Lydia had captured this meeting in writing and, once, with a discreet video of the goodbye. She had expected it to reassure her client, the wife of Mr Black Coffee, and draw the job to a close, but instead the client insisted that Lydia keep watching. Lydia's job often felt like an invasion of people's privacy, mostly because that's exactly what it was, but when they were doing something morally questionable it was easier for her to justify to herself in the small hours of the night, when she stared at the ceiling and wondered which side of the line between good and evil she was currently falling. However, watching two innocuous-looking friends on their monthly catch-up felt undeniably grubby. If they didn't start doing something overtly sexual together or turn out to be the heads of a criminal gang, Lydia was going to tell the client that her part in their little play was over. There was a chance that this was some bizarre fantasy that the husband and wife had together, in which she had him followed by a P.I. and it added spice and sensationalism to their marriage, but Lydia didn't get into this business to be a sex aid, and she had no intention of being one. Not while she had enough other work coming in, at any rate. As a self-employed single person, she recognised that she had to stay flexible. Beggars, choosers, etc.

WITH THE POLICE drawing a blank on the dead man's identity, and Jason nagging her about leaving a lost spirit wandering alone in the ethereal wilderness, Lydia knew she had no choice but to go on a ghost hunt. To be fair, Jason had made an excellent point. If she could just ask the ghost who he was and how he had died, it could be the quickest and easiest case she had ever tackled. Of course, that involved going back underground, something she wasn't over-keen to do. Under the earth was not her natural habitat and she could remember the sensation of the ground above pressing down, threatening to cave in and bury her in its suffocating embrace.

Still, Crows don't flinch, so she pulled on her jacket and boots and headed out. Her London Transport contact, Faisal, was initially unwilling to take her back down to the disused tunnels but she flipped her gold coin high into the air and before it had finished spinning managed to convince him otherwise.

As they neared the unmarked door at the end of the platform, his voice had taken on a quivery tone. 'It's a crime scene,' Faisal said. 'We're not supposed to go there.'

He had repeated this several times. Lydia's mojo clearly hadn't worked as well as it had last time. Or the resistance was higher. 'You don't have to go anywhere near it. Let me through the service door and give me a map. I'll go on my own.'

Faisal shook his head. 'That wouldn't be right, either. Members of the public aren't allowed on their own.'

That gave Lydia pause. 'What was our man doing down here? He wasn't wearing a uniform or high vis, didn't work for you guys, or an engineering crew.'

Faisal shrugged. 'They do tours sometimes. You can pay and they take a small group. Maybe he went on one of those and then came back for a private view.'

'Maybe,' Lydia said. 'How hard would it be to get down here without a guide to open the service door?'

Faisal's eyes narrowed. 'I don't think that's the sort of information I should give out.'

'I'm not going to tell anybody,' Lydia said. 'You can trust me.' She took out her coin and gripped it hard, letting the confidence of the Crows flow through her, helping her to nudge Faisal into compliance. It was a dirty trick to play and she knew it, but it worked.

'There's a code on the door but it's never changed. If you went on a tour or saw someone open it and you were close enough to see, you could use it yourself. Once you're down there, there's nothing to stop you getting back out. The doors are only locked one way. We get urban explorers down there sometimes. Right pain in the neck they are. If we find one and report them, then we get in trouble. They say that we must have left the door open or something, but like I say, you don't need to leave it open. It's not high security and it's not fair to blame us, not our job.'

Lydia nodded and made sympathetic noises, before adding. 'So, what's the code?'

Faisal gave her the four numbers and then said, in a worried tone: 'You can't go on your own.'

Lydia patted his arm. 'I wouldn't get you into trouble, Faisal. I'm not messing about. I'll follow the rules.'

He visibly relaxed and Lydia put her coin back in her pocket.

'Rules are, I need to stay with you. But the police said it was a crime scene, I don't know...'

'Take me near, then. You don't have to go to the actual place.'

As it happened, Lydia didn't need to go there, either. There was nothing. A faint trace of Fox but no sign of the ghost.

Lydia swore under her breath.

Back with Faisal, who was holding a torch and looking miserable, she said: 'We need to go rambling. Sorry.'

If you had asked Lydia which was worse; walking the twisty, dusty tunnels with no idea what she was about to find around one of the blind corners, or walking them looking for the ghost of a man into whose dead eyes she had gazed, she would have said the uncertainty was worse. She would have been wrong.

Every few steps, Lydia felt the hairs raise on the back of her neck and her shoulders hunch. False alarms were everywhere as now that Lydia was expecting a ghost to come screaming out of the wall and envelop her with eternal cold, she kept imagining it. It was exhausting.

They checked the old tunnels, the decommissioned platforms, and every ventilation shaft that was large enough to walk through. After an hour, Lydia was worn thin from the tension and wasn't sure how much longer she would be able to maintain her hold on Faisal. She let him lead her back to the land of the living.

CHAPTER FIVE

Back at The Fork, Angel had locked up and gone home. The floor was freshly mopped and the counter area sparkling clean. Lydia helped herself to a stale croissant from a bag in the kitchen and climbed the stairs to the flat. She knocked on Jason's bedroom door, wishing that she had some good news to share.

He was sitting on the bed, Sharpie in one hand and the new A2 pad of paper in front of him. There was a doodle of a snail surrounded by spiralling greenery, but nothing else. 'Not working?'

'I miss the walls,' Jason said. 'Maybe if I stick these up it will work?'

'Worth a try,' Lydia said. Then, quick like ripping off a plaster: 'I didn't find him.'

Jason shrugged. 'It might take a few attempts. If you keep going back, maybe you'll power him up. Like you do with me?'

That wasn't an entirely pleasant thought. Lydia could still feel the freezing sensation of having the ghost inside her body.

'I was thinking that you could help with this one.'

'Sure,' Jason brightened. 'How?'

'You said it yourself, I could solve this instantly if I could just ask the guy who he is and how he died. Case over. No more Paul Fox. No more hassle. Done.'

'I like the sound of that,' Jason said.

'Right?' Lydia tried to work out how to phrase her next question, but Jason was already speaking.

'Are you going to look into your Family mojo? See if you can find out how to power me up some more?'

Lydia suppressed a sigh. She understood why Jason was so keen on this option, but she wished he could understand how complicated and dangerous it felt to her. 'I'm sorry, I can't ask Uncle Charlie. I don't trust him.'

'What about your dad? Won't he know?'

'I'm not asking Dad,' Lydia said. 'He spent his life protecting me from this stuff. Suppressing his power might be why he's... The way he is, now. And I make him worse. I'm not asking him.' Lydia continued, rushing ahead before Jason could interrupt. 'Why don't you let me look into your life? If we can work out why you're here, maybe it will unlock whatever is keeping you here.'

Jason's expression closed down. Lydia knew that it probably mirrored her own. Two stubborn people refusing to budge. 'But it might unlock me being here at all,' Jason said. 'What if I get all peaceful and shit and just float away to the clouds?'

42

'Look,' Lydia sank down to sit cross-legged next to Jason. 'How about we just talk. It's not like you're going to be able to tell me anything that you don't already know. And if you already know it, then you know it's safe. I mean, if it was going to send you off to the after-life, then it would already have done so. Makes sense?'

'Yes, but then you'll go and do your detective thing and find out more and that might be the thing that kills me.'

'I won't.'

'You will. You won't be able to help yourself. You have to work out the why of things all the time. That's why you chose this job. That's why you're making a decent go of it.'

'Thank you,' Lydia said, touched. 'What if I promise not to tell you what I find?'

'And what would that accomplish?'

'I don't know,' Lydia said. 'But knowledge is good, right?'

'That's not what you say when I ask you to look into your family power voodoo.'

'That's different.'

'It's really not. Why can't you just work out how to abracadabra me into being able to leave the building? That seems like the better option.'

'I've told you, I don't know how.'

'And you refuse to even try.'

'And you refuse to talk to me about your life, even when it might help.'

Jason was shimmering, the edges of his grey suit jacket bleeding in and out of the scenery. That wasn't a good sign, but Lydia was too worked-up to apply the brakes. 'You say you want to help, to change your situation, but you're not willing to take a chance. It's bloody frustrating. You're already dead, how much worse can it get?'

Jason looked at her for a moment, not speaking.

'Sorry,' Lydia said. 'Bit harsh.'

'You're right,' he said. 'I'm bloody terrified, though. I don't know how much worse it can get. I just know I don't want to disappear. I don't know where I go or if that would be the same or different when it happens permanently. My parents were religious and I didn't think it rubbed off on me, but when I close my eyes I see visions of a fiery hell and I'm not anxious to visit.'

'There's no such thing as hell,' Lydia said, with more confidence than she felt. 'And besides, you wouldn't be going there. You're a good person.'

'I died on my wedding day. I wasn't old so it's not likely to be natural causes which either means I'm an innocent victim or I invited trouble somehow. I can't remember anything about it, which makes me worry I don't want to remember. What if I did something terrible?'

'Wouldn't knowing be better, though?'

He smiled sadly. 'Maybe for you. We can't all be as strong willed.'

'I'm not that strong,' Lydia said, but he had already gone. 'I'm scared half the time,' she said to the dead air.

LYDIA FLIPPED open her laptop and navigated to the

births, deaths and marriages registry. She felt guilty, she was going directly against Jason's wishes, but the puzzle was too tempting. Curiosity killed the cat, but what would it do to the Crow? Crows were smarter than cats, in Lydia's book at least.

Jason and Amy had got married and, on the same day, Jason had died. That was all she knew and she had promised that she wouldn't pry. She looked around, now, checking that Jason hadn't re-materialised before typing in Jason's name. She was betraying his trust and going back on her word. There was no way to dress that up as noble. But then, Lydia thought, she had never claimed nobility.

Once upon a time, Jason Montefort and Amy Silver had met and fallen in love. They tied the knot in St Etheldreda's Church just off Holborn Circus. Searching the newspaper archives and obituaries threw up the sad truth within a few keystrokes. Lydia sat back, as if the information were poisonous and she needed to move to a safe distance. 'Hell Hawk,' she muttered.

The newlyweds had gone to The Fork for their wedding breakfast and, at some point during the afternoon's festivities, tragedy had struck. Both Jason and Amy had died that day. The news stories were light on detail. Lots of 'police are investigating' and 'unknown cause'. The obituaries were short and most likely written by the families. They listed date of death and spoke of 'beloved son' and 'beloved daughter' with no reference to the circumstance or cause of death. 'Passed away suddenly'. As if Jason and Amy had simply slipped into another room.

Amy Silver had died at The Fork. Lydia stood up. She felt sick. If that was the case, then surely Uncle Charlie would know about it. He had to have rented the place out for the wedding party. It wasn't strange that he had done so for a Silver, the Crows and the Silvers had long been friendly, and had sided often even before the truce. But a double tragedy on Crow property. That had to have been a big deal. That had to have soured relations.

Lydia frowned as she paced, a tension headache tightening around her temples. *Nineteen eighty five.* Uncle Charlie would only have been in his twenties. It was more likely that Grandpa Crow had dealt with the wedding party. Or one of his people. Grandpa Crow had the whole family empire to run, it might have been too small a deal for him to even know about. Another thought hit Lydia. This was all before she had been born. Which meant that it could just have easily have been her father who had handled the booking. He was the golden boy, after all, primed and trained to take over from Grandpa Crow when the time came. Until he had married Lydia's mother and abdicated his position.

There was no way she was going to ask her dad about Crow Family magic and ways in which she might be able to release a ghost from his earthly prison, but she could maybe face asking him about the old days of the business. If she didn't have any other choice. After doodling on some paper, downing a beer to help her think, and pacing the flat for forty-five minutes, trying desperately to think of another choice, she came up empty.

'Hell Hawk', Lydia said out loud, and went to get another beer.

THE NEXT DAY, Lydia avoided Jason. She felt guilty for giving in to the lure of Google. She felt like she had spied on Jason, even though he was the one who could walk through walls. And she had no idea whether he knew about Amy. He wouldn't talk about his own death and had never mentioned Amy dying on the same day, but that was no guarantee he didn't know. Did she have a moral obligation to tell him? It would reveal that she had been googling his history without permission.

The past was too difficult, so Lydia concentrated on the present instead. She wrote up a client report for a job she had finished the previous week and sent it along with an invoice. When Jason appeared in the kitchen, she pretended to be buried under a pile of urgent accounts work, a strategy which backfired when Jason offered to help her with it. 'I have decent finger control, now,' he said, waggling them in her direction as proof. 'And I have a head for figures.' Which was, of course, putting it mildly.

'If I had another laptop,' Lydia said, putting him off so that she didn't have to reveal that she had been lying about the accounts.

Jason nodded and made her a cup of tea, instead, which made her feel even worse.

LYDIA COULDN'T WAIT for the end of the day to speak

to Fleet and he agreed to meet at their bridge, texting back that he 'needed the fresh air'. With any luck, his department would have made progress on the identity of the dead guy and she wouldn't be tempted to investigate Jason's death any further. Something told her that was a story that might be best left unread.

Lydia knew that the managerial side of Fleet's job had taken over too much of his day-to-day work and that he often had back-to-back meetings which sapped his will to live. It wasn't the policework he had dreamed of when he started as a wide-eyed recruit, but he seemed happy enough to slog onward. As he put it, 'you've got to be inside the system to make it better'. His idealism was yet another thing she found irresistible. She was so accustomed to a world-weary cynicism both from her Family and her own thoughts, that Fleet's attitude was exotic.

Crossing the park, she saw him standing on the bridge to nowhere in his work suit, gazing down at his phone with a slight frown. He looked up when she approached and his smile made her stomach do a flip-flop. Lydia had always assumed that a proper long-term relationship would settle into a comfortable, maybe even slightly boring, rhythm. She was delighted that, several months in, it hadn't happened with Fleet. 'Any news?'

'Still no identification. He's not popping up from DNA or dental records, and we've run searches based on his tattoo and the scar on his abdomen.'

'Tattoo?'

'Neck tat on the top of his spine.' Fleet swiped his phone and passed it to Lydia. There was a close-up image of the back of the dead man's head and shoulders. The word 'cursed' was written in bold script lettering, a thick swash of black extending from the last 'd' to underline the word.

'That's dark.'

'And the scar on his stomach isn't from an appendectomy.'

'Stab wound?' Lydia guessed.

Fleet nodded. He fell silent as a pedestrian approached and they both waited until he had passed the end of the bridge. 'Hard to be certain, but the pathologist says it's not recent. At least five years old, but can't get any more accurate than that.'

'So, what do we do next?'

'Hope that somebody comes forward and identifies him. Given time, a missing person report usually gets filed or a bit of new evidence crops up in another ongoing case which leads to an identification.'

'But not always, right?'

Fleet nodded. 'Some people tread lightly and leave no trace. There are more unidentified bodies in the system than you might imagine.'

'Lovely,' Lydia said, pulling a face. 'What about cause of death?'

'We're still waiting on toxicology. But there's no sign of trauma.'

Lydia closed her eyes. 'Please don't tell me that's a mystery, too.'

'Sorry,' Fleet said. 'Best guess is asphyxiation. There are small haemorrhages and, I'm quoting from the coroner's report 'some visceral congestion via dilation of a portion of the venous blood vessels'.'

'Strangled?'

'No sign of it. No ligature marks, no bruising, no signs of struggle.'

'That makes no sense,' Lydia said. 'What am I missing?'

'I have no idea. The investigating officer is stumped. And we can't exactly tell her that she is dealing with a member of the Fox family. Not without sounding unhinged.'

'Welcome to my life,' Lydia said.

Lydia took the photograph of the dead Fox's tattoo to every tattoo studio in Whitechapel, figuring that a Fox wouldn't go anywhere else to have work like that done. Of course, there was always the possibility that he had gone off-territory, wanting to keep the tattoo secret from his nearest and dearest, but Lydia was hoping to get lucky.

There were more studios than Lydia expected and it took a while. She had sore feet and was lighter by fifty quid in bribe money and had exactly nothing to show for it. Except for the new knowledge that tattooists were a secretive and paranoid bunch. Most of the people she spoke to assumed she was a spy for a rival parlour and the ones who spoke about the photo at all were full of criticisms of the work, as if they were touting for business and wanted to demonstrate to Lydia that she would be better off getting work with them. 'I'm never getting inked,' she found herself saying to the last guy, when her fatigue and frustration got the better of her.

Luckily he didn't take offence. 'It's a big commitment.'

'Are you sure you don't recognise this style? I'm just trying to identify the artist.'

The guy squinted at the picture. 'It's pretty standard work. Nothing exciting. You could try the one on Wentworth street.' Lydia had already drawn a blank at that studio, but she thanked him and left. Outside, Lydia turned right and was going to head to the nearest tube station when a voice stopped her.

The tattooist stood in his doorway, head tilted. 'You're really not from another ink shop, are you?'

'No,' Lydia said. 'Or the police.'

He hesitated. 'I remember the guy. Nervous type.'

'You inked him?'

'Yeah,' he nodded. 'Last year. But I remembered it because it's unusual. Not many people want 'cursed' written on themselves. 'I love my mum' and the name of their pet, mostly. I assumed it was from a book or a film or something. Fan art.'

'Why didn't you want to admit it was your work?'

He looked uncomfortable. 'Guy was jumpy. Paid in cash and gave a fake name. I mean, it happens all the time, no law against it, but then... You come asking questions. Made me think there might be something wrong. That I might be in trouble for some reason, some regulation...' He trailed off. 'It's not a regulation thing, is it?'

'I'm afraid not, sir,' Lydia said. It had been too much to hope that he would have paid in contactless, something traceable, but Lydia still felt the stab of disappointment. 'What name did he give?'

'John Smith.'

Lydia had been planning to ask why the tattooist thought it was a fake name, but she didn't bother, now. She wrote it down, anyway. 'Did he know what he wanted or did he look through your books before choosing?'

'He knew,' the tattooist said. 'Wasn't interested in artwork or a discussion. It was weird because it was his first time and virgins are usually more chatty.'

'Anything else you remember at all? Anything he said?'

'You're really not from another parlour, are you?' The reality of the situation seemed to be finally dawning on him.

'Nope,' Lydia said and dug out a business card. 'Please let me know if you think of anything else. Any detail which might help us to identify the man.'

'I'm guessing something bad has happened to the guy?'

'I'm afraid he's dead,' Lydia confirmed.

'The tattoo healed up nicely, though,' he said, seeming to speak without thinking. 'No blow out.'

CHAPTER SIX

Lydia met her mother across the river and not far from Covent Garden, where she had been doing some shopping. She had booked a table in a low-key tapas joint. It had warm wood, gentle lighting and smelled of garlic, wine, and savoury deliciousness. 'This is nice,' Susan said, looking around with evident satisfaction. 'And it's mandatory that I have a glass of red, isn't it?'

'They throw you out if you don't,' Lydia said, and signalled to the waitress. 'A bottle of the Rioja, please.'

'A bottle? At lunchtime? I'll fall over,' her mother said delightedly. 'Have you been here before? With Emma?'

'Once,' Lydia said 'And I thought it would be better to get away from The Fork,' Lydia said. 'I know it's not your favourite place.'

'Not yours at the moment, either, by all accounts.'

'You've spoken to Charlie?'

'I heard him speaking to your dad. Complaining that you weren't being as helpful as he would hope.'

Lydia smiled knowing that, at least, her mother would be thrilled about this. She had cautioned Lydia against living above The Fork and getting dragged into the Family business.

'I think it's a mistake.'

'What?'

The waiter appeared and asked if they wanted to taste the wine. 'I'm sure it's fine,' Lydia said. 'Fill 'em up.'

'Cheers,' her mother said, holding her glass out.

'Cheers,' Lydia echoed and they clinked. The wine was delicious. Rich and spicy and full of tasty tannins which Lydia knew she would pay for with a heavy head and a black tongue.

Susan was studying the menu. 'I definitely want fried artichokes and the salted cod. Shall we get patatas bravas and some bread and olives, too?'

Lydia's mouth started watering. She had skipped breakfast on account of being asleep and not wanting to be late to meet her mother and her stomach joined in the party with a loud gurgle. Susan began to recount an article from New Scientist about AI and Lydia tamped down her impatience.

Once the table was crowded with little pottery dishes of intensely-flavoured Mediterranean food and they were both half a glass of wine down, Lydia looked around to check the distance to the next table and leaned forward, lowering her voice. 'Why is it a mistake?'

Susan blinked. She looked as immaculately turned out as always, lipstick expertly applied and not a hair in her shiny blonde bob out of place, but there was tension around her eyes. Dark shadows which make-up couldn't quite disguise. She looked tired. Or, Lydia realised with a start, she was just looking older. Mortality was a kicker.

'This is delicious,' Susan said, tearing a piece of bread and dipping it into a dish of seasoned olive oil.

'Mum,' Lydia said. 'I thought you didn't want me to get involved?'

'I didn't,' Susan said. She put the crust down onto her plate and picked up her wine glass. 'I don't. I warned you not to live at The Fork, but you went ahead.' She pulled a face. 'Which is your right. You are an adult. You get to make your own decisions.'

'I'm not joining the business,' Lydia said, trying to reassure her. 'I'm doing my own thing. I'm staying safe.'

'You're Henry Crow's daughter. That makes you next in line to lead the Family.'

It was Lydia's turn to fall silent. Her mother wasn't a Crow, and rarely referred to the Family with a capital 'F' directly. She was Susan Sykes, with a PhD in chemistry, who'd had aspirations to work in research. She had fallen in love with Henry Crow and, loving her right back, Henry had followed her wishes and abdicated his position as head of the Family, moved out to the suburbs and raised their daughter away from that life. Susan had taken a substantial career break to be home with Lydia, spending days baking, crafting, playing games and taking her to swimming lessons and, eventually, to and from school each day, making her feel loved and secure. And then, once Lydia moved on from primary school, Susan had returned to academia. Not easy after such a break, but she was smart and determined and she had clawed her way to a research position at Imperial College London. For a few years, at least.

'Your father made a deal, you know that. Charlie took his position as head of the Family and I got to bring you up in normality. No responsibility, no training, no business. I wanted to keep you safe and I wanted you to have a choice about what you did with your life. I didn't want it mapped out. I didn't want some old system to have chosen for you.'

'And I'm grateful,' Lydia said. Her true feelings were more complex, but she had always recognised the love and care which had gone into her mother's decree and she was thankful for that. Always. 'And you don't have to worry. I'm not working for Charlie. I'm doing my own thing.'

Susan's smile was very small and very sad. 'You can't.'

'What?'

'You chose. You might not have meant to, but you moved to Camberwell. You're literally roosting with the Family. You did a job for Charlie.'

'That was nothing. I just told him the Family of one person,' Lydia caught herself. 'Two people. That's it.'

'And how did you do that?'

Lydia had told the truth without thinking. This was her mother. She was the safest space that Lydia knew, but they didn't usually talk about this side of life. Her dad had never spoken about Crow stuff to Lydia when her mother was around, but that didn't mean they didn't talk privately. 'I can just tell. I don't know how.'

Susan nodded. 'How did Charlie react?'

'I think he already knew,' Lydia said. 'About me, I mean. I didn't reveal anything he didn't already know. Did you know?'

Susan nodded. 'Of course. Your dad was watching out for your abilities since the day you were born. I didn't want to hear about it, but he kept me updated every step of the way. We don't keep secrets from each other. Never have. He never shut me out, never made me feel less for not being part of a Family.'

That punched Lydia in the gut. She didn't mean to make Fleet feel 'less', but was that exactly what she was doing? She was so busy trying to stay loyal to the Family and to make sure she never gave away Family secrets, that she had let it become her default position in all matters. Whether it was her own work, Emma or Crow stuff, she gave away as little as humanly possible. She had always thought she was being smart and careful and a good Crow. Maybe she was just being a horrible girlfriend.

'And now you're in it, you're in danger. You can't stay like this, one foot in the pool.'

'I'll get out,' Lydia said automatically, wanting to erase the expression of pain and worry on her mother's face. 'I'll move back to Scotland. Or I'll come and live with you and Dad. You need help, anyway. With Dad.'

'No,' Susan shook her head. 'You're always welcome, you know that. It will always be your home. But you moved back to London for a reason.'

'I had to get away from a work thing. I didn't choose-'

'Lydia,' Susan said gently. 'You could have gone anywhere.'

She opened her mouth to argue but closed it again, knowing her mother was right. She had been offered free rent above The Fork and was cash-strapped so it seemed like the perfect solution, but she had known it was risky. She could have borrowed money and gone to Europe for a few weeks, instead. She had been curious. She had felt the pull of Camberwell. Feathers, she had been curious. That was supposed to be fatal for felines, not Crows.

'It's all right,' her mother said, now. 'I wanted you to have the choice and you did. Now you have to be smart. Charlie is getting older. Who is going to take over when he is no longer strong enough?'

'I'm not,' Lydia said, properly shocked. 'I don't want that.'

'Does everybody know that? Does everybody believe that? Who might see you as a threat to their own ambition?'

'You're saying I need to worry about Family? I thought loyalty was the number one thing? No Crow would hurt another.'

'Oh, sweetheart,' Susan shook her head. 'You grew up hearing your Dad's stories. But he got out pretty young, really. And the further you get from something, the simpler and more idealised your stories get. It's only natural. It's how nostalgia happens. You're living in the present, now, though. I have no idea if a Crow would hurt another. I have no idea if anyone is looking to usurp Charlie or is viewing you as a threat. I just think it's sensible to consider every logical possibility. Don't you?'

Lydia thought of the range of human behaviour she witnessed in her P.I. work and nodded. People could surprise you.

'And that's before you've considered the more likely threat.' Susan took a sip of wine before continuing. 'The other Families. Again, they will assume you are in training to take over from Charlie. When is the best time to take out a threat? While it's growing or when it reaches its full power and potential?'

'But there's the truce.'

'I'm a realist,' Susan said. 'I was brought up in the normal world by normal parents. I wasn't filled with tales of magical Families and ancient truces. And in the normal world, truces get broken and wars happen. I'm not saying it's going to happen in your lifetime, I just think you should consider it a very real possibility.'

Lydia's head was spinning. Not just from her mother's words, but from the fact that it was her mother, Susan Sykes, saying them. 'What do you know?' Lydia said. 'What's happened? I know Charlie was trying to train Maddie. That went wrong, obviously, which is why he's so focused on me, I think.' She looked around to make sure there weren't any other diners close enough to overhear, leaning over the table and lowering her voice just to be sure. 'I know the Silvers have got their Family cup from the British Museum and they have a statue which is imbued with magic. Something strong enough to send people with no power insane. What else should I know?'

'Eat,' Susan said, pushing a dish of fried potato across the table. 'You're too thin.'

'Mum. What's brought this on? What do you know?'

Susan closed her eyes and took an audible deep breath. Then she looked Lydia square in the face. 'Nothing else. Just that you're Henry Crow's daughter. Your Dad isn't in any state to step back in to help the Family if things get bad. I thought he might get well again. I thought that being a Crow might protect him somehow, but he just gets worse.'

'Mum-'

She shook her head 'It's bad, Lydia. So you need to be strong. For the sake of peace between the Families. For the sake of the Crows, and for your own safety.'

'Mum-'

'I know what I always said,' Susan said. 'But things change. Besides, you made your choice. That was all I ever wanted. For you to have that chance.'

CHAPTER SEVEN

Perhaps it was the wine or perhaps it was the weirdness of the conversation with her mother or some other factor Lydia didn't care to examine, but she found herself calling Paul Fox and telling him to meet her.

The longer Lydia thought about it, the less likely it seemed that Paul Fox was entrusting an investigation into a member of his family to a Crow. Which meant he was being less honest than he pretended. It shouldn't have been a surprise, and the fact that it was brought its own sense of alarm. She was letting her guard down, beginning to trust Paul Fox. And that couldn't lead anywhere good.

Paul answered quickly and agreed to meet. 'I'm in town, as it happens,' he said. 'I'll come to you.'

Lydia went to the relative quiet of St Paul's, the actors' church, behind the bustling piazza and snagged a bench. She watched the pigeons, all of whom kept a respectful distance from her, and enjoyed the autumnal sun on her face.

She had her eyes closed, but caught the scent of Fox as he entered the churchyard. Paul walked down the central path looking like exactly what he was, an expert hunter in a field of prey.

He tiled his chin, not sitting. 'Walk?'

Lydia stood, hating that she was being obedient, but feeling that she ought to pick her battles. He had come to meet her, after all, like a dog when you whistle. Perhaps this was his way of rebalancing his sense of power.

'Nice lunch?'

A cold feeling. 'You were following me?'

He shot her a quizzical look. 'No. It's the garlic and wine.' He tapped his nose. 'Keen sense of smell.'

Well that was disturbing. 'Creepy, much?'

He smiled, flashing white teeth and making Lydia's stomach loop.

Get a hold of yourself, she counselled sternly and silently. It was the Fox magic, nothing else. Nothing she hadn't dealt with many times before.

They walked up the path toward the back of the church. Lydia stopped at the steps into the entrance, with its list of service times to the side of the door, but Paul kept moving. Lydia followed and found herself in a large open space with peach-coloured walls, white plasterwork and elaborate candelabras. It had a faintly theatrical air, but that might have been the power of suggestion. Lydia knew it was the church adopted by the second oldest profession, and that the ashes of Dame Ellen Terry resided below, not to mention the many memorials to actors like Charlie Chaplin and Vivien Leigh.

Lydia followed Paul as he moved slowly around the outer edge, pausing to look at the memorial plaques to the great and the good of the theatre world. Next to Noel Coward's plaque, Paul said. 'I assume you have an update?'

The church was large and almost empty, just a couple of tourists doing the same as they were and nobody was paying them the slightest attention. Still, Paul spoke quietly and that, and the surroundings, gave Lydia an intensified feeling of collusion. Maybe that was his intention? She wouldn't put anything past Paul, or make the mistake of underestimating his capacity for manipulation.

'I know I'm missing something,' Lydia said. 'And I'm trying to work out what. You expect me to believe that you are worried about someone in your family, but you're willing to send a Crow to investigate. It doesn't ring true. So I know you are messing with me, but I haven't worked out how, yet. I was hoping you would just cut the crap and tell me.'

A tourist coughed loudly and Lydia wondered if her voice had raised a little too much.

Paul took her elbow and steered her to a corner at the back of the church, speaking urgently as they moved. 'I think you're good at what you do and, I know you won't believe this, but I trust you more than some random investigator I might find on Google.'

He was right. Lydia didn't believe him. She planted her feet and looked him square in the eyes. 'You must have your own trusted resources. People your family have used before. And you must be able to find out about a missing family member, you must have done already.'

He shook his head lightly. 'I don't know every single member of my Family or where to find them. We don't have parties all together or run a crime syndicate.'

Lydia ignored the jab at her own Family. 'I thought Foxes stuck together?'

'We do,' Paul said, irritated. 'But we're not that organised. It's not like we keep a spreadsheet.'

'But what about chain of command? What about protecting the Family as a whole?' Lydia couldn't imagine they were as free-wheeling as Paul was suggesting.

'We're not like the Crows. We don't care about all that king of the hill, dick swinging shit. We don't even have a master.'

'Somebody should tell your dad. Far as I know, Tristan Fox is the head of the family, same as Charlie is the head of the Crows. Acting like you're so much better than us, doesn't make it true.'

'I didn't say anything about better,' Paul said. 'We're just different. We're a quiet family group, not a minia-ture empire like your uncle is so busy defending.'

'A quiet family group,' Lydia laid the sarcasm on thick. 'That's not how the stories go.'

'Yeah, the stories. We're all sneaking around and tricking people out of their rightful lot and making shady deals. And when we make a deal, even when you think you've checked every aspect, every last detail, you know that it's going to go south because any deal with a Fox goes that way. So you better get in there first. Stab him in the back before he can stab you. That about the size of it? That the measure of the Fox Family?'

Lydia held his gaze.

'Well I don't speak for every Fox. Just myself and those closest. That's two out of my six brothers, in case you were wondering.'

'You're saying I should trust you? That the stories aren't all true and you're not like your father?'

'Are you like yours?'

'Leave him out of this.'

'He tried to keep you out, didn't he?' Paul took a step closer. 'I remember when we spent time together. You were so angry about that. Lost and confused, but mostly really fucking angry. It was one of the things I liked most about you.'

A couple leaving the church heard the expletive and harrumphed.

'You didn't like me,' Lydia said. 'You were playing a game, looking to use me for some advantage. Get some dirt that you could use as leverage. Well, congratulations. You've finally got what you were after.'

'I swear I am not your enemy.'

'Blackmail is a terrible way to convey that.'

'I wish you no harm.'

'I don't believe you.'

'I know.' Paul tilted his head slightly, appraising her. He was a less than an arm's length away, now. Lydia couldn't take a step back if she wanted to, the wall was directly behind. She concentrated on hiding her alarm at being trapped, but must have failed as Paul frowned.

65

Then he took a step back and turned his palms upward in a gesture of peace.

A very small part of Lydia was curious as to what he had been about to do. Attack her? Kiss her?

'Why don't you touch me and see if I'm lying?'

'What do you mean?'

'Right here,' he tapped his chest. 'You're the strongest Crow I ever met and I've spent time with your crazy cousin. I bet if you put your hand right here you'll know that I'm legit. And we can't move forward in this endeavour until you know that. If you're looking over your shoulder, checking I'm not about to stick my claws in you, how are you going to look where you need to be looking?'

This was probably a trap. Or an elaborate scheme to make her look like an idiot. But Lydia took a step forward and placed a hand flat onto Paul's chest. It was very hard and very warm. Luckily, Lydia had had time to acclimatise to the Fox magnetism, or she might have combusted with instantaneous lust. Instead she breathed slow and steady through her nose and reached out with her extra sense. The one which told her whether a person was Fox, Pearl, Silver or Crow. She closed her eyes as a certainty crept over her. Paul was telling the truth. She had no idea why she felt that certainty or where it had come from, only that it felt as true and as natural as when she sensed a person's Family power.

She opened her eyes. There was an even chance that this was his Fox mojo confusing her own, making her experience something that was not real. She had never sensed truthfulness before, but then again she had never tried laying hands on people. Either way, something had shifted in her view of Paul that was difficult to deny. 'All right,' she said, dropping her hand from his chest. 'You're not trying to get me killed.'

Paul flashed white teeth. 'That's the spirit.'

LYDIA WALKED HOME, craving the exercise and movement. It helped her to think and she needed to sort through the tangle of her mind. And to walk off the lust-hangover caused by Paul Fox. She had considered going straight to Fleet, wherever he was right at that moment, and jumping his beautiful bones. But it felt weird. She needed to make sure she had got Paul out of her head, first.

Besides, London was looking its best and Lydia wanted to enjoy it. The air was cool and crisp and the sky a pleasing bright blue. Plus, she was pretty sure that Paul Fox wasn't trying to get her killed, and that was a welcome relief.

Her phone buzzed and she checked it while crossing the road, dodging a large group coming in the opposite direction. It was Emma. Lydia knew she had disappeared on her best mate. Again. Tom, Emma's husband, had recently revealed an illness to Emma, and she had been upset and relieved in almost equal measure. Having decided that his weird behaviour and mood was down to some extra-marital activity, hearing that it was ulcerative colitis was an odd sort of blessing.

Lydia had backed off, reasoning that they needed some space and that Emma wouldn't relish the reminder that she had tried to book Lydia to investigate her own husband. But she had given them enough time, now, and had to admit she was failing to integrate the areas of her life. As usual.

Lydia pressed to answer before she could chicken out. Emma might be upset with her, but she deserved it. And she never stayed pissed off for long. It was one of the many things Lydia loved about Emma.

'We've worked out that dried fruit is a no-no,' Emma said.

Lydia hazarded a guess. 'Archie?'

'Tom,' Emma replied. 'I've got good news, though. His last check-up went really well. Consultant reckons he's on his way to remission.'

'That is brilliant.' Lydia was genuinely pleased for Emma's husband, and the added bonus was that thinking about Tom's bowels was a great remedy for the inappropriate Fox-lust. He had been diagnosed with the ulcerative colitis after a scary few months of tests, and made great improvements as soon as he was on the right medication. Not having the worry that he had the big 'c' and finally talking to Emma about it had helped a great deal, too. Lydia didn't blame him for wanting to protect Emma and to deal with it on his own, but in her line of business she was always seeing relationships which had been eroded by a lack of trust and open communication. It was terrifying how quickly secrecy could poison a good thing.

'How's work?' Emma was asking. 'Have you got enough on? Or too much?'

Emma knew that was the state of the self-employed.

Feast or famine. Lydia was either stressing about not having enough clients and running out of money, or all the jobs came in at once and she had to work twenty-four-seven until she felt like she was going to turn psychotic from lack of sleep. 'It's good,' she said, not wanting to burden Emma with her problems.

There was the sound of heavy breathing and then a high-pitched voice said 'lo!'.

'Hi Maisie-Maise,' Lydia said, realising that Emma's youngest had wrested the phone.

There was a brief scuffle and then Emma came back on. 'Sorry, I'm going to have to run.'

'All okay?'

'Yeah, just-' Emma broke off as a full-blast Maisie-wail began in the background. 'You know.'

'No worries,' Lydia said, but Emma had already gone.

She felt an ache in her chest as she slipped the phone back into her pocket. Paul had been told one story growing up and Lydia had been told another. They were raised to be wary of each other, more than that, to be enemies. But then there was Emma. She had been raised with a different story, again, one in which the magical Families of old London were a fairy story. A myth.

They were all still children, following the paths through the dark forest that they had been set down by their heritage, their parents, their birth, and that made Lydia grind her teeth. She wanted to go off-road.

BACK AT THE FLAT, Lydia was just contemplating a

69

nightcap to help her sleep when Faisal rang. 'You said to call you if I spotted anything weird.'

'I did,' Lydia said, still eyeing the whisky bottle with longing. 'What's up?'

'Driver was just telling me about an empty carriage on his train today. All day.'

'What do you mean?'

'People won't get on one carriage of his train. Even when it's packed. I'm looking at the footage from the last eight hours and people are like, repelled by it. The doors open and its empty inside and they just turn away and go to the next set of doors, even though there are loads of people cramming on.'

'All day?'

'Not a single person got into it. I'm watching the live feed, right, now, and it's still happening. I mean, there aren't as many people around at this time, so it's less obvious, but... Nobody will get on it. I'm telling you.'

'What line?'

'Victoria.'

Lydia cursed Paul Fox, the world, and her own stupid curiosity. 'I'm on my way.'

Faisal sent a text with times and stations for the train over the next hour and Lydia made her way to Kennington and got the Northern line to Warren Street. Changing there to the Victoria line, Lydia was on the correct platform for the designated train. There was a large group of revellers, talking in loud voices about a party that either had been or was about to be 'lit', and a few scattered singles and couples spread out along the platform. Lydia walked to the far end, ready to join the train at the furthermost carriage. She peered down in to the unfathomable blackness of the tunnel, remembering what it had felt like to walk down its disused counterparts, wondering what branching warren of tunnels and passages and ventilation shafts were hidden in the dark.

It was almost eleven o'clock when Lydia felt the familiar whoosh of warm air which heralded the arrival of a train, and then it appeared. Lydia caught the briefest glimpse of the driver, and then the passing carriages rolled past. Each one had passengers inside and Lydia wondered if she had the wrong train. Or whether Faisal had been mistaken. The train stopped and Lydia stepped up to the last carriage. The doors slid open, and Lydia stepped inside as the disembodied train voice told her to 'mind the gap'.

Faisal had been wrong. The carriage wasn't empty. A man was sitting in one of the middle seats, hands clasped loosely in his lap.

CHAPTER EIGHT

A second glance told Lydia something very important. The man was dead. She recognised the long brown hair which hung in knotty unwashed ropes, the strange hazel eyes which appeared yellow in the artificial light, and, perhaps most importantly, the way he was ever-so-slightly translucent.

He was staring at the window opposite but, as the train began to move, slowly turned his head to look in her direction. His expression was bleak. Lydia grabbed a pole as the train shook from side-to-side, gathering speed. She should sit down, show that she wasn't a threat, but her legs had decided to temporarily stop working. Annoying.

'Hello, again.' Lydia pushed as much 'relaxed cheer' into her voice as she could manage.

The man flickered. It was a bit like the vibrating thing that Jason did when he was upset, but more violent. His image strobed in and out, giving Lydia an instant pain behind her eyes. 'I'm not going to hurt you,' Lydia said quickly. 'I want to help.'

He tilted his head very slightly. Listening, Lydia hoped.

'It's interesting that you can move around like this. Ghosts I've known before are usually anchored to one location.'

His mouth opened into a silent scream.

Idiot. She was a complete fool. Throwing around the 'g' word. But surely he had worked out by now that he was dead? She went on, scrabbling for something better to say, some words of comfort. 'I'm so sorry this has happened to you. You must be very frightened and upset. I want to help. I'm on your side.' The ghost was rising, now, his image flickering wildly, his mouth still gaping in an awful way. 'Please don't,' Lydia heard herself say, her voice most definitely not 'cheery'.

The ghost moved closer, a jerky, terrifying motion as the train sped up, shaking and screaming along the tracks. She tried again, babbling in fear. 'You're a Fox, right? What's your name? I'm Lydia. Pleased to meet you.' Hell Hawk. Her mind was racing, the panic rising in her chest. Please don't walk into me again, please don't walk into me again, please don't.

The ghost disappeared and then reappeared at the far end of the carriage. Lydia felt a moment of utter relief. He was further away, not about to jump into her body, not about to attack her. Then he stepped through the back wall of the train and disappeared.

Lydia rode the train all the way to its final destination and then back again, torn between hope and fear. She told herself that she wanted the ghost to appear again, to give her another chance to make conversation, but she was lying.

After a few stops, the occasional person got into her carriage, but not too many. It was at the end, after all, and the platforms were quiet. Lydia fixed her gaze at her reflection in the window opposite and watched it flicker and shake with the movement and changing light of the underground. After a while, she felt a kind of trance-like state descend and found herself with stray and unhelpful thoughts about whether her reflection was how she would look as a ghost. Translucent and transitory.

The cool night air when she emerged from the depths of the earth was a welcome slap in the face, awakening from maudlin thoughts.

Back at The Fork, Lydia went straight upstairs.

'Jason! I need you!' Lydia fast-walked through the flat, calling for Jason to appear. He didn't which either meant he was in the unknown place he went to when he disappeared, downstairs in the cafe watching the patrons enjoy their cooked breakfasts, or he was ignoring her. 'Come on, please! Jason?'

Lydia hesitated in the doorway between her office and the small kitchen. If only there was a way to summon a spirit. Wasn't there a symbol she could paint on the floor and a special candle to light? Some mumbled Latin phrases and a bucket of incense. Or was she thinking of demons?

A quick check of the cupboards didn't yield anything remotely arcane. Not even a standard house-hold candle. She flicked her lighter and yelled as loudly as she could. 'Jason! Get your backside in here, now, or I won't buy you any more stationery!'

The drop in temperature let Lydia know she had been successful even before she turned around and saw Jason standing next to the counter, looking aggrieved. 'There's no need to be bossy.'

'Sorry,' Lydia said, 'it's an emergency.'

'Nobody is trying to kill you, for once, so I don't think it counts.'

Lydia ignored this. 'You know the ghost I found? Well, I met him again today. He was riding the underground.'

Jason stopped pouting. 'He was on a train?'

'Yep,' Lydia said. 'And not even close to where I found his body. Interesting, right?'

'So, the rules don't apply to everyone,' Jason folded his arms. 'I feel special.'

'Or, he didn't die where I found him. Maybe he died on the train and his body was moved after. Although that would be tricky to hide from CCTV.'

'You know that makes no sense,' Jason said. 'Is it just me that's stuck, then? That would be just my luck.'

'It's good not to jump to conclusions. I'm trying to keep an open mind and explore all possible scenarios. I'm trying to improve my cognitive whatnots.'

'Cognitive whatnots?'

'My reasoning skills. Whatever.'

'Right.' Jason picked up the kettle and filled it.

'But if the man did die in the place I found him then you're right. The rule which applies to you isn't universal. Which means we've got an excellent chance of breaking it. It's good news.'

Jason got two mugs down from a cupboard. 'Did you manage to talk to him this time?'

'Not really. Same as last time. I spoke, he did the silent scream thing and then ran away.'

'Ran away?'

'Through the back of the carriage.'

Without waiting for the kettle to boil or adding any tea or coffee to the mugs, Jason poured the water into the mugs. He was clearly distracted. 'If we can work out how you died, then maybe you won't be stuck here, anymore. You could come with me. Maybe you'd be able to talk to the ghost, spirit to spirit, and that could solve the case.'

'Or, I could disappear into the light,' Jason voiced his usual argument, but it didn't have the usual conviction.

He was clearly wavering and Lydia pressed her advantage. 'Freedom, Jason. You could help me on other cases, if you wanted. Join me in exciting hours watching unfaithful spouses meet in by-the-hour hotels. Or go wherever you like. You could attend university lectures or go to the cinema or visit the National Gallery.'

'He sounds scared,' Jason said. 'This other ghost.'

'He looked it,' Lydia said. And he had looked angry, but she decided not to mention that.

'All right,' Jason handed a mug of cold water to Lydia. 'You can take my case.'

'Really? You're sure?'

'Nope,' Jason said. 'But I want to help this other guy. I have to try, at least. We might be the only two ghosts in London.'

'I'll keep you updated every step of the way,' Lydia said.

'Don't,' Jason said. 'I'm going to try not to think about it. Just treat me like a client and come to me when you've got something. I trust you.'

'Thank you,' Lydia said, touched. She walked out of the kitchen, heading for her desk. Then turned back. 'I won't let you down and I won't let anything bad happen. I promise.'

Jason smiled weakly. 'You can't promise that.'

Lydia opened her mouth to argue, but he carried on speaking.

'But I know you'll do your best.' He raised a mug in salute.

She would do her best. She was going to solve the riddle of Jason's death and free him up to leave the building. Then he would talk to the ghost on the train and solve the Fox case. Then she would get back to her normal, paying clients. And keep her business going. Simple.

CHAPTER NINE

When Lydia stepped into the house, she knew instantly that her mother wasn't home. For starters, when she let herself through the front door, calling out 'hello' nobody appeared in the hall to greet her. Secondly, she could hear the rumble of male voices and taste feathers in the back of her throat. Uncle Charlie.

The door to the living room was ajar and Lydia pushed it open. 'Hi, Dad,' she said. 'Uncle Charlie.'

Charlie stood up and kissed her on each cheek. His hands covered her shoulders and his bulk dwarfed everything in the room. Her dad, always thin, looked like a stick next to his younger brother.

He blinked. A hesitation. Then, a small smile. 'Hello, love.'

Lydia leaned down and kissed her father's dry cheek. There was a rasp of stubble and the scent of ozone.

'It's good you're here,' Lydia lied. 'I need to ask you something about The Fork.'

Henry frowned. 'The cafe on Well Street? Didn't we close that up?'

'I'm staying there, Dad. In the flat above. And Charlie has opened the cafe, again.' She looked at her uncle. 'Isn't that right? Angel is running the kitchen. It's doing well, I think.'

'That's right,' Charlie said. 'It's all good. Easy-breezy. What did you need to ask?'

'Do we take bookings for private parties?'

Charlie frowned. 'I don't... That's up to Angel. Did you have something in mind?'

'No, nothing,' Lydia said. 'Someone just asked me, that's all, and I didn't know if we had a policy. Thought I should ask the owner and Angel was busy, anyway. It's mobbed there today.' Lydia knew she was talking too much. She took Henry's hand and squeezed it gently. 'Why did The Fork get shut down, anyway?' Lydia watched her father's face carefully.

'Ancient history,' Charlie said loudly. 'Who can even remember that far back?' Lydia didn't look at him, didn't want to take her eyes off her father.

'I know it was open in the eighties,' Lydia said. 'You used to rent it out for parties.'

A spark of something flared in her father's eyes. 'You look just like my little girl.'

Lydia willed herself not to glance at Charlie. She remained focused on her dad. 'Did you used to handle the bookings back then?'

'Yeah,' Henry said. 'We had lots of parties. The Fork

in the road, choose your path, choose your own adventure. Choose your place... Very important to make the right choice.' His fingers suddenly gripped Lydia's hand, too-long nails digging into her flesh. 'Did you do it, yet?'

'Do what, Dad?'

But Henry's eyes had already unfocused, his grip loosened. The flash of Henry Crow had been and gone. Lydia watched her dad watching the snooker for a few minutes and then said, 'I'm desperate for a cuppa, haven't had one yet, today,' hoping that Charlie would offer to make it, leaving her alone with her dad.

'Magic,' Charlie said, making no move to get up and help. 'You want a tea? Lydia's putting the kettle on.'

Henry didn't respond.

'Right, then,' Lydia went to the kitchen and made two teas. She waited for a few extra minutes, hoping to hear Charlie conveniently get up and go to the bathroom. Weren't men of a certain age meant to pee every ten minutes? Uncle Charlie clearly had a bladder of steel and Lydia had no choice but to go back into the living room. 'Drink up,' she said, passing Charlie his mug.

Fine. She would do this in front of Charlie. Lydia took Henry's hand, again, willing him to come back from wherever he was visiting, willing him to look into her eyes and see her. 'Dad? Do you remember a wedding party at The Fork? Amy Silver's wedding party.'

'Don't bother your dad with that stuff,' Charlie said, quickly. 'It's all in the past.'

Lydia willed herself not to glance at Charlie. She

remained focused on her dad. 'Something very bad happened at that party. Two people died.'

'What's this about parties and bookings? What do you want to know about the cafe for?'

'Just trying to get up to speed on the Family business,' Lydia said. 'Feel like I ought to know more than I do. Now that I'm in Camberwell.'

'I thought you didn't want to be involved.'

'There's not being involved and then there's being wilfully ignorant. I was reading and I saw a news story about a wedding party at The Fork in which the bride and groom both ended up dead. It kind of stuck out.'

'Well, this is a good day,' Charlie was beaming. He rubbed his hands together and, this evidently not enough to release his happiness, pulled Lydia in for a lung-crushing hug, too. 'You're really home.'

Lydia pulled away. 'It's my job to know things, now. I'm an investigator.'

Charlie was still looking annoyingly happy. It made the stone in Lydia's stomach grow several sizes larger. If she had made Charlie this happy, she had probably taken a misstep. Still, she had come this far. 'Do you remember that, Dad?' She ignored Charlie and tried to engage her father, again. 'Why did a Silver book a wedding party at The Fork?'

'Silver has its uses,' Henry said, not looking away from the snooker.

'Who would have wanted to harm Amy Silver and her groom?'

Henry shook his head, his lips compressed into a thin line. He was staring at the television, still, but Lydia caught a new determination in his attention. He wasn't just watching the snooker, he was deliberately avoiding her gaze.

'Your mother will be back in a minute,' Charlie said. 'She's just gone out for some fresh air.'

That got her attention. 'On her own?'

'Yeah. While I'm here to keep your dad company.'

And the penny dropped. Her mother didn't want to leave Henry alone, was worried about him. So she was taking the opportunity to get out of the house. 'She probably just wanted to avoid you,' Lydia said, instead. 'You're not her favourite.'

Charlie smiled his shark's smile. 'I'm everyone's favourite.'

'Not Mum's,' Lydia persisted. She didn't know why she was needling Charlie. Just that the sight of her father's confused expression had made her suddenly, ragingly angry. She wanted to kick something and Charlie just happened to be closest.

LYDIA SAID her goodbyes and left the room, then burst through the front door of the house like she was escaping from a burning building. She doubled over, with her arms wrapped around her body, the pain of seeing her father so confused and shrunken like a physical punch.

'You heading back to town?' Charlie's voice was unwelcome. He had car keys in his hand and waved them. 'I can give you a lift.'

'I brought my car,' Lydia managed.

'Is that what you call it?'

Lydia had no particular love for her old Volvo but she leapt to its defence. 'It's the perfect stakeout car. Roomy.'

'Unmemorable,' Charlie said, making it clear it was a criticism.

'Exactly,' Lydia said. 'Perfect.'

'Well, I'm not going to tell you how to do your job. Speaking of which, I've got another little task. I'm having a meeting later this week and I'd like you to drop by the table. Give me a reading-'

'Right,' Lydia said, a stone settling in her stomach. Her uncle let her live above The Fork rent free and this was the price. Using her gift to tell him the Family background and power, if any, of his business associates. So far she had managed to hide that she could communicate with a ghost and seemed to act like a battery, powering some people's abilities or essential strength, but she worried about him finding out every single day. Uncle Charlie was power-hungry and Lydia did not like to dwell on how he might react. And what he might demand.

'I'm glad we bumped into each other today,' Charlie said, 'I wondered if you were ready to learn a little more. About the business.'

'No, thank you,' Lydia said. 'I'm running my own firm. But thank you.'

'Maybe not the business,' Charlie said. 'But about the Crows. Our legacy. Our abilities.'

'More history?' Lydia feigned disinterest. This was exactly the area she wanted to avoid with Charlie. 'I know our legends, Dad told them to me when I was kid.'

'Come on, Lyds. You know I was working with your cousin. She had a gift.'

Maddie had demonstrated a level of power that hadn't been seen in the Family for generations. Charlie had been very excited. Until Maddie went rogue and then disappeared. Lydia had no intention of being her replacement. The less Uncle Charlie knew about her own abilities the better. 'You know mine,' Lydia said.

'Aren't you curious to know if you could do more?'

'Nope,' Lydia lied.

Charlie looked momentarily disappointed, but he rallied fast and grabbed her into a bear hug. 'Nothing more important than family, Lyds,' he said, speaking into the top of her head. 'And nothing is more important to me than your happiness and wellbeing.'

He pulled back and looked into her eyes with more care and sincerity than she could stand. 'You're my blood and, more than that, you're Henry's girl. I would do anything for you, you know that?'

This was most unlike Charlie, who tended toward the terrifying. Lydia managed to nod and to mutter 'course' like an embarrassed teenager. Then she escaped.

CHAPTER TEN

Lydia was sitting out on her roof terrace on her nice new wicker chair. She had a mug of coffee on the bistro table and was wrapped in Fleet's hoodie. It was so damn cosy.

Jason had wandered around the terrace, looking longingly over the edge and trying to see how far he could lean over before whatever force kept him in the building, snapped him back upward.

'What do you remember about your wedding day?'

'The day I died, you mean?' Jason turned away from the view of the narrow street which ran behind The Fork. 'You want me to tell you how I died? If I could do that, you wouldn't need to investigate.'

'I know that,' Lydia said, trying to be soothing. An unwelcome thought crossed her mind; what if this plan worked, but the dead Fox ghost had the same issue as Jason, and wouldn't be able to remember his death, either? Still. It was the only plan she had, so she ploughed ahead. Forward momentum trumped rational thought every time.

'It was sunny,' Jason said after a moment. 'Dead or Alive was on the radio in the cab.'

'You took a taxi from the registry office?'

Jason nodded. 'It wasn't a budget thing... I don't think so, anyway. Amy wanted everything low key and simple. Her parents would have paid for a limo, but she didn't want one.' His eyes misted a little. 'She was cool, you know?'

Lydia nodded. 'Did you get on with her parents?'

'I think so,' Jason said, after a moment. 'We didn't spend a lot of time together, really. And they wouldn't have said anything if they didn't approve. They were too smart for that.'

'What do you mean?'

'Amy knew her own mind, you couldn't tell her what to do. I think her parents knew that if they had told her they didn't like me, it would have made her marry me even faster.'

'You don't think they liked you?'

Jason shrugged. He was flickering slightly, clearly getting agitated. Lydia sensed she didn't have much time before he disappeared. 'She sounds great,' Lydia said. 'I'm really sorry for your loss.'

Jason's flickering slowed down a notch. 'Thank you. She really was.'

'Did she talk about her family much? The Silvers?'

'Not at all,' Jason said. After a moment, he added. 'I always had the impression that she was rebelling against her upbringing. I never questioned her about it, I was just happy be along for the ride. I guess,' he hesitated. 'I assumed we had time. I thought we would become proper married grown-ups, have kids, and grow old together. There was time to get to know her parents, time for her to reconcile with them, time for us to do everything.'

Lydia put a hand on his arm. His flickering calmed even more and she felt his arm become more solid under her fingers. After a moment Jason gave her a small smile. 'That feels good. It's like I'm really here.'

'You are here,' Lydia said.

'I was always very rational. I didn't believe in life after death, spirits, none of it. But Amy did. She loved ghost stories and those fake psychics who pretend to talk to the dead. She had seances with her friends on sleepovers when she was a kid. If one of us was going to hang about it should have been her.'

'Did they ever work?'

'What?'

'Amy's attempts to contact the dead?'

'Of course not,' Jason said. 'That's all bollocks.' It took a second and then he realised what he had just said. The laughter that followed felt good. Better than Lydia had felt in days. Who knew that living with a ghost could be so therapeutic?

HAVING ESTABLISHED that there wasn't anything in the news stories which followed Amy and Jason's wedding-day deaths, Lydia was pretty sure it must have been hushed up. Probably by the Silvers. They had the power, after all. The obvious person to ask would be Alejandro or Maria, but Lydia didn't think they would be in a helpful mood. She could ask Fleet to look into it, but Lydia knew it wasn't as simple as it used to be in the good old days. Fleet would need a good reason to go digging into an old case or even just running a name through the database. She wondered if there was a more direct method of finding out what happened on that day. There seemed to be more than one ghost in London, maybe she could just ask Amy directly?

Lydia retrieved her phone from the desk, where it was plugged into the charger and pressed to call Emma 'Hey,' Lydia said as the call connected.

'You won't believe what Archie just put down the toilet.'

'Ah. Shall I call back later?'

'No chance,' Emma said. 'You won't.'

Her voice was dry and Lydia felt her stomach drop. 'I'm really sorry-'

'Joking,' Emma said quickly. 'I know you're busy. No worries. Now guess. You'll never guess.'

'Um, is it a live thing?'

'Ew! No! He's not a psycho.'

'Sorry. Right.' Lydia tried to put herself into the shoes of Archie. Cheeky. Six years old. Male. Adorable cheek dimples which even Lydia was helpless against. 'A book?'

'He wouldn't dare,' Emma was laughing, now. Then her tone changed. 'Back into your room, mister.' Then, to Lydia. 'Sorry, he's in a time out.'

'Fruit?'

'Good guess. No.'

'I give up,' Lydia said, smiling and wondering, as she always did, why she didn't live with Emma and feel this good all of the time.

'The little ratbag emptied my handbag down there. My sunglasses, wallet and house keys.'

Oh, that's right. That was why. 'What possessed him to do that?'

'He says he didn't want me to go out again, but that's just a feeble manipulation tactic to get out of trouble. I think he just wanted to see what would happen. Kids are like that. They are inquisitive and have very poor impulse control. Remind you of anybody?'

'Have you been going out a lot?'

'Don't try to change the subject. We're talking about you. Put any other scary and powerful people in jail, recently? Please tell me you're staying safe. Being careful.' Emma's voice was no longer light.

'I'm being careful,' Lydia said. 'I promise.' She knew that her life was terrifying to Emma and a part of her appreciated her friend's concern. It was grounding.

'Right, then. Are you coming round? You owe me a visit.'

'I was actually hoping you could come here. Tonight.'

'Yes.'

'I have an ulterior motive.'

'I already said 'yes'. I'm desperate for a change of scenery. I love these kids but, God, a pause button would be great.'

'Do you still have that ouija board game?' Emma's

dad had brought one back from a business trip to America and Emma had been the belle of the sleepover circuit for the rest of the school year. Lydia had point blank refused to have anything to do with it and she was hoping Emma might have forgotten that.

'The devil's playground?'

Apparently not. 'Yep.'

'Well, this day is full of surprises,' Emma said. 'You provide the wine, I'll provide the cheesy board game.'

THAT EVENING Lydia put Fleet off. 'I'm seeing Emma.'

'When do I get to meet her?'

'Not tonight.'

'I didn't mean tonight. I know you two haven't seen each other in ages. I just meant it more as a general, what is the state of our relationship kind of a question.'

Lydia had wandered over to the window while they spoke and she looked at the street outside, desperate for a distraction from the conversation. If a dozen white horses could just appear trotting down the middle of the road, she would have a legitimate reason to change the subject. Lydia would have settled for some drunks on their way home from the pub getting into an altercation. Sadly, the road remained empty.

'Well, that's my answer,' Fleet said.

'It's not meant to be,' Lydia said. 'I'm a bit... Over-whelmed.'

'By my raw sex appeal?' Fleet's habitual joking tone was back and Lydia felt a flood of relief.

'I was thinking more about work and family stuff. The usual.'

'You're right,' Fleet said. 'I'm sorry if I'm pushing you. I'm used to getting on with things in my personal life. If I waited for everything to calm down at work before having a life, it would never happen.'

'I get that and you're right,' Lydia said. 'Can you just give me a little bit more time to adjust?'

'If you're in, you can take all the time you need.'

'I'm in,' Lydia said. It wasn't until she had hung up that she realised she was smiling.

WHEN EMMA ARRIVED THAT EVENING, carrying the ouija board game in a battered cardboard box and a bakery bag of double chocolate cookies, Lydia had just finished rinsing the takeaway container from dinner and stuffing it into her overflowing recycling crate.

They caught up on the toilet situation and chatted about Tom's health while Lydia poured red wine and set out some jar candles she had bought at the local Tesco. They were 'cotton fresh' scent which didn't feel appropriately occult, but she was willing to work with what they had. She had warned Jason and he had elected to attend. There was a spark of hope in his eyes which made Lydia's stomach hurt.

The board was set up on the living room floor, in the space between the desk and the sofa. Emma sat on one side, Lydia on the other, and Jason hovered on the sofa, overseeing proceedings from what he considered a safer distance. Lydia could see the tension in his expression and the way his body was not quite sitting on the cushions.

'Do you remember how this works?'

Emma gave Lydia a wide smile. 'It doesn't work, as I recall.'

'Yeah, but that was before I was involved.' Lydia caught Emma's eye and held her gaze. 'I honestly don't know. I mean, it might. Is that okay?'

'Of course!' Emma looked more excited than the time she found a beautiful pair of yellow heels marked down from a hundred to a tenner.

'I'm serious,' Lydia said, knowing that there was no way to properly prepare Emma or to convey the feeling that would come from realising that there was more to this world than met the eye. Emma thought she wanted a spooky experience, proof of another plane of existence or the soul or whatever, but the truth was scary. Lydia was a Crow and she was still freaked out.

She checked on Jason. He had his hands clasped and his sleeves pushed up even further than usual. He meant business, in other words.

'What?' Emma had caught Lydia's glance.

'Nothing,' Lydia said. She would save the news that there was already a ghost in the room for another time. Like never.

'Do you need the instructions?' Lydia opened the lid of the box to look.

'I can remember it,' Emma said. 'Honestly, I did this so many times it's ingrained.'

Lydia lit the candles and jumped up to turn off the main light, before retaking her place.

'Okay.' Emma was sitting cross-legged and her face spelled concentration, for a moment, Lydia could see Emma in her school uniform, taking her purple furry pencil case out of her Converse back-pack. Twelve years obliterated in the blink of an eye. 'I call upon my spirit guide to join us. I call her to watch over me and to guide me as I contact the other side.'

'Spirit guide?' Lydia said.

'You have to have a guide,' Emma said. 'It's the rules. Mine is Madonna.'

'But Madonna isn't dead.'

Emma shrugged. 'I was twelve when I created her. She's the astral projection of Madonna. Shut up.'

Lydia smothered her laughter. 'Sorry. Please continue.'

Emma resettled herself, hands on her knees, palm upward like in yoga class. Then she began invoking her spirit guide again. After a few minutes of Emma asking for her guide and then appearing to listen, she nodded. 'It's time. Put your finger on the planchette.'

Lydia placed a finger on the planchette and so did Emma. Lydia felt a chill and she assumed Jason had moved closer.

'Is Amy Silver available? We would like to commu-nicate with her.'

It was typical of Emma to be super-polite, even when contacting the dead. The planchette slid across the board and landed on the word 'yes'.

'Holy shit,' Jason said.

Lydia couldn't stop herself from looking at him. He

was huddled on the sofa, his feet drawn up and an expression of agony on his face.

'Is there someone here?' she said.

'If the board doesn't lie,' Emma said, smiling.

Jason had closed his eyes. 'I don't know. I can't look. I can't.'

'It's okay,' Lydia said.

'Who are you talking to?' Emma frowned. Lydia hadn't looked away from Jason quickly enough and Emma had caught her speaking to the sofa. 'Are you messing with me?'

'No,' Lydia said. 'Sorry. Just saying it's going to be okay.'

'I know,' Emma said. 'I'm not worried. You don't have to worry about me.'

'Shall we carry on?' Lydia made sure she kept her eyes on Emma, although the question was really for Jason.

'Sure,' Emma said.

'Do it,' Jason said in a strangled voice.

'Right, then.' Lydia took a deep breath. Was it her imagination or was the planchette icy cold? Shouldn't it be warm from the heat of her finger? 'Are we speaking with Amy Silver now?'

Again, the planchette slid across the board and landed in on the word 'yes'.

'Are you doing that?' Lydia looked at Emma but knew immediately that she wasn't. 'That really moved.'

Emma's expression was calm. 'It's the ideomotor effect. You really want Amy Silver to be here.'

'Wait, what?' Lydia took her hand off the planchette and sat back. 'The what effect?'

Emma waved her hands. 'It's a subconscious reflex thingy. Your body responds without you knowing and you push the planchette even though you don't think you are. It's how these things work,' she gestured at the board. 'I read up on it so that I'd be better at doing it.'

Only Emma would do her research to be the best at a board game. 'But I want to use it for real. I don't want my subconscious whatnots messing with it.'

'The effect works best when you think you're not controlling it. That's why a group of people joining in is best, because you don't think you're having any individual effect, you can just go with it.'

'So I should plan to control it in order not to do it?' Lydia closed her eyes in frustration. An image of a crow in flight flashed into her mind. 'This was a terrible idea.'

'No, no, don't give up,' Emma said. 'Let's keep going. Don't think so much. Try to just have a bit of fun.'

Lydia wanted to tell Emma that she lived with a depressed ghost and had recently met a screaming, terrifying spirit on the underground, and pushing a plastic triangle around just wasn't doing it for her. Instead she reached for her wine glass and took a healthy slug. 'Okay.'

Emma put her finger back on the planchette and Lydia did the same. It still felt cold and Lydia was about to ask Emma if she had noticed the odd temperature, when the planchette whizzed across the board to the array of letters. It stopped as abruptly as it had started, pointing to the letter 'h'. A beat, and then it moved, again, just tilted very slightly so that the tip of the arrow was on the letter 'I'.

'Hi?' Emma said. 'Did something just say 'hi' to us?' Her eyes were wide.

'Is this what usually happens?' Lydia asked, already knowing the answer. Emma's shocked reaction had already told her that this was not normal. The planchette was moving again and they both read out the letters as it slid across the board.

'S.I.L.V.E.R.'

'Oh god, oh god, oh god,' Jason was curled in on himself and Lydia wanted to reach out and pat him. She wanted to reach out and give him a sympathetic pat, but she couldn't. So she said 'it's okay,' instead, and hoped he knew it was for him.

'Silver?' Emma was pale and the words tumbled out in a panicked babble. 'That's really clear. It's usually just gobbledygook unless you ask something specific. And then, even then, maybe a yes or a no, not this. Are you doing it?'

'I don't think so,' Lydia said. 'I can't be sure, though. I wish I could ask something that only Amy Silver would know.'

'But you would still know,' Emma said. 'It wouldn't prove anything.'

Of course, Emma didn't know that Amy's dead husband was scrunched on the sofa, moaning gently to himself. Jason could confirm the answer after the board had spelled it out. There would be no way for Lydia to do it sub-consciously.

'Prove you are Amy Silver,' Lydia said out loud. 'What's your favourite colour?'

Emma pulled a confused face but didn't argue. For a moment, nothing happened, and Lydia had a split second of feeling daft. Two grown women, one of whom belonged to an ancient magical family, leaning over a kid's board game, and then the planchette moved. Again, it slid swiftly and surely across the surface, spelling out the word 'lilac'.

'That's very specific,' Emma said. 'If your subconscious was guessing, it would have gone with blue. I think that's the most common answer-'

'Amy?' Jason was on his feet. Lydia felt the blast of cold air as he moved closer. She didn't want to take her hand off the planchette, in case it somehow cut the connection to the other side, but she wanted to soothe Jason, too. He was vibrating so fast that his image appeared to flicker in and out of existence. 'You've got to calm down!' Lydia said sharply. 'Breathe!'

That did it. Jason instantly stopped vibrating and turned hurt eyes on Lydia. 'Well, that's just mean.'

'Sorry,' Lydia said to Jason. 'But you need to keep a hold of yourself. You don't want to miss this.'

'I am calm. Who are you talking to?' Emma said. 'Seriously. I'm going to start freaking out if you don't tell me what the hell is going on. Can you see somebody here?'

'Sorry,' Lydia said. 'I'm sorry.' Emma was Lydia's normal friend. She had always kept everything Family-related firmly under wraps. Partly from habit, partly because she was brought up in suburbia and the whole point was that she was meant to have a normal life and partly, if she was honest, from fear. She didn't want to frighten Emma and had never wanted her to look at her differently. All of that had changed, now, of course. She had opened up to Emma since returning to London and they were closer than ever. But old habits died hard. And it was one thing to talk in theory about the Crow Family history and quite another to explain that there was a ghost in the room. A ghost that Lydia appeared to power-up so that he could now reliably make cups of tea.

'Don't be sorry,' Emma said. 'I know it's hard. You can trust me.'

That did it. Lydia felt pricking behind her eyes. Emma had never been anything except a good friend. She was on her side Lydia knew that in her bones. So why couldn't she trust her not to hate her? Be disgusted by her? Frightened of her? She took a deep breath. 'There is a spirit in this building. I can talk to him.'

Emma nodded. 'Is he doing the board?'

Lydia shook her head. 'We don't need it. I can hear him.' She hesitated before adding. 'And see him.'

Emma looked around, as if she would be able to see him, too. 'He's here, now?'

'Yes.' Lydia looked up at where Jason was standing by the board, in between her and Emma. 'He's right next to us. Don't worry. He's really nice.'

'You think I'm nice?' Jason said.

'Of course,' Lydia said.

'What?' Emma said.

The planchette began sliding again. 'S.T.I.L.L.H.E.R.E.'

100

'Jesus H.' Emma breathed out the curse. 'This is surreal. If we were recording this we'd make a packet on YouTube.'

'People would assume it was faked,' Lydia said.

'Ask if she knows I'm here,' Jason said. 'Ask her if she can come here. Why isn't she here with me?'

'Hang on,' Lydia was trying to think, to stay calm. She needed the smart play and this connection, whatever it was, might be lost at any moment. She didn't want to upset Jason but part of being an investigator was putting aside emotion in order to get to the truth. 'How did you die?'

The planchette got even colder, the ice turning to a burning sensation on the tips of Lydia's fingers.

'Ow,' Emma said, but she didn't move her own fingers.

'You might want to leave,' Lydia said to Jason. Adding 'not you,' to Emma.

The planchette slid slowly. It stopped and started, moving jerkily as if the force powering it was uncertain or angry. 'H.A.'

'Ha?' Emma frowned. 'Is it laughing?'

The planchette moved again. To the 'T'. Please don't be spelling out 'hat' Lydia prayed. Death by hat. That was neither dignified nor helpful. Then the planchette moved again, settling on the letter 'E'.

'Hate?' Emma said. She breathed out. 'Bloody hell.'

The burning in Lydia's fingers was worse and she said, 'I'm going to have to let-' just as it began spinning and she could no longer keep contact.

The planchette span around in place, faster and

faster, before whizzing off the board completely and launching across the room, flying through Jason's body and under the sofa.

'That was an unpleasant sensation,' Jason said and disappeared.

Lydia stuck her fingers into her mouth and sucked. They were frozen and the heat of her mouth intensified the pain. Was it possible to get frostbite from a piece of plastic?

'So, that was Amy Silver?' Emma sat back. 'I guess she's finished chatting.'

Lydia took her hand out of her mouth and said something she often thought, but didn't often say. 'I bloody love you.'

CHAPTER ELEVEN

Emma and Lydia moved to sit on the sofa with their wine glasses fully topped up. Emma was still being remarkably calm. 'Tell me about your spirit friend.'

'His name is Jason Montefort. He died here. And now he's stuck.'

Emma pulled a face. 'Well, that sucks.'

Lydia nodded. 'He's nice.' After another moment of hesitation, she decided to go all in. 'I think. Well, we think, that I might be powering him up.'

'What do you mean?'

'He never used to be able to touch stuff and, since I moved in, he can. He even makes tea.'

'That's handy,' Emma said. 'Send him over to my place.'

'He can't leave The Fork. Well, he can move around the building and out onto the roof terrace, but not over the edge or out through the main doors. I'm hoping that if I can find out how he died, it will unlock that for him. Give him some freedom.'

'He doesn't know how he died?' Emma's nose wrinkled when she was thinking hard. Archie and Maisie were exactly the same. 'Was he unconscious?'

'I don't know. He can't remember anything. Except that it was his wedding day.'

'Jesus. That's awful.'

'I know, right? Poor guy.' It felt amazing to talk to Emma about Jason. Lydia didn't know why she had always been so cautious and closed off.

Emma got up suddenly and ran to the kitchen. A moment later she called through. 'False alarm. Sorry.'

There was the sound of the tap running.

'Sorry,' Emma said again, wiping her mouth as she returned to the sofa. 'Thought my wine was going to come back up for a moment, there. It's just all a lot to take in.'

And Lydia remembered. That was why.

'Just a delayed reaction,' Emma said, cheerfully enough. 'Nothing to worry about.'

'I do worry,' Lydia said, feeling like hell. 'I'm sorry, I shouldn't have-'

'Will you stop that?' Emma looked cross which was so unusual that Lydia shut her mouth immediately.

'You don't have to look after me or protect me. Just because I might be freaked out by something doesn't mean I would prefer to be left out. Life is messy and full of things we don't know but then we experience them or learn them. That's the whole point of life.'

'But this stuff-'

'Is really cool,' Emma said. 'It's scary and over-whelming, but it's also amazing and exciting. You don't get one without the other.'

'You are very wise,' Lydia said, keeping her voice light even though she suddenly felt like crying. 'When did you get so wise?'

'Parenthood,' Emma said cheerfully. 'There's nothing like realising you are responsible for moulding tiny lives to make you get your shit together.'

'I think you were the same at school,' Lydia said.

Emma made a finger gun and pointed it at Lydia. 'Don't you dare tell me I was an old soul.'

'Wouldn't dream of it,' Lydia said. 'Although you were. And are. What?' She ducked as Emma aimed a cushion at her head. 'It's a compliment.'

'The word 'soul' suddenly seems very real,' Emma said, once she'd stopped laughing. 'We have actual proof that there is life after death. That there is a spirit part to us, not just electricity and neurons and biology.'

'I think we always knew that. Really.' Lydia had never thought she was just flesh and blood. Being a Crow had always given her a strong sense that there were things in this world other than the purely physical, her Family powers for starters.

'There's a difference between believing it and knowing for sure, though.'

'I guess,' Lydia said.

'Is he here, now?'

'No,' Lydia shook her head.

'Where does he go?'

'His bedroom,' Lydia said, smiling at how mundane

the phrase sounded. 'Or the kitchen in the cafe. Sometimes the roof terrace. And sometimes he disappears completely. He doesn't know where he goes when that happens, he can't remember anything.'

'That sounds scary,' Emma said. 'For him, I mean.'

Lydia nodded. 'It is. He's terrified he won't come back.'

'It's strange to think about a ghost being afraid of death, but it makes sense.'

'While he's a sentient ghost, he's not really dead. He's terrified of oblivion. And being so close to it, he has the sense that there is something else. It might just be peaceful quiet, true oblivion, or it could be something different. Something worse.'

'Or something better?' Emma pointed out. 'Is he religious? A nice vision of heaven would be comforting right about now.'

'I don't think so.' Lydia decided not to mention Jason's fear of a fiery hell dimension. Emma was dealing with quite enough as it was.

'You could be on the brink of solving the big question. The whole life, universe and everything thing. What happens when we die? What's it all mean?'

Lydia had never thought of the wider ramifications of Jason's existence. She felt a little bit ashamed.

'Although it could be counterproductive,' Emma was thinking out loud. 'I mean, isn't that the point of belief? That it's something you take on faith, not requiring evidence. Once you have evidence, it's fact instead?'

Lydia didn't know. Just that this line of thought gave her a headache. And made her want to do something physical and simple. Either hit something or bang someone. She was not as evolved as Emma, that was for certain.

Emma took a healthy sip of her wine and shook her head. 'Is it weird that I want to go home and jump Tom?'

'Oh, thank Feathers,' Lydia said. 'I was just thinking that I felt weirdly in the mood.'

'It's probably our animal instincts jumping in because we've reached the limits of our conscious understanding. Or just thinking about death this much reminds us to seize the day.'

'Either way,' Lydia said, and took another slug of wine. It warmed her from the inside and highlighted the other feelings that had stirred. She shifted and Emma stood up. 'I'm going to head home.' She blushed. 'For completely unrelated reasons.'

'Yes,' Lydia said. 'I'm going to call Fleet. Also for unrelated reasons. Something completely different.'

Emma kissed Lydia's cheek and left, phone in hand and a determined look in her eye. She hoped Tom was feeling energetic.

After Emma had gone, Lydia wasted no time in calling Fleet. 'You know I said I couldn't see you tonight,' she began.

'On my way,' Fleet replied, a smile in his voice. 'Unless you want to come to my place?'

Lydia hesitated and he said 'no worries' and finished the call.

There was a flutter of guilt, but since she couldn't

quite explain her reluctance to visit his home to herself, let alone anybody else, she ignored it. A Crow, roosting in the home of a copper. It felt like a statement and she still wasn't sure she was ready to make it. However much she wanted to wander off her given path.

He had been to the gym after a late finish at work, and his tightly curled hair was still damp from the shower. He was wearing a t-shirt which meant his biceps and forearms were available for her viewing pleasure. And it was a pleasure.

All was going very well, when the conversation took a turn. Lydia had made the mistake of mentioning her fruitless ghost-hunting expedition. Which put Fleet back onto the subject of Paul Fox. His brows lowered and a deep crease appeared between them. 'I don't know why you're doing his bidding.'

Lydia stamped on her irritation. 'Putting aside your feelings about Paul,' Lydia caught herself, 'our feelings. There is a distressed spirit underground and it feels like I ought to try to do something about it.'

'Fair enough, but you don't have to interact with him. You don't need to do this for him.'

Was he? Could he be? 'Don't be jealous,' Lydia said. 'You've got nothing to worry about.'

'I'm not,' Fleet said, annoyance clear on his face. 'This isn't about that. I don't trust him, though. And I'm worried that your judgement is clouded.'

'By what? My lust?' Lydia felt herself blush. Which was irritating. She did feel lust for Paul Fox. He was a Fox. In every sense. But she was smart and knew to allow for that reaction. Knew to account for the animal magnetism that blessed the Fox Family. Besides, she had literally been there and done that. 'I exorcised that long ago.'

Fleet winced. 'Thanks for reminding me.'

'Sorry.'

'I'm not talking about that. This isn't about us. It's about you being seduced by his charm into taking risks. Trusting whatever line he's feeding.'

'I'm not an idiot. And you said 'seduced'. Freudian slip?'

'Stop being defensive,' Fleet said, frustration bubbling through. 'I'm on your side.'

'I know,' Lydia forced herself to stop reacting. To take a moment and a deep breath. 'I'm sorry. And you're right. He is very persuasive. But I am being wary. I don't trust him, I promise.' Lydia heard a high-pitched caw. A warning sound. She looked around, but it must have been in her mind. Tinnitus?

'You don't trust anybody,' Fleet said. 'Not even me.'

'I do trust you,' Lydia said, trying to placate him.

Fleet shook his head. 'Don't try to handle me. I want you to take me seriously. Believe it or not, I'm quite good at this stuff. It's my job.'

'I know,' Lydia said. He didn't know the Families the way she did, though. And he didn't know Paul Fox. 'This stuff, though... It's kind of my area.'

'Just because you're a Crow and I'm not doesn't negate my opinion.'

'Of course not,' Lydia couldn't work out how to stop the argument.

Fleet blew out a sigh and ran a hand over his head. 'I'm tired. Think I'll head home.'

'If you want.' Lydia knew her voice had come out toneless. Almost sulky. She tried again. 'You don't have anything to worry about. With Paul, I mean.'

Fleet flinched. 'Every time you say his name I feel sick.'

Lydia hesitated, trying to choose her words. 'I understand how you feel and I'm sorry. But I'm doing this job for him. I don't have a choice.'

Fleet shook his head. 'You always have a choice. And I want you to stay away from him.'

'Don't give me orders,' Lydia said, her patience snapping. 'He could make trouble for me, trouble for my Family. And besides all of that, it's my professional reputation. I've got to do my job.'

'You are your own boss,' Fleet pointed out. 'Which means you are doing exactly what you want. As usual.'

Lydia opened her mouth to argue, but Fleet had picked up his coat and was halfway to the door. She closed her mouth. She couldn't think of anything to say, anyway. Nothing that wouldn't be a lie.

CHAPTER TWELVE

The next day Lydia woke up with a sore head. Which wasn't fair since she'd only had one whisky after Fleet had gone. Two at the most. But she never got hangovers; it was one of her favourite things about herself. Lydia downed a glass of water and headed out in search of fresh air and a bucket of caffeine. She often mooched some from The Fork, but Angel was looking particularly fierce this morning and Lydia decided to walk to the bagel takeaway place on the corner, instead.

She took her biggest mug with her so as not to get a disposable cup. She might be a terrible girlfriend and a disappointment to the Crow Family, but she could do her bit for the environment. On her way back to her office, she distracted herself from her failings by mulling over the case. An unknown victim with an unknown cause of death. The police weren't even treating it as murder, at the moment, so resources weren't exactly being thrown at the investigation. But what if it was murder? And what if the method of murder was magical? That would explain why the police didn't have a clue. There were magical objects which could affect people, like the silver knight statue which had sent Robert Sharp and Yas Bishop around the bend. And her Crow Family coin definitely put a bit of whammy on susceptible people. She hadn't found anything on the body, but the murderer could have retrieved the object after the Fox had died. Or there might be other kinds of magic, stuff she didn't know about.

Lydia knew that Uncle Charlie was the obvious person to go to for a magic lesson, but her nightmares with Maddie and the sense that Charlie had bigger plans, ones she might not approve of, stopped her. The less she revealed to Charlie, the better. Her mother was right: her uncle loved her, but the Family business came first. He would manipulate her, use every piece of information for his own agenda, and not even think twice.

She tapped out a quick text message, carefully not admitting to herself what she was doing until it was too late. There was a strong chance she was also reacting to Fleet telling her to stay away from Paul. She had clearly never grown out of her teenage rebellion phase and it wasn't a fact she was particularly proud of.

Paul Fox replied in seconds, as if he had been waiting. Just two words.

The Den.

When Lydia had been young and stupid and had

dated Paul Fox, he had always suggested they go to The Den for drinks. Lydia had always refused. It was one thing to date a Fox, but drinking in their Family bar was just asking for trouble. It had been one of the things he had always teased her about. Underneath the teasing had been an annoyance. Lydia had sensed that Paul wasn't used to people saying 'no' to him and that had just cemented her resolve. He was getting his wish, which was irritating, but Lydia didn't feel she had much of a choice. She wanted information and perhaps giving him this small victory over her would loosen his tongue, put him in a sharing mood. Whatever Fleet might think, her mind was focused entirely on the job. And justice for the unfortunate in the tunnel.

The Den was slap bang in the middle of Whitechapel. Fox territory. Knowing that she could just as easily have gone to see her father to ask about magical murder methods and not wanting to think too hard about the reasons why she wasn't, Lydia was distracted enough to walk past the number of The Den. Turning around and retracing her steps, dodging past a large family pushing a double-stroller which was taking up the entire pavement, she forced herself to concentrate. Standing in front of number thirty, she realised why she had walked past it in the first place. Rather than the entrance to a bar, she was standing in front of a barber shop. The classic red-and-white striped pole was spinning and an illuminated neon sign said 'open'. Lydia would have assumed she had the wrong place, if it hadn't been for the name. Red Brush.

Pushing open the door, a bell jangled and a man sitting in one of the old-fashioned barber's chairs looked up from the newspaper he was reading. He was clean shaven and had the neatest, shiniest hair Lydia had ever seen on a man. It was styled with a quiff at the front, which matched the fifties style of his cream-and-black fine knit bowling shirt and narrow trousers. And the honest-to-Crow matchstick he had gripped between his teeth. 'Help you?'

'The Den,' Lydia said. 'I've got an appointment with Paul Fox.'

Fifties-Throwback tilted his head and for a moment Lydia thought he was going to be tiresome. She slipped her hand into her pocket, felt the edges of her coin. Whether he saw something in her eyes or name-dropping Paul Fox had done the trick, Lydia didn't know, but he stood up, unfolding long legs and walking to the back of the barbershop. He held open a door and gestured for Lydia to pass him. The door led to a straight flight of stairs leading down to a wall with a framed poster of Elvis.

'Push on the right'.

Lydia glanced back up, but Fifties-throwback was already shutting the door. The small expanse of wall between the poster and the adjoining wall was smudged with hand prints. She reached out and pushed the flat of her hand and felt the wall swing inward smoothly. Instantly, she could hear low voices and ambient electronica. The secret door and surrounding walls had some serious sound insulation.

The Den was decorated in classic speakeasy style with 1920s decor, low lighting, and rows of inviting-looking glass booze bottles behind the bar. It was mid-afternoon and not busy, the man behind the bar was wearing a crisp white shirt with the sleeves rolled up and a black velvet waistcoat and tie, complete with a looping watch chain and sleeve garters.

'He's in the back room, Miss,' he said when Lydia approached.

Lydia felt the hairs on the back of her neck rise and the urge to fly was very strong. The place smelled of Fox, which she had steeled herself for, but the choking taste of earth in the back of her throat was making it hard to swallow or breathe. She was going to pass out if she wasn't careful. Forcing a breath through her constricted airway, she threaded through the clusters of tables and chairs to the open doorway in the far corner. Inside, was a smaller space. Same decor, same scent of Fox, but with one important difference. This space held Paul Fox.

He was sitting with his back to the wall on a tufted dark green velvet sofa, one arm stretched out along the back. His impressive biceps were clearly visible and he had the knowing look, complete with an almost-smile, which used to flip her stomach. It had no effect, now, she told herself. Thank Feathers.

Paul didn't stand up but he indicated the seat opposite. 'I took the liberty.'

For a moment, Lydia didn't know what he meant. She was light-headed from the lack of oxygen and focusing on damping down the insta-lust which was part

Fox magic and part memory. Paul had been excellent in a physical sense and Lydia's first sexual experience. From a purely technical point of view, it had been an excellent decision. Now, however, she was wishing that every nerve in her body wasn't insisting on reliving his touch, the feel of his lips and tongue and hands. Hell Hawk. She had to focus. Paul picked up a glass and Lydia realised there were two. He had got her a drink. Whisky by the look of it.

There was, of course, a slim possibility that Paul had poisoned or drugged the drink, but Lydia grabbed it and knocked it back, anyway. The alcohol immediately hit her system, calming her mind and helping her to take the first proper breath since she had walked into the joint.

'You still like that, then?'

Before Lydia could say something cutting and witty like 'duh', the bartender appeared at the table. It made Lydia jump, which was annoying, but props to the man. He had the light-footedness and stealth of a cat. Or, more accurately she supposed, a fox. He was carrying a small tray with several glasses. 'Same again, Miss?'

Lydia nodded and watched as the empty glass was replaced by a full one. Not taking her eyes off Paul, in the way she would watch any dangerous animal, she lifted the fresh glass and took a more measured mouthful.

'What do you think?'

'Of this place?' Lydia forced herself to put the glass back down on the table. Out of temptation. 'It's very vintage. Attention to detail is excellent. And the whisky is good.' Credit where it was due.

Paul's almost smile quirked up at the corners and his eyes crinkled. 'I'm so happy you're finally here.'

'I have an agenda,' Lydia said.

'Naturally.'

Glancing around to check for listeners, purely out of habit, Lydia took a breath and said: 'What sort of magic could kill a man?'

Paul's smile vanished. 'Are we talking about the case?'

'Police have no cause of death. Nothing.'

'That doesn't mean-'

'I know,' Lydia broke in. 'But I'm exploring every possibility. Keeping an open mind. You want answers, right?'

'Right.' He glanced behind Lydia and she turned around just in time to see a figure in the doorway, moving out of sight.

'Friends?'

'Brother,' Paul said, pulling a face. 'Just watching out.'

'For me?' Lydia was fighting the urge to fly, again. What had possessed her to walk into The Den? Fleet was right. She was being reckless.

'You can't blame him,' Paul said. 'Your cousin did this.' He lifted his black t-shirt and Lydia had to stop herself from reacting. Apart from the abs, which were just as beautiful as she remembered, there was a burn mark in the shape of a handprint. It was red and slightly raised and in a splayed shape, the fingers reaching from next to his navel to the bottom of his ribs.

'Madeleine did that?'

Paul nodded, dropping his shirt and taking a drink.

Suddenly Paul inviting Lydia to put her hand on his chest made more sense. He had been showing her that he trusted her. Or, perhaps, checking to see if she was as powerful as Maddie. Which just went to show he had a reckless streak all of his own. 'I thought you two were friendly. You helped to hide her.' Maddie had gone missing and Lydia had been tasked with finding her by Uncle Charlie, on behalf of John and Daisy, Maddie's parents. When Lydia had tracked her down, Maddie had been hiding on a canal boat in Little Venice, courtesy of Paul Fox.

'I'm not sure your cousin has friends,' Paul said. He hesitated and then, seeming to think better of whatever he was about to say, drained his glass instead.

'What?' Lydia leaned forward slightly. 'Say it.'

'Have you heard from her?'

Lydia thought about the series of nightmares which had, thankfully, stopped. In them, Maddie had showed up, shoved her over the railing of her roof terrace. It hadn't been pleasant. 'No,' she said.

'Okay, then.'

'What?' Lydia couldn't keep the impatience out of her voice. Truth be told, she wasn't really trying.

'She reminded me of you,' Paul said, after a pause. 'At first, anyway. But I soon realised you are very different.'

'Damn right,' Lydia said. 'I'm one of a bloody kind.'

He smiled, flashing white teeth, and Lydia felt the call of woodland and earth. 'She's a fan of chaos. That's never been your bag, has it? Not even when you were taking a walk on the wild side with me.'

A piece clicked into place. 'You thought it was Maddie? That's why you wanted me to take the case. Because I found her before. Because I'm a Crow, so you couldn't have anyone else go after her or there would be a war.'

Paul shrugged. 'It crossed my mind.'

'Well it wasn't her,' Lydia said.

'You came in here thinking it was magic. Maddie's gifted.'

'Yeah, but I would have been able to tell.'

Paul still didn't look completely convinced.

'And no marks, remember?'

He nodded. 'Not consistent with her previous work, I agree.'

Lydia wondered how much Maddie had told him when they had been together. Then she wondered how *together* they had been and felt a spurt of jealousy. Feather and claw, she was losing her mind. 'So, you thought my cousin was involved in something Fox-related, which was why you blackmailed me into working for you. Why did you send me down to the tunnels? What did you expect me to find?'

'I didn't know about him,' Paul said quickly.

'I believe you,' Lydia said. 'But what, then? Why send me underground?'

Paul blew out air through his nose. He picked up his glass but didn't take a drink, putting it back down on the table and leaning forward. 'Okay. There were a couple of disappearances in the Family.'

'Who?'

'My cousin Jack. My brother.'

Lydia wanted to take out her notebook but she knew this wasn't the time. A Fox was admitting a weakness. And this was after showing her that he had been hurt by a Crow. It was unprecedented. At this rate, she was going to forge a new alliance with the Fox Family and the threat of war would be a thing of the past. Or, more accurately, she would have balanced out the fact that she had pissed off the Silvers. 'I'm sorry to hear that,' she said. 'Why didn't you give me names and descriptions? And why the tunnels?'

'They aren't lost anymore. They've both come home.'

'I don't understand. They're back?'

'But they seem different,' Paul said. 'Something isn't right with them. I can smell it.'

Lydia kept quiet. Paul wasn't focusing on her, anymore. He was seeing something else. 'Luke got drunk one night. He hardly touched the stuff before, but he was knocking vodka back like it was water. Before he passed out, he said he'd been underground. On the tracks, but not with the trains.' His gaze snapped back to Lydia. 'So, I thought it wise to check it out.'

'You thought it wise to send me to check it out,' Lydia corrected.

Paul nodded. 'You're strong enough to withstand whatever is in the air down there.'

He was flattering her to distract and disarm, Lydia knew. It still worked a little bit. 'So, who is our unknown victim? I assume you've asked around to find out who else has gone missing?'

'I didn't recognise him,' Paul said. 'I wasn't lying.'

'I'm not saying you were, but you haven't exactly rushed to enlighten me. This trust thing is only going to work if you share information.'

Paul almost smiled. 'Says the open book, Lydia Crow.'

Lydia wasn't going to get distracted. She slid her glass away and made as if to stand up.

'All right, all right,' Paul made a conciliatory gesture. 'It's Marty. I asked around and he went missing last week. He matches the description.'

'Marty?' Lydia rested a hand on her hip and waited.

'Benson,' Paul said eventually. It was clearly an effort and Lydia sympathised. It wasn't easy to break the habit of distrust. Of guarding information like it was plutonium. 'Not central bloodline, but still family. As you identified.'

Lydia ignored that fishing expedition. 'Any idea why someone would want him dead? Was he in trouble?'

'A bit,' Paul shrugged. 'Did a bit of dealing. Weed and some coke. Nothing major, though. Just to friends and friends of friends.'

'In Camberwell?' Lydia's thoughts had swung to Uncle Charlie. He was not a fan of the drug trade on his turf.

'Nah, just locally. He was a stoner but he wasn't that stupid. Or suicidal, as far as I know.'

'Any link between Marty and the others who went

missing? Also, I'm going to need to speak to Jack and Luke.'

Paul's attention was caught by something behind Lydia. 'I can look into that. We should wrap this up,' he said.

'Fine by me,' Lydia downed the rest of her drink and got to her feet. She had the strange sensation of not being ready to leave Paul's company. Her life just got odder and more complicated by the day.

CHAPTER THIRTEEN

Lydia walked into the cafe just past mid-afternoon. Her mother's words about becoming the head of the Crow Family had been simmering at the back of her mind and the sight of The Fork, complete with the current leader, brought a rush of panic. She understood her mother's concerns, but had no intention of taking over anything, least of all the infamous and slightly-dodgy Crow Family business. Perhaps it was time to lay down some boundaries, again?

Uncle Charlie was sitting in his favourite table by the large window of The Fork. He had one arm resting along the back of the banquette of the booth and was reading a paperback. Or pretending to read, you could never tell with Charlie. He looked up when Lydia arrived at the table. 'You're early,' he spoke approvingly. That wasn't going to last. Lydia swallowed hard before launching into her prepared speech.

'I can't do today,' she said. 'Something's come up with work.'

'No worries,' Charlie said, his eyes cold. 'We can do it later. Five?'

Lydia forced a headshake.

Charlie paused, clearly weighing up his next words. 'It's important to me, Lyds. I wouldn't ask otherwise.'

'No.' The word came out before her brain had time to finesse it. 'Sorry,' she said, forcing herself to look Charlie in the eyes, terrifying as that was. 'I'd rather not.'

'You'd rather not,' Charlie said slowly.

'I'm really busy, back-to-back clients and I can't spare the time. Besides, I can afford to pay rent, now, and I would rather do that than...' She hesitated, trying to work out the least offensive phrasing.

'Than be at my beck and call?' Charlie supplied. 'Rather give me money than your help. You'd rather pay off your family than be a part of it, than be a help. You don't want to sully yourself with Crow Family business, while you're happy to be one when it suits you. That about right?' Charlie's tone was mild, but it contained more fury than most people could manage with full-on yelling.

Lydia wanted to take a step back, to put a bit more distance between her and her uncle. 'It's not like that,' Lydia said. 'I'm just really busy. It's hard to be a solo operator. When I make enough I'll hire some help and that will free me up a bit. It's nothing personal.'

Charlie smiled thinly. 'It's always personal, Lyds, you know that.'

Wanting to prove to herself that she wasn't playing

favourites, or losing her critical edge when it came to Paul Fox, she called him. She certainly wasn't going to admit that she sort of wanted to hear his voice. He picked up after one ring and Lydia launched straight in. 'Aren't you best placed to find out about Marty's life?'

'It's my favourite Crow. Lovely to hear from you so soon.'

'Do shut up,' Lydia said, but her lips were turned up in a half-smile. Hell Hawk.

Paul was still speaking. 'Everyone knows I'm Tristan's son, they won't say anything negative.'

'Everyone knows I'm a Crow,' Lydia argued. 'They're as likely to punch me in the face as talk to me at all.'

She could hear the smirk in his voice. 'Good thing you're quick, Little Bird.'

'Don't call me that,' Lydia snapped.

'Okay, Lyds.'

'Or that.' Paul had always been excellent at getting under skin. It was a talent he clearly still possessed which annoyed Lydia more than she cared to admit. She shouldn't care what he thought or what he said. He was a Fox.

'Anyway, not everyone knows you. The Crows aren't as important as they once were. You might be surprised how many members of my extended family neither know nor care about the old Family stories.'

'It's a brand-new day?' Lydia laid as much sarcasm into her voice as she was able, which was a lot.

Paul sounded utterly unperturbed. 'Exactly.'

Infuriating.

ARMED with an address for Marty Benson, Lydia went in search of answers. The quicker she finished this job, the faster she could get Paul Fox out of her life and her head. On the way it occurred to her that she hadn't updated Fleet, yet. Before she could examine why she hadn't thought to speak to him, yet, she called his mobile.

'Marty Benson,' Lydia said when he answered. 'I got a name for our unknown murder victim.'

'Great. How?'

Lydia hesitated. Fleet was not going to take this well. 'Paul asked around for missing people in the wider family. Came up with that name.'

'Checked description matches?'

Lydia was walking fast and she slowed down so that she wouldn't sound out of breath. 'Yep.'

'And why didn't Mr Fox come forward with this information earlier? And to the police?'

'You know the answer to the last bit. And he only just found out about Marty. He didn't know before. He had some closer family members go missing and then show up again, changed, which was why he hired me to check out the tunnels.'

'I don't follow,' Fleet said.

Lydia gave him a full recap of the conversation with Paul. After a second of hesitation, she included the bit about Paul suspecting Maddie's involvement.

'Your cousin?'

'The very same. And there's something else.' Lydia wasn't exactly sure how to tell Fleet that her cousin had branded Paul Fox by simply placing a hand on his skin, but she knew she couldn't keep on hiding everything from him, trying to keep everything safely in compartments. He had proven that he trusted her and could be trusted. He had dealt with the existence of a magical statue and barely even blinked.

'That's interesting,' Fleet said, his voice even. 'Is that a common ability in your family?'

'Not as far as I'm aware,' Lydia said. She suddenly wanted the comfort of her coin, but resisted the urge to produce it. 'But Maddie is really strong. She showed more ability than anybody has for years and years. My uncle was very excited by the possibilities.'

'I bet,' Fleet said. 'So you went to talk to Paul, again? In person?'

'He asked to meet. He had information. You know how it goes.'

'I do,' Fleet said. And Lydia couldn't tell what he was thinking. She wished she could see his face.

'It's good news, though, right? It will help the case?'

'If it's true, it might.'

Lydia bit down the urge to get angry. He didn't trust Paul and that was fair enough. She reminded herself, that was bloody sensible.

THE ADDRESS TURNED out to be a dud. The person who opened the door to the unprepossessing tenth floor flat said that Marty Benson had moved out six months earlier and no, they didn't have a forwarding address. After Lydia had produced her Family coin and pushed a little harder, the weasel-faced man revealed that Marty had been chronically short of funds and, his best guess, was that he was sleeping at his place of work. 'Which is?' Lydia said, not bothering to conceal her impatience.

'Not official work, like,' the man said, eyes darting nervously from Lydia's gold coin to her face.

'Dealing,' Lydia said, trying to move the conversation along.

'Bar work! Collecting glasses and that. At the theatre.'

'The theatre?'

'Cable Street,' the man swallowed visibly. 'Don't tell them I sent you there.'

'Tell who?'

'The Foxes,' the man whispered, clearly terrified. 'Please.'

'Interesting,' Lydia said, pocketing her coin. 'Tell me everything you know about Marty and the Fox Family.'

Having ascertained that weasel-face knew nothing else of interest and that he had recently wet himself if the smell emanating from his person was any gauge, Lydia left.

LYDIA WAS ON FOOT, not in the mood to descend into the stale air of the underground, when her phone rang.

'I've got news,' Fleet said. 'Toxicology report has come back on Marty.'

'And?'

'Decent amount of Ramipril and bisoprolol in his blood.'

'And what are those?' Lydia stepped off the pavement and into the shelter of a doorway, sticking a finger in one ear to better hear Fleet's voice.

'ACE inhibitors and beta blockers. Heart medications, basically.'

Marty had been early thirties. Didn't seem like a likely candidate for heart problems. 'Enough to kill him?'

'No. Enough to suggest that he was taking a regular prescribed dose. Consistent with treatment for congestive heart failure, according to our guy. Running his name came up blank on the health service but that doesn't mean he wasn't getting it some other way.'

'Foxes look after their own,' Lydia said. 'They don't like to be part of the main social order, so they see their own doctors and all that. He was young for heart failure, though. That's bad luck.'

'How do they prescribe without it coming up on the system?'

Lydia didn't answer. Black market medications, underground surgeries, favours pulled in from hospital employees; Foxes had their own way of handling things. 'Did it kill him?'

'His heart condition? That's what they're putting on the certificate. A pre-existing condition resulting in heart failure. Of course, the coroner isn't writing down the most important piece of the story.'

Lydia was still thinking about Marty's weak heart. She was suddenly uncomfortably aware of her own, thumping away in her chest. 'What's that?'

'I had an informal chat and the coroner said that he most likely received a massive shock which triggered the heart attack. His condition wasn't likely to kill him for many years, particularly as it was being managed with medication.'

'Fright?'

'Probably. It could also have been intense physical exertion, but neither the scene nor the position of the body are concurrent with that hypothesis.'

Lydia tried to remember the body. His expression. 'He didn't look frightened.'

'Body relaxes after death, he would have lost muscle tone and that would have altered his expression.'

'Lovely.'

'Scared to death, though,' Lydia said. 'That doesn't sound like a real thing.'

'People are easier to kill than you might imagine,' Fleet said.

'You really shouldn't say things like that,' Lydia said. 'You'll end up on a government list.'

LUKE WAS the youngest of the seven Fox brothers. He hadn't long turned eighteen and Lydia could understand why Paul was worried about him. There was something delicate about him, something Lydia couldn't quite put her finger on. Perhaps it was just his youth. Or the fact that he seemed to have a more skittish Fox energy than the rest of his Family. He was attractive, with the animal magnetism common to the Foxes, but Lydia was getting images of darkness and fear, along with the usual taint of earth, fur, tooth and blood.

'Thank you for speaking to me,' Lydia said, taking

the seat opposite Luke in the anonymous branch of Costa on Whitechapel High Street. She had been surprised when he had agreed so readily to the meeting and had assumed that Paul had told him to cooperate.

'Haven't yet,' Luke said. He smirked as if mightily pleased with himself.

'Paul said that you disappeared for four days. Where did you go?'

Luke looked away. 'I've told him.'

'You said 'underground'. That's not very descriptive. Do you mean the tube?'

He shook his head. 'No trains.'

Lydia decided to try a different tack. 'Why don't you like talking about it? Did something bad happen?'

'Nah, not really. It was boring.'

'No phone signal?'

Luke became animated for the first time. 'Don't use mobiles. They're a conspiracy. Government mind control.'

Lydia nodded as if this was perfectly reasonable. 'How long have you felt this way?'

Luke slumped back, the energy draining away. 'Dunno. Years. My whole life.'

'So, it's not a new conviction? I wondered if you saw something in the tunnel-'

'Who said I was in a tunnel?'

'Have you had experience of government harassment? Surveillance?'

Luke perked up. 'Nah, too smart for them. Keep moving, keep off the grid, keep away from their systems of control.'

This was familiar territory for a Fox but, somehow, hearing it come from Luke made it sound standard-crackpot. When Paul had mentioned the Foxes' penchant for living outside the system, it had seemed almost reasonable. 'We can look after our own,' Paul had said. 'Why would we need to be a drain on the social systems which are there to protect the helpless?'

Lydia wanted to put Luke at his ease, so she tried a neutral topic. 'Are you working? Studying?'

He gave her a pitying look. 'Are we done here?'

'How have you been feeling recently? In yourself.'

'What do you mean?'

'Happy, sad, anxious, chilled, excited, energetic, depressed, aimless,' Lydia counted off the words on her fingers.

'Why do you want to know? Are you a therapist?'

'Definitely not,' Lydia said. 'But Paul's worried about you. He asked me to check on you.'

'Paul's not worried,' Luke said, but there was uncertainty in his voice. 'I'm good. I'm chilled. I'm-' Luke broke off, staring to the left of Lydia for a few seconds as if hoping inspiration would appear there. 'Dunno,' he eventually finished. 'I'm normal. I'm the same as everyone else. I'm fine.'

'People often use that word,' Lydia said. 'But they don't really mean it. And it covers a lot of ground.'

When he focused on her, his face was anguished. Just for a split second. In that moment, Luke looked about five years younger, heartbreakingly young and vulnerable. And in the next second he was no longer a frightened kid, but a young adult Fox with all the accompanying swagger. He stood up. 'Time for you to go,' he said. And then, like the good little apprentice he was, he waved his hands. 'Fly away, now. Shoo.'

THAT EVENING, Fleet came round after work and they managed an enjoyable evening. Mainly by not talking about either of their jobs. Later, in bed with Fleet, feeling pleasantly satisfied and a little bit sleepy, Lydia found herself setting fire, once again, to domestic harmony.

She didn't consciously decide to talk about the case, but without agreement from her brain began telling him about her failure to get Luke to open up. They were lying on their sides, faces close and speaking quietly so there was no way she could miss the tension which suddenly appeared. The set of his mouth.

'What?'

'You shouldn't have spoken to a Fox on your own.'

'Paul asked me to investigate.'

'And you're just doing whatever Paul asks, now, are you?'

Lydia turned onto her side, away from Fleet. She was too tired to argue. And still felt a dragging sadness from meeting Luke which was back after a brief respite. She knew what Paul had meant. There was something broken about him. And it was another thing she didn't know how to fix. Her dad's mind was dissolving and her presence made it worse, Jason was stuck in the building and she couldn't work out how to free him, and she had no idea how Marty had died or even if it was murder.

And she was sharing a bed with a copper. A copper who didn't trust her instincts when it came to the Families which was adding insult to injury.

'Lydia,' Fleet said quietly. 'I'm just worried. Please let me help.'

Lydia turned back to Fleet and touched his face. The orange glow of a streetlight was struggling through the curtains and she could see enough to see anguish and uncertainty. 'I'm sorry,' she said. 'I know that.'

He smiled. 'Take me with you next time. I can be your bodyguard. Pretend I've got an earpiece and mutter things like 'the eagle has landed' into my collar.'

'You're an idiot.' Lydia smiled despite herself. 'But you can come with me next time, if you want.'

Peace restored, Lydia curled up to sleep. There was still a nagging sense of foreboding but she pushed it down. It was just this case. Once she had worked out the mystery of Marty's death, everything would settle down.

CHAPTER FOURTEEN

Lydia's phone had been buzzing for the past three hours and she had successfully avoided it, while pretending to herself that she was just too busy writing up some case notes and updating her accounts. In any previous relationship, Lydia would have assumed this was a sign the dalliance was as good as over. It would have been a fatal sign that she was willing to procrastinate with financial records, her least favourite part of running her own business, but this felt different. She wasn't avoiding Fleet's messages and calls because she was bored of him, or no longer liked him in that special after-hours, between-the-sheets, kind of a way. It was quite the opposite. She was scared of how normal and comfortable their relationship had become. How steady. And how frightened she was at the small rift that had opened up between them.

She could see his point of view and knew that he was only worried about her, but the sting of his mistrust was sharp. It felt like a criticism and that was unbearable. Not to mention the fear that he might decide dating her was a step too far from his world, after all. Her stomach clenched and she felt her chest go tight, her breath stopped with the mere possibility of Fleet no longer being hers. Her phone buzzed again, the phone moving on the flat surface of the desk like a frustrated beetle.

She picked it up and tapped out a quick message, apologising for not answering. She didn't actually lie and say that she was doing surveillance or something which required silence, but strongly indicated it. And promised she would call later.

Her second phone, a basic pay as you go model whose selling points were its chunky indestructibility and cleanliness - no stored numbers, no personal information - rang. The tones available were limited and already quaintly retro in style. So the pace of the modern world span; faster and faster. Lydia checked the number and answered. 'Hey, Mum. You okay?'

'I need to see you.'

It wasn't her mum. Henry Crow's voice was the one she knew from childhood. Warm, but fast and definite. Not a voice to argue with.

LYDIA DROVE to Beckenham in her ancient blue Volvo. It was making some interesting noises when she braked or changed gear, suggesting that its tank-like indestructibility might be coming to an end. It was boxy and the dark blue paint had a dusty sheen, even when freshly washed, and the inside smelled of late-night stakeouts and the fake-pine air freshener that the previous owner had favoured, but Lydia would be sad to see it go when the time came. The Volvo represented freedom. She had bought it and driven to Scotland. A decision which had led to her training as a P.I with her old boss in Aberdeen and, for the very first time in her life, a sense of purpose. The feeling that she was doing something she ought to be doing and was good at. Or, at least, had the potential to be good at.

Getting parked in suburbia was marginally easier than it was in Camberwell, but Lydia still had to circle the street with The Elm Tree a couple of times before snagging a spot large enough. Henry Crow spent Thursday evenings at his local, regular as clockwork. That he had proposed a meeting there on a Friday afternoon, meant only one thing; he wanted to discuss something he didn't want Lydia's mother to hear.

Her dad was sitting at his usual spot, his back to the wall and a pint of bitter and a folded newspaper on the small circular table. Lydia dragged a stool to the side of the table and kissed her dad's cheek before sitting down.

'Lydia,' Henry said. His eyes were clear and piercing. 'I need to get right down to it.'

'Okay,' Lydia said.

'Write this down,' he said, 'I don't know how long I've got.'

'What do you mean?' Lydia felt a spurt of pure terror. 'What's wrong?'

Henry gave her a look which sent her straight back to childhood. Henry had been a kind and funny father, quick to hug and softly-spoken, but there was a core of steel. When he had been displeased, Lydia had never felt a fear like it. She hurriedly dug her notebook and pencil from her bag.

He nodded. 'I had a little charm, something your grandpa gave me back in the day. It helps people think. For someone who isn't suffering cognitive degeneration it turns them into a stone-cold genius. For an hour or so, anyway.'

Lydia realised that her dad had used some magic. Something he had promised years ago to stay away from. A promise that he had kept, as far as Lydia was aware. She had her father back in his full mental capacity and that felt like a miracle, but she knew that he probably didn't have another shot of brain juice sitting around. She couldn't waste time getting emotional. 'Do you remember a Silver wedding at The Fork. Amy Silver and Jason-'

Her dad interrupted. 'Don't derail me. Please. I've got lots to tell you. Got to keep it all straight.' He tapped the side of his head for emphasis.

She nodded, and placed the nib of the pencil on a fresh sheet of paper. 'What did you want to tell me?'

'Alejandro was always ambitious. He was obsessed with researching the old ways, thought that we could be so much more powerful than we were. That we deserved to be back on top, as he put it.'

'The Silvers haven't exactly been suffering,' Lydia couldn't stop herself from saying.

'It's all a matter of degree,' Henry said. 'And Silvers like things shiny. Alejandro told me he couldn't stand to have his family's treasure in the British Museum. Burned him up inside, it did. He had a plan to get it out.'

'He succeeded,' Lydia said.

Henry nodded. 'I didn't say anything at the time. Would have sparked a riot. All the Families rushing to grab their artefacts, everyone running around worrying that the sky was falling, that Alejandro was planning some kind of takeover of London.'

'And you probably didn't want to draw attention to the fact that we didn't put our coin there in the first place.'

Henry smiled. 'Exactly.' He leaned forward. 'Don't say it out loud, though. Never admit it to anybody else. Did you ever wonder why there are only four of us?'

Lydia struggled to keep up, Henry's right hand was tapping on the table, drumming a beat and she longed to reach out and put her own hand over it, to still him.

'Four Families with a little... something extra? Grandpa told me that we are just the only ones left. That back before there were written records, that it was common. Not everybody had something, but everybody knew somebody who did. The ones who survived are the ones who raised their next generation with the knowledge, passed on what they knew. We did it through stories. Silvers found a way to capture it in metal. Pearls, feathers knows what they did, and the Foxes did it by inbreeding.'

'Is that true?'

Henry shrugged. 'Who knows? That's the story. And none of us can get too sniffy about that subject. Go back far enough and everybody was at it. Like royalty, it was the only way to keep the power close.'

Well that was a thought to haunt her nightmares.

'But we passed it through stories. Those tales I used to tell you? Those bedtime stories? That was your inheritance,' he smiled. 'I hope you were listening.'

And then, as if running a race he knew he couldn't win, he began running through them, again. 'I know the stories, Dad,' Lydia broke in at one point and he smacked the table. 'Write.'

There were ones she knew well, half-remembered tales or ones which had a few more violent details than she recalled, details he must have left out when she was a little girl, and stories she didn't recognise at all. There was the Night Raven, of course, and the time the Fox flattered the Crow into dropping her piece of cheese, and more prosaic ones like the story of how Great-Grandpa Crow had outwitted council objections and secured funding for the Camberwell College of Arts in the eighteen-nineties, and ensured its doors would be open to talented people of all classes. Then there were the other stories of Grandpa and Great-Grandpa and Great-Great Grandpa that were less wholesome. Protection. Extortion. Racketeering.

'I thought I'd have plenty of time,' Henry said as his voice grew thin with speaking so intensely and quickly. 'Once you'd decided to join the Family, I thought there would be time.'

'You were sure I would?' Lydia's pride was pricked. She hated the thought that she had been so predictable.

'It's in your blood, but more than that, it's in your

head.' He looked sad, almost ashamed. 'I made sure of that.'

Lydia didn't realise that she had produced her coin until she felt the edges digging into her palm. She was gripping it tightly and she forced her hand to relax.

Her dad changed mood abruptly and began laughing with a hoarse, wheezing sound. 'Sorry, sorry. Just having you on.' His accent had gone full south London. 'I wasn't sure of anything. I just wanted you to have the choice. Didn't feel right not to pass it on to you.' The laughing stopped. 'It's all I've got. It's my legacy.'

ONCE SHE HAD NAVIGATED the appalling traffic and made it back to Camberwell, Lydia rang Fleet, as promised. She had good intentions of having a proper, grown-up conversation to patch over the recent awkwardness in their relationship, but her mouth seemed to have other ideas.

She had tried to ask her dad, again, about Amy Silver, but the charm or mojo or whatever it had been had worn off abruptly. One moment, Henry Crow had been clear-eyed and laughing and the next he had been painfully confused, thrown back into tangled confusion.

'Can you look Amy Silver up on your database?' Lydia knew it wasn't a romantic or conciliatory opener and she mentally kicked herself. Self-sabotage; one of her strongest abilities. 'She died in the eighties..'

To his credit, Fleet took the conversation in his stride. 'Who is Amy Silver?'

'Someone who died at The Fork,' Lydia said. 'In the

eighties. I've researched the newspapers but the stories were light on detail. I can't find a follow up with a cause of death'

'Right,' Fleet said slowly 'What has she got to do with Marty? Or is this another case?'

'No case,' Lydia said,

'What aren't you telling me?' Fleet asked.

'She died at The Fork. I'm just interested.'

'In the history of the building?' Fleet said, scepticism laid on thick. 'I could do with a reason to be poking around the files. Everything is recorded these days, you know, I'll have to justify the search.'

'Isn't there a way to bypass the system?'

'No,' Fleet said, clearly exasperated. 'That's the whole point.'

'It's stupidly restrictive,' Lydia said. 'Why don't they just trust you?'

'It's about the public trusting us,' Fleet said. 'And making watertight cases with a clear trail for every single investigative action taken. Means fewer cases lost at court on technicalities.' He paused. 'At least, that's the theory.'

'I know all that,' Lydia said, 'but I think it's ridiculous.' She was still annoyed and unable to let go of it. It seemed like a safe thing to be cross about, something manageable in a world which was increasingly complicated and confusing and full of insurmountable issues.

'I'll see what I can do,' Fleet said.

'Thank you,' Lydia said.

'Did you want to come round to mine tonight?'

'How about my place?' Lydia said automatically.

'Not tonight,' Fleet said. 'You're welcome here, but I'm going to have an early one. I want to be at home.'

'Right.' Lydia knew it was a perfectly reasonable request and completely unfair to keep making Fleet come to her place. She had to make concessions, compromises, all of those good and sensible and mature things. 'I'm knackered, too,' she said. 'See you tomorrow?'

'Sure,' Fleet said. 'Sleep tight.'

Hell Hawk. Lydia finished the open bottle of whisky and went to bed in a foul mood. She knew it was her own fault and that made it worse.

CHAPTER FIFTEEN

After a poor night of sleep and the required caffeine shot to get her moving, Lydia went looking for Jason. She realised she hadn't seen him since the séance and, with a stab of guilt, that she ought to have checked on him before. Her father's stories had left her with the lingering impression that the Crows had not always been the sharing and caring type, and she was determined not to follow blindly in their footsteps. Not without good cause, at any rate.

After checking his bedroom and the kitchen, Lydia went out onto the roof terrace. Jason was next to the railing, staring out, his head tilted to look down the alley which ran behind their building, toward the main road.

'Hey,' Lydia said gently, not wanting to startle the ghost. Which was funny, if she thought about it.

He turned slowly and Lydia saw, with a twinge in her own heart, that his eyes were sad. He folded his arms, tucking his hands into the large turned-up cuffs of his voluminous suit jacket.

'Any luck?' Lydia knew that Jason spent hours trying to lean out over the railing that ran along the edge of the roof terrace. Either that, or attempting to step outside the back door which led from the kitchen to the alley where the wheelie bins were stored.

He shook his head and Lydia pulled a sympathetic face in response.

'Any luck your end?'

'I've asked Fleet to look into Amy's death,' Lydia said. A pause. 'I'm really sorry about that.'

'What? Her death or the séance?'

'Both.'

He nodded. 'I just feel stuck. I know I've been saying that for ages, but now I really feel it. I knew she was gone, before, but now I know she's somewhere else. She's continuing on, in some form and in some way, but not with me. It's worse.'

'You want to be with her.'

He nodded. 'So much.'

'I'm sorry,' Lydia said, again, wishing it wasn't so inadequate a sentence. She stepped forward and put her arms around Jason, ignoring the freezing cold and slight buzz of electricity that seemed to jump along her skin when she touched him, and hugged him as tightly as she could.

'I've got bad news,' Fleet said, calling her later.

146

'There's a reason the journos didn't report many details on Amy Silver. It's a cold case.'

'Unsolved?'

'Amy Silver died on her wedding day. She had just married a Jason Montefort and the happy couple, plus selected family and friends were celebrating at The Fork.'

Lydia bit down on the urge to say 'I know, what else?' as Fleet continued: 'Amy Silver was aged twenty-three and her new husband was twenty-four, neither had any health problems, no enemies that the investigation turned up, and no connections with organised crime or, for that matter, crime of any kind. Which makes their selection of The Fork as a wedding venue extremely peculiar.'

'Hey!' Lydia said. 'That's my family you're maligning.' With good reason, but still. 'Cause of death?'

'Unknown,' Fleet said. 'No marks on the bodies. No signs of struggle. Nothing in the toxicology report or the post-mortem.'

'Nothing?'

Fleet shook his head. 'It makes no sense. Young healthy couples don't just drop dead for no reason. There must have been a mistake.'

'With the investigation?'

'It's possible,' Fleet said. 'This was before the integrated database system was brought in. The investigation records aren't as thorough as they would be now. And it's possible that something got lost interdepartmentally. Or even through poor communication with another borough.'

'Can I see the post-mortem reports?'

Fleet sighed. 'May as well be hung for a sheep as a lamb.'

WHEN HE ARRIVED LATER he tapped in an access code and then passed across his laptop. The documents had all been hard copy originally and had been scanned in. It was odd to read handwritten notes and Lydia had the weird sensation that it had all happened a very long time ago. The past was another country. Weirder still, she was reading about the corpse of the person she shared a flat with. The accompanying photographs made her draw her breath in. Jason was laid out on the examination table, his face a mask. It was both familiar and different. No matter how many dead people Lydia saw, the initial shock was the same. The emptiness of the physical body without its soul intact, the essential wrongness of it. She looked around, making sure Jason hadn't appeared. He definitely shouldn't see this.

'Are you okay?'

Lydia glanced up and found Fleet looking at her with deep concern. 'Fine,' she said quickly.

'You don't look fine. What is it?'

I'm looking at my friend's dead body. 'Nothing. What can we do to work the case?'

Fleet shook his head. 'I'm not sure, it was a long time ago. I can't imagine we'll turn up anything new.'

'Cold cases do get solved though. Sometimes.'

'This isn't even a murder, though. It's two tragic, unexplained deaths. Suspicious, but with no cause of death, no motive, no suspects.' Fleet spread his hands. 'I'm sorry. I don't see where to start.'

As he spoke, Lydia looked back at the image of Jason on the screen. She pushed her emotions to the side and focused on detail. On fact. There had to be something. The screen went blank and for a second Lydia assumed Fleet's laptop had suddenly run out of charge. Then the screen came back to life but instead of the image of Jason, there was a black screen with a text box in the middle which said 'error, file not found.'

Lydia looked up. 'That doesn't seem like good news.'

'Just a bug,' Fleet said, but he didn't sound sure. 'I'll pop into the office, see what IT say.'

'You'll go, now?'

'It's obviously important or you wouldn't have asked.' Fleet put his laptop back in its sleeve and kissed Lydia goodbye.

Once he had gone, Lydia went and had a hot shower, then spent some time tidying and cleaning the flat. It wasn't normal behaviour and she didn't feel like examining the reasons why, she just went with it. The place was disgusting, anyway.

A COUPLE OF HOURS LATER, Fleet returned. The sky had darkened and Lydia's stomach was rumbling. 'Takeaway?' She asked the moment Fleet had taken off his coat.

'It's a cold case,' Fleet said, 'but that's not the issue.' His skin had gone the grey-ish colour it did when he was extremely worried.

'What's wrong?' Lydia's hunger fled.

'I had a call from a well-spoken man from the NCA.'

'National Crime Agency? Bloody hell.'

Fleet nodded. 'And he explained that the case had been handled by them, and then had been taken over by the intelligence service. And that any further questions I may have regarding it should be directed to their office.'

'Well that's good,' Lydia said. 'Did he give you a contact name?'

'No. And I got the distinct impression that I wouldn't be having any further questions.' Fleet ran a hand over his face. 'He made it very clear that my curiosity had been entirely satiated. Should I wish to continue with a policing career.'

'Hell Hawk,' Lydia said quietly.

'I've come up against security before, but never like this. Usually it's a redacted file and you have some warning. I've never had a file disappear while looking at it.'

'Did you get an inkling as to why it had gone to the NCA?'

'Organised crime, most likely. Especially given The Fork link.'

'When he said intelligence service...' She paused. 'Did he mean MI5?'

Fleet nodded. 'I don't wish to state the obvious, but the chances of us getting access to the complete case files are zero. Less than zero, actually.'

'Thank you for trying.'

'After the phone call, the entire file disappeared, not just that report. Even searching their names showed an error message saying the link was temporarily unavailable. That's quick work. It must have been flagged as an immediate priority, which is alarming for something so long ago. What possible relevance can it have?'

'And there was nothing about Amy? Nothing you saw before this?'

'Redacted,' Fleet said. 'The phone call interrupted me and then it was all gone.'

Lydia looked around nervously. She had the sudden feeling that they were being watched and half-expected a government spook in a long coat to be eye-balling them as they spoke.

'Don't worry,' Fleet was saying. 'I convinced him I was just an idiot copper. Not hard to do. The intelligence services don't have the highest regard for our mental capabilities. They refer to us as the brawn. Or cannon fodder. And a few other names I won't repeat in polite society.'

Lydia smiled. 'Well, I am a lady, after all.'

'Exactly.' Fleet returned her smile, but Lydia wasn't convinced. He was shaken and that was a scary sight. Fleet always appeared utterly unflappable.

CHAPTER SIXTEEN

The Fox Family were known for two things; giving you a good time and robbing you blind while doing so. Nobody knew how many nightclubs and bars they controlled, but if you were on a bender in the Whitechapel area of London, it was safe to assume you were drinking with the Foxes. Lydia wasn't very familiar with the area which was enough to put her on high alert. Add in the fact that she was visiting with the express purpose of finding out more about one of their own, and Lydia felt distinctly jumpy. Marty Benson had apparently had a job collecting glasses at the theatre on Cable Street and Lydia was hoping to get chatting to some people who knew him. If she could find out more about how the man lived, perhaps she could find out how he died.

She had wanted to bring Emma. Both for moral support and to make sure she actually saw her best friend, aware that, as always, her personal relationships were at the bottom of her priority list and that wasn't a good way to live. At least, according to the entrepreneurial podcast she had listened to while running around the park. She had been looking for tips on growing her small business and had, instead, been treated to lots of touchy-feely self-development bollocks. It had clearly got under her skin, which was annoying.

Her second choice had been scoping the place out on her own, but she had the mistake of mentioning it to Fleet and he had insisted on tagging along. 'I don't need baby-sitting,' she said as she swiped mascara over her lashes and applied red lipstick. She was wearing a silky black top which had a subtle sparkle, black skinny jeans and had swapped her usual Dr Martens for heeled boots. She wanted to blend in with the party crowd, but this was as far as she was willing to go. 'You don't need to come.' Lydia was still annoyed with Fleet for not trusting her judgement and issuing orders. It was a good thing she liked him so much.

'I know that,' Fleet said, crossing the room to stand behind her, his hands resting on her hips. 'It's not a hardship to go drinking with you. Have you looked in a mirror?'

Lydia was, in fact, peering into one at that very moment, but she got his meaning. She looked over her shoulder. 'If this look is working for you, just be here when I get home. You don't need to escort me into the Foxes' den in order to get lucky. I'm easy like that.'

He laughed and Lydia watched his eyes in the mirror. His pupils were dilated and she thought she might be successful in her distraction technique. He dipped his head and kissed her neck, sending shivers through her body. But then he straightened up and said. 'You're still very resistant to this whole relationship idea, aren't you? I like you. I want to spend time with you out of the bedroom, too.'

Lydia rolled her eyes so hard she thought they might not return to normal. 'This is work, and you are being gallant. Unnecessarily gallant. Weirdly gallant.'

Fleet chose to ignore this and continued with his earnest conversation. 'We're a team. At least, I think we're a team. Am I wrong?'

Lydia forced herself to engage with the conversation. She knew she couldn't keep pushing Fleet away. It wasn't fair and it wasn't kind. He had proven himself trustworthy, now it was her problem that she wasn't letting him in. Damn it. That self-development stuff had really taken root. She spun around in his arms and put her hand on his face. 'We are a team,' she said. 'I trust you. I'm glad you're here.'

Fleet looked like he wanted to laugh.

'Shut up,' Lydia said. 'I'm trying, here.'

He grabbed her in a hug and then kissed her lipstick off, leaving them both breathless and wide-eyed. There was a bubble of hope in Lydia's chest. That the weirdness that had been growing between them had been an illusion, banished in an easy instant.

LIPSTICK REAPPLIED and an uneventful train ride later, Lydia and Fleet emerged from the station on Cable Street. Lydia had been very happy that it had been an over ground journey for a change. She was sick of descending underneath the city and fantasised about boycotting the tube entirely. They walked along Cable Street, the relative quiet broken by the clatter of an occasional train running along the overhead tracks. The street was narrow and had the ubiquitous mix of modern block buildings interspersed with Georgian townhouses with creamy stone work and classic London brick facades. The Jack The Ripper museum, a reminder of the area's insalubrious past, sat next to a mini-mart. Hitting Royal Mint Street, Lydia knew they had gone too far, and they doubled back to find the venue. The theatre was an old music hall. It had been in business since eighteen forty-eight and generations of local kids had grown up sneaking into the shows. The management team didn't carry the Fox name, but they had intermingled plenty, and everybody knew that Tristan Fox's name was on the title deeds for the property. Lydia sensed Fox before she saw the understated doorway to the theatre. It had been painted crimson, once upon a time, but that colour had faded. A couple of framed billposters were on the wall next to the door and the only indication of the wonders within was the over-sized wrought-iron hanging light which curved out from the brickwork and cast a perfect yellow circle on the ground.

The show that night was a burlesque act, opened by a hipster accordionist with a cult following. Lydia had bought tickets online and she showed them on her phone to the woman in topcoat and tailcoat who was standing at the bottom of the stairs. 'Drink first,' Lydia said, following the sign for the bar.

Dominating the room was a boat-size bar made from intricate curling ironwork and topped with polished Verdigris copper. The walls were peeling and cracked plaster and the bar was actually a series of interconnecting rooms, through the doorway Lydia spied an upright piano with a vintage marquee sign above it. The word 'Vixen' was picked out in large metal letters, lit with bulbs.

'Subtle,' Fleet said, looking around. 'I'll get the first round.' He headed to the moderate crush at the bar and Lydia took a quick tour of the rooms, getting a feel for the scope of the place. In the back rooms, every detail wasn't just in-keeping with the building's status as a grade-two listed piece of cultural history, it appeared to be original. If you removed the modern hairstyles and clothes of the patrons and swapped out the electric light, Lydia would have believed she was looking at a Victorian drinking den.

In the last room, an intimate space with ochre-coloured walls and a red-velvet sofa, Lydia was hit with a fresh wave of Fox magic. Luckily, she had been swimming through the stuff since arriving and was fully prepared. There was the momentary urge to rip her clothes off and rub against the stranger who had just got up from the sofa and was heading for the doorway, but she managed to contain it by squeezing every muscle in her body. The figure was a woman. Anywhere from Lydia's age to mid-forties, with long, curled auburn hair like a pre-Raphaelite painting, and eyes which, in this light, looked pale green. She was very beautiful and Lydia wasn't entirely sure if it was her desire for information, the Fox magic, or basic human attraction which made her touch the woman's arm and smile. 'Which way to the stage? This place is a warren.'

The woman smiled back, taking in Lydia's form with a subtle up-and-down look. 'I'll show you,' she said.

Lydia followed the woman through the rooms and out to the main stairs. 'Back down to the main entrance and straight through the double doors on your left.'

'Ah, sorry. I'm an idiot. I thought it was somewhere up here.'

'Nah. Unless you've got a gallery seat?'

Lydia shook her head. The woman was turning away so Lydia took a punt. 'Can I buy you a drink?'

She looked back over her shoulder. 'Sure.'

Lydia spotted Fleet, holding two glasses and heading in her direction. She caught his eye and gave a small head shake. She saw him take in the sight of her companion and change course, heading for the doorway to the next room as if he had always been going that way.

Once Lydia had a gin and tonic for her new companion and a whisky for herself, she looked around the packed room for a quiet corner or spare seat.

'We could go into the hall early, if you like? Get a good spot.'

Lydia realised that she had assumed her ticket would have a seat number. It would be quieter in the hall, she assumed, too. Better for chatting. She followed the woman down the stairs and into the hall. It smelled of greasepaint and cigarettes, with an undertone of spilled alcohol, and had the shabby charm of a Victorian theatre but in miniature. The gallery seating was just a couple of rows with a low balustrade. The stalls had one central aisle and they went right up almost to the edge of the stage. The proscenium arch had plaster mouldings depicting twisting vines and flowers and there were chandeliers hanging from the ceiling, casting the scene in a warm glow.

They weren't the first inside, several people were already seated in scattered groups. 'I'm Alex, by the way. Cheers.'

Lydia raised her glass in return. 'Becca.'

'First time here?'

'That obvious?' Lydia took a healthy sip of her whisky, hoping it would encourage Alex to do the same. She had about twenty minutes before the curtain went up and had to make them count.

Alex sipped her gin and tonic before speaking. 'Play your cards right and I'll show you the secret passages.'

Lydia bit her tongue to stop an inappropriate joke from passing her lips. She was trying to walk the line of flirty, just in case Alex was interested, but not overtly so, so that she could back off to 'just friendly' if her gaydar turned out to be broken.

'Under the floor,' Alex tapped the ground with one high-heeled foot. There are hidden trapdoors and passages which lead from the cellars to the river. Used to be, drunk sailors were robbed and then dumped in the Thames.' She raised an eyebrow, waiting for Lydia's reaction.

Lydia obliged with an avid expression. 'History was

never that colourful when I was at school. I might have done a bit better in my exams if it had been.'

'How long ago was that?'

Lydia smiled. 'If you want to know my age, just ask.'

'Fair enough. How old are you?'

'Young enough not to be offended by that question,' Lydia said. 'You?'

'Older than I look,' Alex said.

'The Holy Grail,' Lydia said. 'And, at the risk of sounding cheesy, do you come here often?'

'Fairly,' Alex said, a smile playing around her lips.

Lydia knew that Alex was a member of the Fox Family, but she didn't know whether she was deeply affiliated. The Fox vibe was pretty strong, enough for her assume Alex was main bloodline, and they were in a Fox-owned emporium. Still, Lydia didn't want to make assumptions. Especially after Paul's little speech about his Family and how loosely they were organised. She needed a seamless and non-suspicious way to ask about Marty. Quickly. People were filing into the theatre ready for the show to start. 'I bet this would be even better with a little chemical enhancement.' She blurted the words out and Alex frowned. *Smooth, Lydia. Really smooth.*

'You're into that?'

Lydia shrugged. 'Nothing serious.'

Alex looked at her for another moment, clearly calculating something. 'Did you speak to me because you assumed I'm a dealer?'

'No!' Lydia said. 'I just thought you'd be the person to ask. You strike me as a woman who knows how to get things done.'

'Flatterer.' Alex's tone was deadpan, but her eyes were smiling.

Lydia didn't have time to breathe out in relief, as Alex was on her feet, holding out a hand to Lydia. 'Come on, then.'

'What? Isn't it about to start?'

'No time to waste, then,' Alex towed Lydia down the aisle toward the stage. She turned right and marched past the front row of seats and to an unmarked door, tucked in the corner. Behind this was a short passage which smelled of drains and cigarettes. Lydia was right behind Alex and not at all prepared for what happened next. Alex turned swiftly and grabbed Lydia by the neck with both hands, pinning her against the peeling and slightly damp wall so hard and so strong that she was forced onto tiptoe.

'Who are you?'

'Becca,' Lydia managed and was rewarded with renewed pressure on her neck.

'What do you want, Becca?' Alex's tone clearly conveyed her disbelief in Lydia's pseudonym.

Lydia managed to make a strangled sort of sound. She hammed it up in the hope that Alex would release her neck. When she felt the grip ease a little, she brought her hands up between Alex's outstretched arms and used them to break her hold. A swift knee to the stomach brought Alex over and Lydia moved behind to get an arm around her neck, forcing her chin up. She had never been so glad to have been taking Ju-Jitsu classes at the gym.

'I'm looking for Marty Benson,' Lydia said. 'He owes me money and I heard he deals around here sometimes.'

Alex sagged, the fight going out of her body. Lydia wasn't fooled. Foxes were excellent at playing dead. Tricksy. She maintained pressure with her arm and braced herself for action.

'Why didn't you say,' Alex said, her voice strained and quiet. 'I can take you to him.' On the last word she bucked her body and attempted to throw Lydia, her hands pulling at Lydia's arm.

Lydia had been prepared, but she still wasn't going to be able to maintain control for much longer. She still wasn't exactly an action hero, despite the gym. And her size was never a help in these situations. There were definite downsides to being a short arse.

'I don't think that's likely,' Lydia said, in between gasps for air. Holding Alex was getting increasingly difficult. 'He's dead.'

CHAPTER SEVENTEEN

Instantly the fight went out of Alex. For real this time. Lydia still wasn't going to let her go, but then the door at the end of the passage opened and Fleet appeared. He took in the scene and closed the gap with a couple of long-legged strides.

'I'm fine,' Lydia said, letting go of Alex.

Fleet crouched down and peered at Alex. 'Are you all right? Do you need medical assistance?'

Alex shook her head. Lydia was rubbing life back into her sore arm and she took in Alex's expression. It was blank with shock. And grief. 'I'm sorry,' she said. 'Was he a friend of yours?'

Alex nodded.

'What happened here?' Fleet said, touching Lydia's face briefly. His fingers were warm and she felt the warm gleam from his skin seep into her cheek. 'Do I need to arrest anybody?'

Alex's eyes widened and she struggled to stand up.

'No,' Lydia said. 'I'm not intending to press charges for assault. And I don't think we breached the peace.'

'You assaulted me,' Alex said. 'Not to mention committed fraud. *Becca.*'

'Lydia Crow,' Lydia said, holding out a hand. 'Pleased to meet you.'

'A Crow?' Alex closed her eyes. 'This just gets better and better. I should have known.' She glanced at Fleet. 'What are you doing with a copper?'

The Fox Family were even less keen on the law than the Crows. Historically, the Foxes were free spirits, priding themselves on living separate to the social systems. It was one of the reasons Lydia hadn't been particularly surprised they hadn't found Marty Benson in any databases. Foxes stayed below ground in every sense.

'I'm sorry for your loss,' Lydia said. 'I'm investigating his death at the request of Paul Fox.' She fished in her pocket for one of her business cards. The image of the crow on the front was a bit on the nose, but Emma had designed it for her and assured that it was her 'USP'. Lydia didn't particularly want her unique selling point to be her Family heritage, but she knew beggars couldn't be choosers and she had bills to pay.

Alex took the card and stared at it for a few moments. She still looked slightly stunned and, Lydia knew this was a window of opportunity, before her thought processes properly came back online. 'Can you think of anybody who would want to hurt Marty?'

Alex raised hollow eyes to focus on Lydia. 'He didn't kill himself?'

Lydia shook her head. 'Why would you think that? Was he depressed?'

'Marty had a lot of problems. He wasn't always happy, but who is?' Her mouth twisted. 'He'd become pretty paranoid, though. I thought he was maybe sampling his own stash a bit too much. The grass that comes over now is stronger than it used to be. It can really mess you up.'

'What was he paranoid about?'

Alex hesitated.

Fleet had melted to the side, displaying his enviable ability to appear completely absent and non-threatening. It was impressive considering the sheer size of the man. Lydia held herself still, leaving a silence for Alex to fill.

'Did you see him?'

Lydia nodded.

'You know about the tattoo, then?'

'Cursed,' Lydia said. 'Pretty bleak.'

Alex shuddered. 'He really believed it. Some bastard cousin of his told him he was marked and that's when he really...' She trailed off before straightening and looking Lydia in the eye. 'He was always a bit cracked. A bit... Nervy. But after that he went full paranoia. Thought that he was going to die.'

'Because someone in his family told him he was cursed?'

'I know it doesn't sound like much, but we're a superstitious pack.'

'It sounds like plenty,' Lydia said. 'Crows are the same.'

Alex nodded at the admission. 'I don't know why he

165

was so sure it meant death, though. I mean, that's a pretty big conclusion from 'cursed'. He wasn't usually so dramatic.'

'Did he ever explain what he was afraid of? Specifically?'

'Not really,' Alex gave a small shrug.

The colour was returning to her face.

'Did he mention being afraid about a particular person or place? Was there any trouble that you know about?'

'He did say he deserved it,' Alex said. 'But I just thought he was being negative. He did get down sometimes. Wasn't the most confident person underneath it all.'

'Anybody new in his life? Any threats made?'

Alex shook her head. 'Same old, same old. He wasn't much for socialising. Just his usual crowd, half of whom were his customers. Other half were people he'd known forever.'

'Significant other? Girlfriend? Boyfriend?'

'Not since Katy.'

'Katy?'

'I never met her. She died a couple of years before I knew Marty. He never got over it.'

'How did she die?' Lydia felt ice run down her spine. She felt she knew what Alex was going to say before the words were out of her mouth. It was a weird moment of premonition and it made her feel vaguely nauseous.

'Bad luck, really,' Alex said. 'Marty was getting into recreational drugs, even then, and he persuaded Katy to take MDMA with him. She died.'

'Bad pill?'

'The opposite, premo grade, very pure. They took a whole pill each, rather than pacing it with a quarter or a half. Marty was fine and Katy had a heart attack.'

'I'm amazed he was doing drugs with his heart condition.'

'That's a recent thing, I think,' Alex said. 'He developed a weak valve or something through doing too much speed and other stuff... He went in hard after Katy died. Kind of ironic, really.'

'Tragic, I would say,' Lydia said. 'You got a last name for Katy?'

Alex blinked. 'No, not that I remember.' She seemed to take in the card Lydia had passed her properly. 'This is your job?'

'Yep,' Lydia said. 'One more question. Who else knew Marty was sick?'

'You mean his heart thing?' Alex gave a short laugh. 'Everyone. It wasn't a secret.'

'Did you know he was sleeping here?' Lydia said.

Alex hesitated and then nodded. 'You know the passages I told you about? There are cellars and store rooms underneath this building.'

More underground. Fabulous. Lydia shivered.

Alex, sandwiched between Fleet and Lydia to stop her from losing them, directed the way to a store room with a hessian mat in the middle of the floor and metal shelving lining the walls filled with bar supplies and sundries.

After a little more encouragement, a reluctant Alex kicked the mat away revealing a trapdoor. 'It's not fit for human habitation,' Alex said. 'Marty showed me once and I told him he would get pneumonia from the damp. He didn't listen, though.'

Fleet lifted the door, revealing a short metal ladder bolted just underneath the opening. Lydia used the flashlight on her phone to look around. The floor was quite far below the end of the ladder and the beam of light from her phone was too feeble to see very far around the cellar. The light from the room they were in didn't make much difference, either, it was as if the space below was repelling illumination.

'You're not really working for Paul Fox, are you?'

'He's paying me for this particular case, yes.' Lydia thought she could see a sleeping bag and a lumpy shape which might have been a duffel bag. She looked at Fleet. 'We have to go down.'

He nodded. 'Me first.' He reached down and grabbed the top of the ladder, giving it a good shake. The metal screeched and rattled in answer. 'Not sure about that. I'm a bit heavier than Marty.'

'Have you ever been down here?'

Alex shook her head. 'Gives me the creeps.'

Fleet hung his legs over the edge, placing them on one of the rungs of the ladder and then manoeuvred himself around so that he was facing the right direction. He was stood on the ladder, now, his legs under the floor and his torso above it. From a certain angle, it would have made an interesting photograph. Adonis rising from the floor. Or somebody who had been miraculously cut in two but was still smiling.

He descended quickly, the ladder complaining all the way.

'That's not encouraging,' Lydia said.

'It's fine,' Fleet called up. 'And I'll catch you.'

'You first,' Lydia said to Alex.

'No way,' she shook her head. 'It's haunted. I'm not going down there.'

'I doubt that,' Lydia said, but she mimicked Fleet's technique and climbed down. It might be easier to have a good poke around without Marty's friend breathing down their necks, anyway.

The ladder was cold under her palms and the air was musty. She felt her lungs tighten against the damp in the air and she began to breathe in shallow sips.

Fleet had clicked on a small torch which gave more light than Lydia's phone. She immediately added it to her growing list of wanted gadgets. The walls of the cellar were rough brick, with patches which looked as if they might have been skimmed at one point in history with a wash or thin plaster, which was now patchy and diseased. The greenish mildew coated the walls at the base, spreading more thinly as you went up and blooming thickly again where the walls met the ceiling. It was much higher than Lydia expected and studying the walls revealed the reason. It looked like the current floor was lower than the one put in originally. As if they had decided to dig a little deeper.

Fleet was looking around, playing the torch beam across the ceiling.

'Maybe they had plans to stash stage sets down here

at one point? Seems awkward, but would account for the space.'

'Not sure I've been in enough basements to make a judgement,' Fleet said. 'Not ones that haven't been converted, anyway. This is probably the last bit of undeveloped space in Whitechapel.'

Lydia crouched down next to the sleeping bag. It was very light and, to her untrained eye, seemed like a good one. She took a note of the brand name and snapped a couple of pictures. Under the sleeping bag, there was a bright blue mat. Also thin and light. Also probably 'technical' gear of some kind. 'Either Marty was a keen hiker, or he knocked off a camping gear shop.'

'Or he borrowed this stuff,' Fleet turned his face up to the rectangle of light, where Alex was visible. She was kneeling and peering in. 'Did you lend him this kit?'

'No, he brought it with him. I think. Why? Does it matter?'

'Probably not,' Fleet said.

'Is there anything down there?' Alex said. 'Have you found his stash?'

'Not yet,' Lydia called back. She unzipped the sleeping bag, and spread it open. There were a couple of balled-up socks at the bottom and a pair of boxers which Lydia had no desire to touch.

Fleet had snapped on a pair of gloves and was unzipping the duffel bag. He tipped it upside down and a twist of clothes fell onto the dank floor. Lydia made to look through them and Fleet said. 'Gloves. And go easy, there might be sharps.'

'Needles?'

'Or a blade.'

'Did he inject?' Lydia called up. There was no answer and Lydia couldn't see Alex anymore. Then the trapdoor closed, cutting the available light. Instantly the corners of the room disappeared and Lydia could only see what was illuminated by their torchlight.

'Hell hawk,' she swore quietly. Then, loudly. 'Alex! Open the door!'

There was a scraping sound and Lydia realised that Alex was dragging something on top of the hatch. Marvellous.

'Well, we probably should have seen that one coming.' Fleet sounded remarkably calm and Lydia decided to believe that was because he had a wonderful plan.

'Is there a lamp? He can't have lived down here in darkness.' The torch beam swept the floor around the sleeping bag and pile of clothes until it hit a candle stuck in a bottle.

'How Dickensian,' Fleet said. 'I don't know if I want to use a flame down here.'

'It's too damp to go up,' Lydia said with more conviction than she felt. The mix of odours was varied as well as terrible, and she could easily imagine that some sort of marsh gas was seeping into the basement.

Fleet handed Lydia his torch and bundled up the scattered clothes back into the bag. 'We'll look through it when we get out of here.'

Something scrabbled in the dark and Lydia let out an involuntary squeak. Which was embarrassing. 'How are we going to get out?' She handed Fleet his torch and then used her phone to play light over the walls, refusing to think about rats running over her feet. It wasn't promising and Lydia felt a bubble of panic inflate inside her chest. Her fingers began to tingle. 'It stinks down here.'

'It's okay,' Fleet said. 'Does your phone have signal?'

Lydia checked. 'No.'

Fleet moved away, holding his phone up, and Lydia moved with him, not wanting to be standing alone.

'Nope,' he said after a moment. 'But it might be intermittent.'

He was trying to reassure her, which was sweet, and just the fact of it helped Lydia's pulse to return to normal. They would work it out.

A second later, Fleet said. 'There's a door.' He walked closer to the far wall and shone his torch on a most welcome sight. It wasn't locked and behind it was another cellar room, much like the one they were stood in. At the far wall of that room, there was an open archway with a passage leading off. 'Alex was telling me that there was a passage to the Thames. They used to use it to move illicit goods from the river to the bar back in the day.'

'Seems unlikely,' Fleet said. 'But I hope she's right.' He moved toward the next room.

'Hang on.' Now that there was the possibility of escape, Lydia's mind cleared. 'I'm going to check in here, first. See if Marty left anything interesting.'

She systematically shone the torch beam around the room, taking it in sections and looking for more of Marty's personal objects. She checked the walls as well

172

as the floor, looking for writing or things pinned up. Maybe it was living with Jason, or maybe it was the insanity-vibe she was getting from Marty's abode, but she half-expected to see disturbing drawings scrawled across the brickwork.

Fleet had Marty's duffel bag over his shoulder and he scooped up the unzipped sleeping bag so that Lydia could check underneath. Apart from a couple more jars and bottles with half-melted candles, a few plastic lighters and a pack of Rizla papers, there wasn't anything to see. Unless you counted the few wet patches and piles of what was almost certainly rodent droppings.

There was a small locked cashbox. The kind that used to be used by small-traders that was, essentially, useless as somebody could simply nick the whole thing. Lydia pulled on a pair of gloves and picked it up. Instantly, a flash of silver obliterated her vision and there was metal on her tongue.

'Swap,' she said, not elaborating. Rather than hand over the duffel bag, Fleet just took the box from her and stuffed it into the bag, before slinging it back over his shoulder.

Satisfied that she wasn't missing anything else, Lydia followed Fleet into the next room. The air smelled even worse and Lydia swept over the room quickly with her torch beam. There was a pile of rubbish in one corner, including old takeaway containers and empty bottles of booze. A drip of moisture landed on her outstretched hand and, playing the light over the ceiling revealed rampant mildew and what looked like moss.

Fleet ducked his head to go through the archway.

The ceiling of the passage was much lower than the rooms, and there was moisture running down the walls. 'Even if this doesn't go to the river, it looks like it could be under it.'

'Can we get out?' Now that she wasn't studying Marty's living space, Lydia could feel her panic returning. The air was full of moisture and she was painfully aware of the amount of mould spores she was probably inhaling with every breath.

Fleet's body obscured the end of the passage and she put a hand out to touch his back, wanting the connection. 'There's a door,' he said, squeezing to the side so that Lydia could see. He tried the handle 'Locked. Doesn't look very strong though,' he was studying the hinges and lock, rattling the handle and knocking on the wood. 'Stand back.'

Lydia retreated down the passage to give Fleet space. He aimed a powerful kick at the bottom corner of the door and it shuddered. Another one and it gave way, swinging open.

Lydia thought she had never found a man so physically attractive as Fleet was in that moment. That might have been the effect of the cooler, fresher air flowing into the passage, though.

Narrow steps led up, finishing with another door. This one closed with a bolt on the inside. Sliding it open proved trickier than kicking the inner door, as the metal was rusted and stuck, but then they were outside, enjoying sweet freedom.

Lydia had never been so happy to hear the evening sounds of London or to see the light-polluted sky up above. They weren't at the river, but in a back alley. Looking at the building they just exited from, it appeared as if they had walked along the row of connected properties, probably travelling no more than a hundred feet. It had felt much further. There was far too much time spent under the earth in this case for Lydia's liking.

FLEET SLUNG an arm around Lydia's shoulders as they walked away from the theatre. 'Well, that was an enlightening experience.'

'Why didn't Marty assume that the curse meant his girlfriend dying? That seems like pretty bad luck to have.'

'Maybe he did. Maybe it made him feel guilty.'

'It didn't exactly narrow our list of suspects. Everyone knew he was ill, and he had that tattoo, so he was broadcasting that he had a touch of paranoia.'

'Can you look into his ex-girlfriend?'

'Okay,' Fleet said. 'I'm not promising anything, though.'

'I know, databases, security. It's okay. Whatever you can find, would be great.'

Fleet gave her a funny look. 'You mean right now, don't you? I was thinking we could go back to mine...'

Lydia shook her head, glad to have a reason other than her weird resistance to a normal relationship. 'I want to look through his stuff, write a report on tonight before I forget stuff.'

'Fair enough,' Fleet said. 'I'll head to the office, now.

You want me to let the investigating officer know you're looking into Marty's death?'

'Nope,' Lydia shook her head so violently she gave herself a crick in the neck. 'Bad idea.'

'You're probably right,' Fleet said. 'I just feel like you should get some recognition for the work you're doing. It's good stuff.'

'I don't want any recognition from the police, thank you. I would like to stay firmly off their radar.' She paused. 'Present company excepted.'

'Of course,' Fleet said, smiling down at her. She felt her stomach flip and stopped walking to press herself against Fleet and kiss him thoroughly.

'Well, now I don't want to go to work,' Fleet said, running his hands over the silky material of her top.

'Me neither,' Lydia said, feeling her nerve-endings respond and her skin tingle. 'But I feel disgusting, so a shower is definitely on the cards.'

Fleet groaned. 'Now I'm going to be thinking of you naked in the shower, too.'

'Good,' Lydia said, smiling.

BACK AT THE FLAT, Lydia spread out the contents of Marty's bag onto the floor of the office and sat back on her heels to survey it. She had laid out a bed sheet first. Partly to protect the floor from anything oozy or infectious and partly to make sure she didn't miss or lose anything. It was a sad collection, made all the worse by the knowledge that this was, likely, the sole possessions of Marty Benson, only grandchild of Blackthorn Fox, estranged daughter of Tristan Fox's great aunt. She had made Paul spell out the family tree to the best of his knowledge, but it had plenty of gaps.

She reached for the whisky bottle and then remembered that she had deliberately left it on top of the filing cabinet and that there was a mug of coffee by her side instead. Better habits. She had never found that alcohol particularly dulled her senses, always feeling that it made her sharper and more awake, if anything, but she didn't feel in the mood to take any chances.

Marty had two grey t-shirts and a pair of branded jogging trousers, all very bobbly and old. Three pairs of socks, not clean. Two pairs of boxers. Ditto. A comb with a few straggly brown hairs ensnared in its teeth, a toothbrush and almost-empty tube of toothpaste and a bar of soap comprised his personal toiletry kit, housed in a ziplock plastic bag.

There were four plastic lighters, like the ones which had been strewn around his sleeping area, and an old tobacco tin with a packet of papers, the cardboard cover torn away, nestling on top of a small quantity of weed. There was a blister pack of medication, too. Heart-shaped yellowish white tablets, half used. Presumably his beta blockers.

Surveying the items, Lydia felt sympathy for Marty. She knew that the Fox family code prevented them from being part of the wider social system, for registering for benefits or even state-sponsored healthcare, but she couldn't stop feeling that this was what happened when a person fell through the cracks of the world. Of course, the Foxes looked after their own. Marty had been given a place to lay his sleeping bag, after all. And it was entirely possible that she was viewing his possessions from her own biased position. Maybe she was too middle class, too conventional, too suburban to appreciate the true quality of Marty's life. But she doubted it.

There was one item which didn't seem to belong with the others. For starters, because she couldn't see how often Marty would have the opportunity to have a long leisurely bath. A plastic yellow duck with a red bill.

Lydia picked the duck up. It was softer and more pleasant to hold than she expected. Slightly squishy rubber rather than cheap hard plastic. She squeezed it experimentally, then turned it over. There was a thin cut along the base of the duck which opened when she squeezed. Jumping up and heading to the bathroom to fetch her tweezers, she put the plug into the sink and dug around inside the duck with the tweezers. With a bit of work, she got hold of something and managed to pull it through the slit. A bit of a clear plastic. Once there was enough of the plastic through to grab hold of, she pulled the rest out. A small plastic bag filled with pills.

If this was the extent of Marty's drug empire, Alex had been telling the truth. He wasn't playing in the big leagues. Lydia held the bag up to the light and tried to guess what the pills might be. They were assorted colours and sizes and there were eleven in total. At least one of them looked like a paracetamol caplet.

She called Fleet. 'I found Marty's stash.'

'What's it like?'

'Small. Just pills and weed and not a lot of either.'

'You want me to get it tested? Find out what we're dealing with?'

'I guess,' Lydia said. 'Seems like a waste of resources, though. This is not the supply of a king pin.'

Lydia took the duck and the bag back to the living room and placed them on the sheet, along with the clothes. 'His stuff is not exciting,' she said. 'It's just kind of sad.'

'You want me to come round and cheer you up?'

Lydia smiled. 'Now, that's a good idea.'

'Or you could come here? I've got white in the fridge, red by the radiator and a full bottle of Talisker. Not to mention nice sheets.'

'Nice sheets?' Lydia said, playing for time. It was getting harder and harder to say 'no' every time Fleet invited her round to his flat. She couldn't explain her reservations as they sounded daft at this point. It felt like a step too far. Too intimate. Too serious. A Crow sleeping over at a copper's home. Just wrong.

'Egyptian cotton,' Fleet said. 'Eighty thousand million thread count.'

'Is that good?'

'I believe so,' Fleet said. 'Want to test them out? Let me know if they were worth the price tag?'

'Tempting,' Lydia said, 'but I haven't finished my notes, yet. Think it's going to be a late one.'

'Course,' Fleet's voice was casual, but Lydia thought she could detect hurt in there. And the new tone of reservation that had been cropping up more and more recently. *Hell Hawk.*

CHAPTER EIGHTEEN

Fleet called Lydia to meet in their favourite pub, The Hare. 'As soon as you can. I'm on my way there right now.'

'What's happened?'

'I'll tell you when I see you.'

Feathers. That didn't sound like good news. Lydia pulled on the cleanest clothes she could find in the pile on her bedroom floor; a stretchy black vest top, skinny jeans, and a checked shirt open over the top to keep her arms from freezing. She made a half-arsed mental note to do some laundry in the near future and grabbed her leather jacket from over the back of her office chair.

The Hare was a popular joint. Not pretentious, but clean and friendly, with comfy seats and the kind of cosy nooks which make London pubs irresistible. A group of women in office wear were sitting in their usual spot, so Lydia walked around the back area of the bar. Fleet had snagged a table in another corner and was sat facing the room, the wall to his back. He stood as she approached and kissed her in greeting. He had two pints in front of him. 'If you don't fancy this, I can get something else.'

'Nah, that's perfect. Thanks.' Lydia sat down next to Fleet, so that she also had a view around the pub. 'What's up?'

'You haven't seen the news?'

'No,' Lydia said, trying not to let impatience bleed into her voice. And failing. 'Tell me.'

'Maria Silver is out.'

There was a second when everything seemed to stop. Lydia could hear the blood rushing in her ears. 'What do you mean?'

'You know she's been waiting for a trial date? Well, the CPS has dropped it. She was released this morning.'

'No.'

'Yes.'

'I don't-' Lydia broke off. She had nothing. Gobsmacked just didn't cover it.

'I know. I'm sorry.' Fleet looked miserable. And nervous. As if he was dealing with a skittish horse and he wasn't sure what it was about to do.

'Can they do that? Just drop it. I mean, it's murder. We're not talking about a minor misdemeanour. She didn't clock up too many parking tickets or nick a mobile phone.'

'If there isn't a strong enough case, like when a witness goes AWOL or problems with the management of the investigation, then the trial can be shelved. Even in a serious crime case. Much as I complain about them, it's why we have so many systems and checks and balances. To try to prevent this from happening.'

'You can't get away with murder because of an administrative technicality. I refuse to accept that.'

'No,' Fleet took a drink. 'You can't. But if the case against you is built upon a piece of physical evidence and that evidence, and all records of that evidence, disappears. Then you can get away with murder.'

'The clothes?'

Fleet nodded, his face grim.

'Hell Hawk.' Lydia swallowed a mouthful of pale ale and wished it was a whisky. She could do with a short tumbler of 'numb' just about now. She felt too stunned and too miserable to even rant about it. That would come later, no doubt, but in this moment Lydia just wanted to drink in silence and pretend the world was not as it was.

'It's not game over,' Fleet said. 'Just because CPS didn't follow through this time, doesn't mean we can't approach them with a new case. It's not finished.'

Lydia nodded and then drank a little more. The main problem, something which Fleet either hadn't thought of, yet, or was too removed from her life to consider, was that there wasn't going to be time to build a new case against Maria. Maria Silver knew that Lydia had been investigating the deaths of Robert Sharp and Yas Bishop. Whether Paul Fox passed on his suspicions about Lydia's involvement in Maria's arrest or not, Maria was likely to be bearing a grudge. Being Maria Silver's least-favourite Crow was one thing, but being the Crow who tried to put her in jail for murder, was likely to end badly. Very badly. She took another sip of her pint and then pushed it away. 'Maria is going to kill me.'

Lydia expected Fleet to say something comforting, and she was strangely pleased when he just nodded. 'She's going to try.'

THE NEXT DAY, Fleet kissed Lydia goodbye and made her promise not to go anywhere dangerous, attempt contact with Maria Silver or any member of the Silver family, and to get some sleep. Lydia thought that she had hidden her tossing and turning from Fleet very well and was irritated to find that he had noticed. Crows weren't weak. Even though she had been brought up away from the Family business, she had still absorbed the central tenets of their identity; Crows were the most talented of the magical Families, and Crows were strong, stoic, and steadfast. When Henry Crow had abdicated his position as head of the Family he had tested this last truism but, as he had always drilled into Lydia, they were still loyal to the Family. Even if they weren't active members. Lydia knew not to talk about the Family, business, or its history, with anybody outside. She knew that whatever she did reflected on the Family as a whole, and that Family came first.

Before she could decide whether to obey Fleet and try to nap or to get up and face her day, Lydia's phone buzzed with a text. It was Emma asking if she was free to chat. Lydia hit the call button and curled on her side with the phone tucked under one cheek. This was what she needed. A little R&R from her normal best friend and her normal family life. No magic. No murder. 'Hey.'

'I saw the news. Are you okay?'

'I'm fine,' Lydia said. 'Don't worry about it, honestly.'

'She must be furious with you, though.'

'Maria Silver isn't coming after me,' Lydia said firmly. 'She's not that stupid.'

'Maybe she's that angry,' Emma said. 'That might cloud her judgement.'

'She just got out of a jail cell. Trust me, she's not going to risk going back inside. Tell me what's up with you. How are the kids?'

Lydia closed her eyes and enjoyed the sound of Emma's voice and the window into another world. A world of playdates and school jumpers and papier mâché. Archie had, apparently, made a T-Rex model and had proceeded to paint his sister in green poster paint to 'match'.

'I'll come round this weekend. If you're free.'

'Always for you,' Emma said. 'Although you might want to make it Saturday as Sunday you'd have to tag along at a six-year-old's birthday party.'

'Saturday it is,' Lydia said.

'Are you sure you're okay?'

Lydia could hear traffic in the background and then a small voice. Maisie. 'Tell Archie and Maisie-Maise that I'll see them soon. Love to you all!'

She cut the call and put a hand over her eyes. She felt like crying which clinched it. She needed some sleep. Everything would look better once she'd had a bit of shut-eye. A sound outside her window made her sit up. It was a scraping sound, like somebody was trying to pick the lock on the door which led from the bedroom to the roof terrace. If someone was out there they had to have climbed up the outside of the building which showed an alarming amount of motivation.

'Jason,' Lydia attempted a loud whisper. It was a contradiction, of course, and she had no idea if it would travel any less than just speaking normally. Her bedroom door swung open and Jason appeared. 'What's wrong?'

'Outside,' Lydia whispered, pointing to the exterior door. She put a hand to her ear, miming listening.

They waited for a few moments, both tilting their heads to better hear. Lydia held her breath and Jason moved silently closer to the door, looking poised for action. A siren split the air, making them both jump. It passed quickly and the normality of it, along with the absence of any further suspicious scraping sounds, made Lydia's anxiety reduce a notch. She reached over the side of the bed and retrieved a checked flannel shirt, buttoning it up to save Jason's blushes, before joining him. The door had an obscured glass panel and was locked. If somebody was outside on the terrace, they were safer inside. Jason widened his eyes in a question and Lydia shrugged.

'I don't hear anything,' he whispered, leaning close with a blast of cold air which made Lydia glad she had put on the shirt.

She stepped into her Dr Marten boots and turned the key in the lock.

'Is that a good idea?' Jason said in his normal voice.

'Crows don't hide,' Lydia said. 'And there are two of us.' She grabbed her phone and tapped in the first two 'nines' of the emergency services, gripping it tightly as she levered the handle down and pushed open the door.

The sky was grey and the air held both the memory of rain and the promise of more in the future. Lydia had overcome her misgivings about her terrace and begun to use it. She hadn't got as far as planting up pots or anything drastic, but she had ordered a couple of steel and synthetic rattan chairs and a bistro table and a globe-sized solar-powered light which sat on the slabs next to the broken terracotta pots which had been there when she moved in. It was a work in progress, but at least she was using the space and not having nightmares about being thrown over the railing every night. Baby steps.

She went ahead of Jason, scanning the small space for intruders. She was so intent on checking for immediate danger that the full horror didn't hit for a split second. There was a black shape on the railing which ran along the edge of the terrace. It was a crow, wings spread unnaturally wide and its small head lolling down, crucifixion style. Lydia took a step closer, taking in the plastic zip ties which had been pushed through the wing and wrapped around the wrist and shoulder joints and then attached to the metal railing, pinning the bird in place. She felt bile rising and swallowed it down. She would not be sick. She would not look away. She would not forgive.

One thing was clear; Maria Silver was intent on waging war.

CHAPTER NINETEEN

After another night of broken sleep, in which Lydia never seemed to fall asleep enough to dream, her eyes were gritty and her head felt as if a giant hand had her skull in its palm and was slowly squeezing. Lydia had messaged Charlie the night before and he had responded that he was going to be at The Fork for lunch. His terse message made it abundantly clear that he wasn't making a special trip and had been planning to visit The Fork for his own reasons. The freeze-out was still in full effect, in other words.

Lydia sat at her desk in the vest and shorts she had failed to sleep in. She did a bit of half-hearted admin work and mainlined some terrible coffee to get her synapses firing. Fleet messaged her to check-in and called her half an hour later. 'Distract me,' Lydia said.

'I looked into Marty's girlfriend,' Fleet said, obligingly. 'Story seems legit. Probable, anyway. I found a

Katherine Mason in system who died of heart failure after taking MDMA on a night out, right time period.'

With a name in hand, Lydia spent some time with Google until she found a news story. A smiling school photograph of a seventeen-year-old Katy Mason. Not surprisingly, the article was heavy on the evils of drug-use and light on details of Katy's life. Lydia saved the picture and added it to the case file.

Jason's head appeared around the doorway of the kitchen. 'Tea?'

'I'm swimming, thanks,' Lydia said.

Jason drifted over and looked longingly at her laptop. 'Busy?'

'Just found Marty Benson's deceased girlfriend.' She swivelled the computer to show Jason.

'That's sad,' Jason said, but his voice sounded funny.

'You okay?'

Jason shook his head. 'Not really.'

'Anything I can do?'

He shrugged, his body rippling strangely. 'Any news on Amy?'

Lydia closed her eyes as the guilt washed through.

'I know you've got more pressing matters at the moment,' Jason was saying, speaking fast. 'It's okay. You'll get to it. Don't worry.'

Lydia opened his eyes and saw that Jason was peering worriedly at her. 'Don't do anything stupid, will you? You've got to lie low and let this Maria thing blow over.'

Lydia tried a reassuring smile but it obviously didn't

work, as Jason's frown just intensified. 'I mean it. I need you and that means you have to stay safe.'

After Jason had gone back to his room, Lydia couldn't settle to work again. She changed into her least-grubby jeans, added the hoodie Fleet had left, and went downstairs. Lydia found Uncle Charlie eating lasagne at his favourite table in the cafe. Angel was behind the counter, putting pastries from an oven tray out on display plates with a large pair of tongs. A boy Angel had hired, who wore his hair in a bun when he was working and let it fly the moment his shift was over, was carrying plates to another table.

Lydia slid into the seat opposite. 'We've got a problem.'

'There's a 'we', now?' Uncle Charlie didn't look up from his food.

Lydia had wondered if her Uncle Charlie was still going to be bearing a grudge after her decision not to help him out with any more of his business meetings when he wanted her to use her power-sensing abilities to identify Families. Now she had her answer. 'You said we had to stick together.'

'How convenient,' he said, and put a forkful of pasta into his mouth.

'Maria is out.'

'So I heard,' Charlie still wasn't looking up. He forked some more food.

'The case has collapsed completely. No trial.'

The waiter appeared at the table. 'You want some-

191

thing?' He didn't look pleased to be asking and Lydia guessed that Angel had sent him over, even though you were supposed to order at the counter.

'She's fine,' Charlie said, glancing at the guy with an expression which sent him back to the kitchen in double-quick time.

Lydia waited, watching Charlie finish his meal and push away his plate. She sat back, and rolled the too-long sleeves of Fleet's hoodie up so that they were no longer flopping over her hands. And then she flipped her coin over the backs of her knuckles to pass the time. Charlie had to put her in her place, exert his authority. It was Crow Family politics 101 and it didn't faze her.

'Why do you care?'

'About Maria?'

Charlie folded his arms on the table, sitting forward and fixing her with the full force of his gaze. 'You told me you had nothing to do with her arrest.'

Lydia pocketed her coin and retrieved her phone. 'Someone sent a message.' She found the picture she had taken and placed it on the table in front of Charlie's folded arms.

After a beat, he glanced down. When he looked up, his eyes were blazing and the black tattoos on his arms had begun to writhe. 'When?'

'Last night. I heard them do it, but didn't catch them in the act.'

'Should have been quicker,' Charlie said.

'Evidently.' Lydia kept her voice even.

Charlie sat back and looked Lydia in the eyes for the first time since she had arrived. 'Silver?'

'I didn't sense a Family when I took it down.' For a moment, Lydia relived the experience. She had put on a pair of the evidence gloves that Fleet had given her and sliced the plastic ties with a pair of kitchen scissors. Her instinct was the bury the crow, but she had managed to stop herself and put it into a plastic bag in the freezer instead. It was evidence. She had salved her conscience by reasoning that crows didn't bury their dead, they would just be left out in the open, consumed by carrion feeders. How Angel would feel about her using the cafe's freezer as its temporary resting place, was another matter entirely, but the ice compartment in her tiny kitchen fridge wasn't big enough so it wasn't like she had a choice. She marshalled her thoughts. 'Although that doesn't mean it wasn't a Silver. They are the most likely to be pissed off with me at this moment, and they could have easily hired a non-Family member to do their dirty work.' The image of Maria Silver's assistant, Milo Easen, flashed into her mind. He was pretty devoted to his boss. What would he be willing to do at her command?

'I think you need to tell me everything about the Maria Silver case.'

'Okay,' Lydia said and proceeded to do just that.

When she'd finished, Charlie's tattoos were no longer writhing. They remained in new positions, though, which meant he was still pretty rattled.

'You shouldn't have done that.'

'What?'

Charlie was giving her his full shark stare. It was unnerving. 'Any of it. Silvers are our allies.'

'I thought we didn't trust anybody,' Lydia said.

'Don't be smart,' Charlie said. 'If the Pearls and the Foxes decide to get pally, we've got no chance.'

'The Foxes aren't pals with anyone. And the Pearls are dispersed. There's nothing to them anymore.' As Lydia spoke she knew she was talking nonsense. That had been true, after a load of in-fighting in the sixties which led to a dispersal of their Family and a loss of their heritage, but the Pearls had opened a grocery on Well Street. It didn't sound like much, but a Pearl trading openly in Camberwell was a clear sign that they weren't completely toothless. The question was, were they squaring up for a fight, or just minding their own business. Maybe the old days were so firmly in the past for them, that the current generation of Pearls weren't even considering the old areas and rules. 'They just mind their own,' Lydia said. 'The Pearls were never aggressive, were they?'

Charlie shook his head. 'They kept to themselves, that's true. Doesn't mean things haven't changed. Who knows what they want these days?' He leaned back. 'Leave it with me. I'll have a word with Alejandro.'

'Is that a good idea?'

'He'll listen to reason,' Charlie said, cloaked in confidence.

Despite herself, Lydia felt reassured. Then she remembered something. 'Be careful of the cup.' When Lydia had visited Alejandro's office, she had seen the Silver Family Cup. A relic which ought to have been housed in the British Museum along with the other Family artefacts. It had been part of the terms of the truce drawn up between the Families back in the nineteen-forties.

Charlie smiled, looking dangerous and certain. 'Alejandro and I go way back. We'll agree terms and this will all be over.'

There was something about that phrase which chased the feeling of security away. Lydia knew that her uncle loved her, but what would he be willing to do for the sake of the Crow Family as a whole? Who would he be willing to sell down the Thames in return for making the best deal?

CHAPTER TWENTY

Having reassured her Uncle Charlie, Jason, and Fleet that she wasn't going to do anything stupid, Lydia loaded up her crappy car with supplies and headed to Maria Silver's home for an old-fashioned stakeout. Lydia knew that many investigators bemoaned the long hours of a surveillance operation, but when she felt this motivated there was nothing better. Since the dead crow, Lydia had felt low-level fury simmering in her gut. Laying eyes on Maria via her high-power binoculars, as Maria moved around her well-lit polished kitchen, nibbling on olives and drinking from a large glass of white wine, soothed the fury in a way that nothing else had. She was doing something. She was fighting back. Maria's little gift had made her feel threatened. Just for a second, she had been a victim. Watching Maria put her firmly back in her professional capacity.

After snacking while staring at her phone, taking a call and pacing the room while she spoke, Lydia watched as Maria settled on the couch at the other end of the open-plan room. She watched Maria watch television for almost an hour, keeping herself alert with sips of cola and working through a large bag of salted peanuts.

Once Maria had headed up to bed, Lydia drove home and slept for a few hours herself, her alarm set for four the next morning. Back at Maria's the next day, she watched her target drink coffee and leave for work. Expecting Maria to head to the nearest tube station, she was surprised when a black car pulled up outside the house instead. Maria Silver had a driver. Or a regular hire car account, at least. How the other half live.

Having not long been released from jail, Lydia would have expected somebody with Maria's resources to take a holiday somewhere warm and luxurious. Or, at the very least, to spend a few days eating in nice restaurants, swimming at the spa, and generally enjoying all the things she had been denied while detained at her majesty's pleasure. Instead, Maria was striding into the offices of Silver & Silver, leather briefcase in hand, just past eight in the morning. Having followed the car through the rush hour traffic, Lydia's nerves were shredded. She had to pay for parking at an extortionate cost and cross her fingers that Maria hadn't done something interesting in the time it took her to walk back to Fetter Lane and get settled in a coffee shop on the ground floor of the building opposite, where she had a view of the reception area.

Lydia had her laptop and she half-heartedly updated her accounts, while keeping an eye on the office. Maria didn't leave all day and when she did, the car took her straight home. At least, as far as Lydia knew it did. By the time she had retrieved her car and headed back to Fitzrovia, she was too late to tail the car and see the drop-off in action.

Finding a space across the road from Maria's white-stuccoed detached house, a building that Lydia had initially assumed must be split into flats or maisonettes, but seemed to be owned entirely by Maria, Lydia settled in for another dull wait. She ate the cheese sandwiches and apple she had packed that morning and drank luke-warm tea from a flask, while watching Maria sit at her kitchen island and read documents.

The next day was similarly unrewarding and Lydia would have been tempted to knock off early if it hadn't been for the simmering fury than she still felt every time she thought about the crow's corpse in the freezer at The Fork. She watched as Maria stood and crossed to the fridge in her showroom kitchen. She poured a glass of white wine and put it on the counter, replacing the bottle in the fridge. Lydia stretched, the bones in her neck and spine cracking. She had just decided to give it another hour, when a grey car drew up outside the house and a figure emerged. Lydia took pictures with her tele-photo lens, as the man rang the bell. He was average height and had a slight build, short dark hair and he wasn't familiar to Lydia. She got a good shot of the car number plate and wrote it down for good measure.

Maria answered the door, and the man passed across a padded envelope. Smaller than A4 and light brown. They spoke for a moment and then the man turned and walked back to his car. Lydia hesitated, trying to decide whether to follow the mysterious delivery guy or stay on Maria. The idea of watching Maria drink wine and watch television for another few hours swung the vote, and she pulled out into traffic a few cars behind the courier.

Lydia was being ridiculous, she knew, and a little reckless. She had the car's plate, she could head back to her office and ask the DVLA for the owner's details. Driving through London traffic wasn't easy and she was bound to lose the car. Besides which, he was a courier, and probably had a series of drop offs which were of absolutely no significance whatsoever.

He drove back towards the City and Lydia followed, arguing with herself all the way. The courier drove along Chancery Lane and parked on a yellow line next to the once quaint alley called Chichester Rents, which was now filled with glass office blocks and home to the mysterious company, JRB. He got out of the car and headed down the alley. Lydia had driven past a little way and pulled over down the street. She had little choice but to follow on foot. She just had to hope he wasn't trained in looking out for surveillance. Most normal people were completely oblivious, especially in London when you knew that a thousand other lives were being lived alongside your own and you had no desire whatsoever to become involved in them. Don't look, don't ask, don't tell. That was the London way.

Sending a prayer to the parking Gods that she didn't get a ticket, she doubled-back to the alley and was just in time to see the courier waiting outside the door to the building that Lydia had visited before when trying to track down the people at the top of JRB. After a few minutes' wait, he let himself inside. Lydia was too far away to see if anybody had opened the door.

He wasn't in the building for long and Lydia followed him back to his car, walking past to her own vehicle and trying to get a look at whatever he had picked up.

'Hello?'

Damn it.

'Yes?' Lydia feigned a guarded confusion, the sort of response she would give to any stranger getting her attention on the street.

'You are following me I think?'

Lydia hesitated. Then decided to cut to the chase. 'You're a courier?'

He tilted his head, waiting.

'Do you deliver things often to that address?'

He didn't answer, just stared at her with a look that was neither challenging nor amused.

'May I have your name?'

He smiled. 'Dmitry.' A little ironic head bow. 'At your service.'

'Russian?'

Dmitry had a boyish, open face. He looked to be in his early twenties at most. 'Yes, I'm Russian. What of it? Or are you one of these bigots who think we're all secret police, bad guys, mafia?'

'The last Russian I met was a hit man. He tried to throw me off my roof.'

A beat. Then he spread his hands wide. 'You meet one bad apple, you throw out the whole pie?'

'The pie?'

'Apple pie. Yes. Yes, you English love apple pie.'

'I think you're thinking of Americans.'

'No, that fruit dessert. With the cooked apples and the topping that looks like a mistake. You all love it. Had it at boarding school along with the cricket and the ritual beating.'

'Crumble.'

'That's it! Apple crumble. And custard, yes?'

'Yes. No boarding school for me, though,' Lydia said. 'No beating.'

'I would love some pudding right now,' Dmitry smacked his lips. 'Do you have a sweet tooth? I am a slave to my sweet tooth. There is a cake shop in Soho which should be illegal. It's that good.'

Lydia broke into the flow of words. 'Do you work for JRB?'

Dmitry shook his head. 'Why do you ask?'

'You just visited their registered office.'

'Did I?' Dmitry said.

Lydia tried another tack. 'How do you know Maria Silver?'

'You are barking up the wrong wood. I just met Maria Silver today. First time. I delivered a package to her door. You know this, I think. You were watching.'

Lydia controlled the urge to punch him in the throat. 'Fine. Who do you work for? And what is your job?'

Another smile. 'I am odd job man. I work for myself.'

'Odd jobs. Like what?'

'Putting together flat-pack furniture, painting,

driving van, gardening, all sorts.' He shrugged. 'Whatever you need. I'm very good.'

'What did Maria Silver hire you to do?'

'She didn't. A gentleman from a firm called Phoenix Logistics hired me to deliver a parcel to Ms Silver's address. Into her hands specifically.'

'And what was in the parcel?'

'I have no idea.' He gave her a steady look. 'I wasn't hired to open it. Just collect and deliver.'

'And I could hire you to do the same? You're not, how shall I put it, allied with any particular client?'

'I'm freelance,' Dmitry said. 'The emphasis is placed on "free".'

'Fair enough,' Lydia said. 'Can I get your number? Never know when I might want to send a message.'

His smile widened. 'Give me your phone.'

'Write it down,' Lydia passed him a business card and a pen. He took out a mobile and tapped her number into it, referring to the card, then pressed the call button. Her phone rang. 'Now you have it.'

Lydia nodded and waited while Dmitry got back into his car and drove away. He tooted his horn and waved cheerily at her and Lydia was left with the impression of a friendly smile and the sense that she was teetering on the edge of a world she did not understand.

GOING BACK to her own parking space, Lydia couldn't find her car. It couldn't have been towed in the time she had been away from it, the most she would have suffered was a parking ticket, which meant somebody was messing with her. Or sending a warning.

Her brain was ready to explode. Fury at the idea of someone touching her stuff, fear that they felt able to, and curiosity over another mystery. Was this bad luck? A vendetta by the local council that she had been caught up in? Or a personal message from JRB, the Silvers, or the police? A quick search on TRACE – the website which listed all the cars that had been towed away – settled the last question. It had not been towed by the authorities.

Lydia began searching the side streets, hoping that someone had simply moved it as a terrible practical joke. The car itself she would happily set on fire, but her binoculars were in the glove compartment and they were worth more than the vehicle.

While she walked, she distracted herself with work and called Paul.

'All right?' Paul picked up on the second ring and his voice had an edge of anxiety. He was worried about her. Or, he was worried about something else and she had just caught some by accident, like worry shrapnel.

'Bit of progress,' Lydia said.

'Okay,' Paul said. 'Good news?'

'Depends on your definition. Marty thought he was cursed. He thought something bad was going to happen to him, maybe that he would die young or be attacked or that he didn't deserve a long and happy life. I'm not sure exactly, but he had a death wish. He'd lost his girlfriend to MDMA a couple of years back, had never got over it.'

204

'Are you telling me he committed suicide, because that doesn't seem...'

'No, no. He had a heart attack. That's what killed him, but I'm pretty sure that somebody gave him that heart attack on purpose. Someone frightened him to death.'

'You're serious?'

'He had a heart condition. Something he developed from one too many big nights out.'

'Speed?'

'And coke. And the rest.'

Lydia could hear voices in the background and Paul said 'hang on' and the sound went muffled for a few seconds. Lydia could imagine him holding the phone against his chest. Then he was back.

'Who would want him dead?'

'That I don't know.' Without thinking Lydia said, 'I only sensed Fox down in the tunnel.'

A silence.

'But that leaves a hell of a lot of London in the mix,' she added.

The noises in the background – angry voices, a banging – were louder. 'Gotta go,' Paul said.

He hadn't called her 'Little Bird' and Lydia felt strangely bereft.

CHAPTER TWENTY-ONE

The sky was dusty blue, lit with the reflected glow from the electric lights all over the city. Lydia had been walking the area for an hour and had failed to locate her car. Now she was just walking, absorbed in her own thoughts, with a side-order of thirstiness. It had been a long day and she could almost taste that first sip of whisky. She paused outside an off-licence which had a tempting display of spirits in the window. They had been artfully arranged with lots of foliage and oak casks, which probably meant it was well out of her price range.

'Long time no see,' a familiar voice from behind made every hair on Lydia's neck stand up. A split second after she realised that there was a metal tang in the air she ought to have noticed. Cursing herself she turned to face Maria Silver.

'You've been seen around Holborn. Not very smart.' Maria was dressed for business, as if she had just stepped away from the office. Well-cut dark trousers, a slash-neck silk top in pale grey and spike-heeled boots. Her hair hung in perfect waves and her skin was even and glowing. Either prison had agreed with her or she was wearing expertly-applied make-up. Or it was just lucky genetics.

'You look well,' Lydia said. 'This is a bad idea, though. Revenge isn't going to solve anything.' Lydia looked around, wondering how many of the people passing on the street would stop to help if Maria took out a knife. Forget that, how many would call an ambulance when she was lying on the pavement bleeding to death.

Maria seemed to read her mind and she smiled broadly. 'I'm not going to kill you, Lydia.'

'Maybe not here,' Lydia was doing a quick mental inventory, hoping to remember a weapon of some kind that she had forgotten she was carrying. 'You probably don't want to rush straight back to jail.'

Her eyes narrowed. Oh that's clever, Lydia. Make her even more angry.

'I'm not going to kill you,' Maria took a step closer and it took everything in Lydia's power not to back away. There was a light in Maria's eyes which made her next words carry real conviction. 'I'm going to destroy you.'

Well that was a downer. Lydia spread her hands, trying for reasonable. 'If you hurt me, your father is going to want to know why. You'll have to tell him the extent to which you fucked up. The whole point of killing Yas was to keep that little secret. Or is everything out in the open between you two, now? Is all forgiven?

It's just, I always thought failure wasn't an option in the Silver Family.'

Maria wasn't smiling, but there was a cold excitement in her eyes. 'My father won't always be the head of the Family,' she waved a hand. 'Just as your dad isn't the head of yours. The old men will move along sooner or later and I can wait.'

That was not an encouraging thought. Maybe it made Lydia a bad feminist, but the idea of avaricious Maria taking over the Silvers was not a pleasant one. 'I'm not going to lead the Crows. I run a small investigating business. That's it. I'm out.' She remembered what her mother had said, and added. 'I'm not the future of the Crows. I'm just a P.I.'

'A P.I. who doesn't know when to keep her nose out,' Maria said. 'And a liar. You are Henry Crow's daughter.' Maria's gaze shifted and Lydia realised, a second too late, that there was somebody close behind her. Hands gripped her arms and pulled her against a slab of human muscle. Lydia aimed for the instep and stamped with all her weight. Nothing. Twisting and bucking, trying to loosen the iron grip around her biceps, Lydia felt her mind go very clear. It was the fear, she knew, but she tried to welcome it. They were in public. A busy street. Maria had to just be putting the frighteners on her, nothing more. The thought was followed by the realisation that she was being dragged backward, toward the road. There was a white van, its back doors open. Maria had planned this all out far too well. She was being moved, no doubt to a quiet location where Maria would have plenty of time and privacy for her revenge scenario.

This was very bad. Lydia's senses were firing as her mind panicked. She felt wings beating wildly against a window, could feel feathers in the back of her throat, and a harsh crow call was getting louder and louder, until it was all she could hear. Her feet were off the ground, the giant had lifted her up as easily as if she were a child, and Lydia kicked again and again, hearing a satisfying 'oof' of pain as she connected well.

Time was moving oddly, and everything was very sharp and clear. The back of the van was in front of her, now, and the sound of traffic flowing past seemed deafeningly loud. Surely someone would see that she was clearly being abducted and would stop? Surely someone was calling the police right at this very moment?

Lydia felt herself lifted higher, preparatory to being shoved into the bare interior of the van. She tensed her core and lifted both legs, ready to brace against the edge of the door frame, to push back against her captor. Perhaps, with enough leverage, she would be able to topple the mountain. Before she could execute the move, she felt herself abruptly released. She fell, stumbling away as quickly as she could, turning away from the open doors of doom. In that moment, she saw the person who had been holding her. A giant of a man with thinning blond hair and sunburned cheeks and nose. He was looking warily at several figures, all recognisably Fox by both their familial resemblance to Paul, and Lydia's extra sense screaming that it was so. Maria was nowhere to be seen.

'Get out while you can,' Lydia heard one of them say and, surprisingly, the big guy slammed the back doors of the van shut, crossed obediently to the front and drove away. Now that was impressive. Lydia had managed to take several deep breaths, but the shaking of adrenaline and fear had begun in her body. She was in no fit state to deal with what came next. Before she could say 'thanks' or, more pertinently, inquire as to how Paul Fox's brothers just happened to be passing at that moment, she was floored by a punch to the side of the head. A face swam into view, a Fox that Lydia didn't recognise. Female. Angry. 'Stay away from us,' she said. And then aimed a couple of kicks into Lydia's side and stomach. Lydia curled over, trying to protect her middle, which might have been a mistake as the final kick was to the head. Pain exploded in her ear and the sound of traffic and voices was replaced by roaring. And then nothing.

A VOICE SPEAKING. 'Are you all right, love?'

Lydia came to. By the angle of the body arched above her, and the buildings and slice of sky, she knew she was lying down. Her brain was rebooting and she could feel the pieces physically clicking back into place. There was a burst of music from a passing car and the sound of footsteps hitting cement. She was on the ground. It was uncomfortable. She was no longer being kicked, which was good, but she had passed out, which was bad. She felt sick. She hurt in various places she didn't want to examine too closely at this point in time.

She could smell the tarmac of the road, and the special pavement bouquet of rubbish, urine and day-old takeaway food.

'Shall I call an ambulance?' The face resolved into something understandable. An older man, maybe in his sixties. A creased face with kindly wrinkles around his eyes, indicating a person who smiled often. Of course, that wasn't always good. Maybe he smiled at other people's misfortune. Finding the world humorous was no guarantee of essential goodness. Lydia was getting side-tracked, she knew, but her brain seemed intent on thinking about physiognomy rather than her current situation. It was painful. And she had been so scared. She couldn't think about that. She had to answer the kindly/maybe psychotic gentlemen in the Adidas T-shirt who was hovering and looking increasingly uncertain.

'No, I'm fine,' she managed. 'I'll be all right in a minute.'

The man rummaged in his bag and produced a well-used water bottle. Lydia pulled herself into a sitting position, moving very slowly. She thought she could hear wings beating, but figured her ears were still ringing from the blows. The water was tepid but welcome. Plus, she felt absurdly proud of London for conjuring a helpful stranger. Okay, a stream of people had no doubt walked past, averting their gaze as she took a beating, and who knew how many had stepped over her prone body, but here it felt like a good time to focus the positive. She was alive, after all.

'If you're sure,' the man said. He glanced around and Lydia knew he was wondering at what point his responsibility ended. 'What about a taxi?'

Lydia didn't want to shake her head so she said. 'Nah, mate. I'm all right. I'll call my uncle in a minute.'

Where had that come from? She must have been kicked harder than she realised.

'I dunno,' the man was saying. 'I don't feel right-'

Lydia closed her eyes and watched the flashing lights for a few seconds. It was less painful than the light of the world, but she couldn't stay there. Sadly. She forced them open, and was treated with the sight of her good Samaritan hailing a cab. 'You got cash, love?'

'I think so,' Lydia said.

'Here,' he shoved a twenty at Lydia and offered an arm to help her into the cab. 'Take care of yourself, now. Right?'

Tears prickled behind her eyes and it was suddenly hard to speak. 'Thank you. I can return this,' she held up the twenty pound note. 'If you give me your-'

'Nah, love. It's fine. Pass it on to someone else in need. Karma, innit?'

He patted the roof of the taxi and disappeared into the throng of people on the pavement.

'Where to?' The cab driver was twisted around in his seat and giving Lydia a suspicious 'don't you dare throw up in my cab' look.'

Now that she was no longer lying on the street and was sat in the relative comfort and safety of the cab, Lydia had no desire to get chucked out, so she tried to pull herself together. The words out of her mouth surprised her, though. Fleet's address.

CHAPTER TWENTY-TWO

s soon as the words were out of her mouth, she knew why her subconscious had thrown them into the air. She didn't want to go anywhere familiar. Until she knew who and why she had been attacked, she needed to hide out somewhere safe. Trusting her instincts, she called Fleet and asked if she could go to his flat to clean up.

'Clean up from what?'

'I'm okay,' Lydia said. 'Just a scuffle. I'm a bit shaken. Just need to get off the street and somewhere different.'

'You have my key?' Fleet's voice was calm and it helped Lydia's jangling thoughts to settle.

She searched her backpack for her own keys and found Fleet's, hooked on the keyring, where he had put it. 'Yeah. But-'

'Not the time, babe,' Fleet said. 'Go. I'll be there as soon as I can.'

He gave her the code for the front door and rang off.

Fleet lived on the fifth floor of a new-build block overlooking Camberwell Green. It was six storeys high and in good condition. Balconies ran around the building and the flat stairwell didn't smell of piss. It was very upmarket, in other words. And each unit must have cost half a mill. Lydia usually favoured stairs, but knew there wasn't a hope in hell of making it up them today. She took the lift to the fifth floor and distracted herself by wondering how Fleet afforded the place on a copper's salary. He was a DCI and there would be London weighting but, still.

Lydia's head was pounding and her body hurt all over. She could still taste blood in her mouth. Her top lip felt swollen and she knew without looking in a mirror that she would be developing an impressive black eye. She checked that the hall was clear and then unlocked Fleet's front door, stumbling inside.

There was a short entrance hall leading to an open-plan living space. For a moment Lydia stood still, unable to process what she was seeing. It was, without doubt, the tidiest home she had ever set foot inside. Lydia couldn't believe that Fleet didn't perform a full-body wince every second he spent in her messy flat.

It was also, undeniably, *decorated*. Not just filled with an accidental collection of acquired objects and furniture, there was an actual, thought-out design aesthetic throughout. From the distressed wood and metal industrial-style sideboard and bookshelves, to the sleek cabinets in the kitchen area, and the cluster of artfully mis-matched photograph frames. A text from

Fleet. 'Make yourself at home. Clean towels in hall cupboard.'

Grateful for the distraction, Lydia proceeded to obey Fleet's instruction and look over every inch of the place as if it were her own. The master bedroom was painted in neutral shades and had a small en-suite. There was a landscape painting over the bed which was original art and not a print. The built-in closet revealed suit jackets, and a neat row of perfectly ironed shirts, hung according to colour, and shelves of sharply-folded sweaters and T-shirts. If Fleet ever decided to leave the force, he could get a job in Gap. Lydia reached out and touched the sleeve of a charcoal suit jacket. The closet smelled of washing powder and Fleet's cologne. It was something citrusy with a hint of wood smoke and sea air.

After sloughing off the worst of the blood in the shower, Lydia wrapped herself in an enormous towel that was as soft as down, and had a look through the cabinet in the bathroom. She told herself that she was looking for Fleet's brand of aftershave so that she would know what to get him for Christmas, like a normal girl-friend, but that was a lie. She was just snooping.

The bathroom cabinet yielded all the usual suspects, toothpaste and wrapped bars of soap, dental floss and paracetamol. Lydia downed a couple of tablets and moved back to the main living area. The kitchen cupboards were as neat as the countertops and the main thing Lydia discovered was that Fleet didn't cook a great deal. At least, there they were similar in that way. She located a bottle of whisky and poured a small measure.

Now that the shock was wearing off a bit, the pain was increasing.

She sat on the sofa and leaned back, taking shallow breaths and closing her eyes, concentrating on riding out the pain. It would pass. She would be fine. She was fine.

LYDIA MUST HAVE DOZED off or entered some kind of trance state as she was startled by the sound of the door opening. She got to her feet, not wanting to be caught lying on his sofa like an invalid.

'It's me! Have you been through all my cupboards, yet?' Fleet's voice was filled with false cheer, and when he walked into the living room and saw her, his smile fled. 'Jesus, Lydia. What happened?'

'This place is so tidy. How do you do it?'

'I always put stuff away,' Fleet said, distracted. 'You're hurt.'

'That can't just be it,' Lydia tensed as Fleet approached. His expression of anguish and concern was giving her a sharp pain in the chest.

He stopped moving and stuck his hands in his jacket pockets. 'I clean twice a week. What? It's relaxing.'

'Cleaning isn't relaxing, it's annoying.' The pain was blooming outward, making it difficult to breathe. That look in his eyes. It made it all real. It brought on something like panic.

'You don't surprise me,' he said lightly. 'Is there any point in me suggesting a trip to A&E.'

'None whatsoever.' Lydia said. 'But back to my housekeeping. Are you calling me a slob?'

He shook his head, his face serious. 'I'm letting you distract me. Stop deflecting and tell me what happened.'

Lydia wasn't ready to do that, so she dropped the towel.

Instead of the instant lust she had been bargaining on, Fleet sucked in his breath and began examining her body with a forensic frown. 'We have to go to hospital. I'm serious, you need to be checked out.'

'I'm fine,' Lydia said, trying not to gasp as his exploring fingers gently touched the bruises on her ribs. She had always enjoyed a high pain threshold, and had once played the second half of a school football match with a broken collarbone, but this was still tender.

'You are evidently not fine,' Fleet said, ducking his head to look into his eyes. 'Please let me look after you.'

Lydia closed her eyes briefly. 'I want to feel like me again. I need to feel something other than scared.' Having been so honest she suddenly didn't want to open her eyes. She couldn't bear the look of concern in his eyes for a moment longer.

She felt his hand on the back of her head, cradling and then tipping it back before lips were on hers. She responded enthusiastically, diving into the sensations with relief and gratitude.

'I don't want to hurt you,' Fleet spoke against her mouth, and she pulled him hard against her, wanting all the good feelings and to obliterate the bad.

HAVING an enjoyable horizontal time with a large, well-muscled copper, while nursing several injuries took a great deal of concentration on Lydia's part and a goodly dose of skill from Fleet. Luckily, he was blessed in that department and Lydia found that although she was still in physical pain, she was at least thirty per cent more relaxed than before she distracted Fleet. Unfortunately, he was also tenacious. Lying next to her, naked and beautiful, Fleet put a hand very gently on her cheek and turned her face so that he could stare deeply into her eyes. 'Two choices, Lyds. Tell me what happened. Truthfully and completely. Or I arrest you and take you to the hospital on the way to the station.'

'You can't just arrest me,' Lydia said.

'Try me.'

His brown eyes were serious and Lydia read the intent clearly enough. She took a breath and then told him. 'I got jumped. It's embarrassing.

'Being attacked is not embarrassing. It's a criminal offence. And it's not your fault.' A quick pause. 'It wasn't your fault, I assume?'

'You're not supposed to blame the victim,' Lydia said, smiling. 'You must have had training on that.'

'I didn't want to jump to any conclusions,' Fleet said. 'And I thought you were allergic to the word "victim".'

Lydia made a finger gun and shot him. 'You thought right.'

'So?'

Lydia gave up and told Fleet about her encounter with Maria and her sunburned goon. 'He was going to put you in a van?' Fleet's skin had taken on an ashy tone and he sat up. 'That's really bad. I've got to call it in.'

'It won't help,' Lydia said.

'You can't let them get away with it,' Fleet argued, he had grabbed his phone and was gripping it tightly. The fear on his face was morphing quickly into anger. Lydia understood. He had felt fear and now he wanted to hit something. 'How did you get away? You fought off the guy who was trying to abduct you?'

The word 'abduct' made Lydia's flesh crawl. 'A few members of the Fox family showed up.'

'I don't understand. They saved you?'

'Not exactly,' Lydia said. She yawned widely, her jaw cracking.

'They gave me a kicking.' Lydia stretched gingerly. 'I should probably send them a thank you note.'

'I'm going to kill them,' Fleet said.

'It's fine,' Lydia said. 'Just a warning shot. And better than the alternative.'

Fleet shook his head. 'You don't have to put his tougher-than-nails act on in front of me.'

'I do,' Lydia said. 'I can't think for a single second that I'm not okay or I'll break apart. That's the truth.'

He must have read the honesty of her statement, as he just leaned in and kissed her very gently. 'We'll talk about this tomorrow. Get some sleep.'

Now that was a suggestion Lydia could get behind. She took another couple of pain killers and dived into unconsciousness with relief.

WAKING up wasn't as bad as Lydia had expected. For starters, Fleet had got up in the night and put more painkillers and a glass of water next to the bed.

Secondly, his bed was extremely comfortable and the sheets deliciously soft and clean. Thirdly, the man himself was sitting up in bed reading files for work and he looked both adorably studious and incredibly hot. And, yes. There was a part of Lydia which found his presence comforting. She blamed her fragile state.

'Hey.' He had noticed that she was awake.

'Morning,' Lydia said and struggled to sit up. There was a very sharp pain in her left side which she was pretty sure was a broken rib, but everything else wasn't too bad. She reached for the painkillers and popped a couple. Lifting the t-shirt she had slept in, she inspected her torso. Impressive black and purple bruises reflected the vigorous attention she had received from the Fox brothers' boots. They hadn't done serious damage, though. They might have cracked one rib, but definitely not more than that, and they had miraculously not broken her nose, either. There were two possibilities; either she possessed a kind of super-human skeleton or powers of healing. Or, more likely, they had been out to frighten and hurt, not seriously damage, and they had the skill to execute that desire.

The next question, was whether Paul Fox had set her up for that encounter, or whether his brothers had been acting on their own initiative. She was surprised to realise that she believed it to be the latter. Just because the Families shared a bloodline and a name, didn't mean they all acted the same, thought the same. Just look at her and Uncle Charlie.

At that moment, Lydia realised that Fleet had put

down his paperwork and was regarding her steadily. 'You really ought to get checked out.'

'It looks worse than it is,' Lydia said. 'I've got such pale skin, I bruise like a peach.'

'I can't tell if you're just being stoic.'

'Honestly,' Lydia lied. 'They hardly hurt.'

He changed tack. 'Are you going to tell me what happened?'

'I already did.' Lydia said. 'I could murder a cup of coffee.'

'I'll make you a tea,' Fleet said. 'When you've told me.'

'Hard ball? I like it.'

'I'm serious.'

'Okay. Tea, then I'll talk, and then we have coffee. And food.' Suddenly, she was ravenous.

Fleet got up and Lydia enjoyed the sight of him in his boxers. He shrugged into a T-shirt and left the room.

It was quiet in Fleet's flat. They were high up enough and the windows were good enough quality, that she couldn't hear the traffic. Lydia could see why he had been so keen to get her to come round to his place. She looked around, testing herself to see if she felt envious of his domestic life, the way she did sometimes with Emma's home and family. Just checking that she was still on the right path. She felt fine, although she might get some better bedlinen and maybe a new mattress. A comfortable bed was a seriously good thing.

Fleet returned with a tray. There were two mugs of tea, more pain killers, a stretch bandage, and a pile of heavily buttered toast. Good man.

Lydia sunk her teeth into a piece and closed her eyes in pleasure. There were few things in life more pleasurable than buttery toast when you were really hungry. When she opened her eyes, she caught Fleet smiling at her. He looked fond and it pierced her right through with happiness and a strange longing. The familiar undercurrent of fear was there, too, but perhaps it was a little reduced. The realities of physical danger had put things into perspective.

Fleet settled back into bed next to her and took a slice of toast. 'Are you going to give me a description of your attackers? I'm not going to say I told you so, but you said they were Fox-'

'Not Paul,' Lydia broke in. 'We can't assume he had anything to do with it. Not yet.'

Fleet must have seen something in her expression because he dropped it.

'There's something else I've been thinking about,' Lydia said, dabbing crumbs up from her plate with a fingertip. 'I went to see Dad and he told me family stories. Loads of them are clearly myth, or exaggerated in the retelling, but it has made me wonder. I mean, what is possible? And then there's someone like Maddie...'

'Not to mention you,' Fleet said. He raised an eyebrow at her carefully blank expression. 'I'm not a complete idiot.'

'I know,' Lydia said. She could feel all her carefully maintained boundaries crumbling. She had told Emma about Jason, Paul had told her about Maddie, her dad had used magic, she had run to Fleet's flat. And there was Fleet's own strange vibe, too. The gleam she caught from him which was unlike any of the four Families. It gave her flashes of midnight on a white-sand beach. The smell of the sea and the sound of waves on the shore.

As if reading her mind, Fleet settled more comfortably against his pillow and said, 'Family stories are mad, though. Mum used to talk about a cousin who could light candles with his fingers.'

'What?'

He gave her a lopsided smile. 'Probably nonsense. You know what family's like. The talk around the table always got more outrageous as the rum flowed.'

Lydia had avoided touchy-feely conversations with Fleet but, over time, had picked up a few details here and there. For example, he mentioned his mum, aunts, and cousins, and that her side of the family were from Sierra Leone, but never referred to his father. 'What's she like?'

'Who? My mum?'

'Yeah, she sounds like a force of nature,' Lydia said, keeping her fingers crossed that she wasn't walking into an invitation to family dinner.

'Dead,' Fleet said.

Well, now she felt like a dick. 'I'm sorry. I didn't know.' Another horrible thought occurred. What if he had mentioned it and she hadn't noticed? Sadly, she could believe that of herself. She had a tendency to disappear into her own thoughts. 'I didn't know, right?'

Fleet shook his head, his smile gentle and eyes sad. 'You're not on the hook. She died five years ago. Ovarian cancer.'

'I'm really sorry,' Lydia said. 'That sounds like a bad way to go.'

'It was,' Fleet said, staring straight ahead. He took a visible breath and Lydia snuggled in, putting a hand on his chest. Her arm was bright white against his skin.

'She was, though.'

'What?'

'A force of nature.' He flashed her a quick smile. 'Proper matriarch. Anybody needed something, needed help or to borrow a drill or to find someone who could sort out their flooded kitchen or hem a pair of trousers or get somebody put back in their place, they came to Mum.'

Lydia was reminded, suddenly, of Uncle Charlie. She kept her mouth shut, though, as she wasn't sure Fleet would appreciate the comparison.

'There was this one guy, a second or third cousin, something like that. I could never keep track of how people were related, the flat always had at least three aunties in it at any time, but this guy's son was going down a bad path. He had got in with a bad crowd and his dad thought he was joining a gang. He knocked on the door in a complete state, wanting mum to advise him. To tell him what to do.'

Fleet's lips twitched as he remembered. 'She put on her coat and hat, she always wore a hat outside the house, not just for church, she was a very traditional lady like that.'

'Is that where you get your snappy dressing?'

'You think I'm a snappy dresser?' He smiled properly, his eyes crinkling. 'That's just because you're sloppy.'

'Hey,' Lydia punched his arm. 'I dress for comfort. I'm practical.'

'I don't care what you wear,' Fleet said. 'Although I prefer you naked.'

Lydia felt the breath stop in her chest. The lust was a wave and she dived straight into it, kissing him hard. Half-lying on Fleet was very enjoyable but it also set off the pain in her ribs. Fleet caught her wincing. 'You're hurt,' he said, gently disentangling her.

'I'm fine,' Lydia said, taking shallow breaths while she waited for the pain to calm down. 'But I do want to know what your mum did. Did she give the guy some good advice?'

'She asked him where the gang hung out, where she would find his son and she went to speak to him.'

'In front of the gang?'

'Yep,' Fleet said, shaking his head slightly. 'Stripe of crazy running through my mum, it must be said. She never showed fear, never backed down from what she thought was right. She marched right up to the kid, he was standing with a couple of bangers on the street, and she grabbed him by the ear lobe and dragged him home. She was short, like you, and this kid was over six foot, but she dragged him back home and whatever she said to him stuck. He straightened up, started going to school again, stopped with the drugs.'

'Impressive,' Lydia said, deciding to ignore the 'short, like you' comment. 'It's hard to picture, though.'

'I know,' Fleet said. 'Trust me, though, that ear pinch was bloody effective.'

'So, your mum was from Sierra Leone? What about your dad? You never mention him.'

A slight pause. 'That's because I don't know him.'

'He wasn't around?'

'Not even a little bit,' Fleet said flatly. 'Mum wouldn't even tell me who he was. She said I was her miracle baby and that was the end of the conversation.'

'Miracle, huh?' Lydia kissed his shoulder 'I can see that.'

'You had better not be laughing at my dead mum,' Fleet said, raising an eyebrow. 'I might not bring you breakfast ever again.' He threw off the duvet and got out of bed, smiling down at her. 'I would just eat toast in front of you. And drink coffee.'

'You wouldn't be so cruel,' Lydia said, sitting up gingerly.

'Not to you,' Fleet said. The look he gave her before heading to the kitchen was so full of affection Lydia felt something give in her chest. And she didn't think it was her broken rib.

CHAPTER TWENTY-THREE

B ack at The Fork, Lydia showered again and changed her clothes. Her phone rang and she saw it was Paul's number before answering. She hesitated for a second but wasn't going to run scared. She had to show strength.

'Are you all right?' Paul sounded distressed. At least, not entirely composed. Which was probably the same thing where he was concerned.

'Perfectly,' Lydia replied. She was glad this conversation was taking place over the telephone and he couldn't see her impressive array of bruises.

'I had nothing to do with this. I have spoken to those responsible and it will not happen again.'

Lydia could hear the world of pain that sentence encompassed. 'I'm trusting you,' she said. 'I'm trusting that you did not order the attack.'

A sharp intake of breath. 'However low you think I

am, I hope you do not seriously entertain the possibility that I would set a pack to harm you.'

'But that's exactly what happened,' Lydia said. 'Your family-'

'My family are not a unified army. I told you that before. They are laws to themselves, every Fox is free to make their own choices, to walk their own path.' He paused. 'That being said, they wish to apologise. And to explain.'

'That isn't necessary,' Lydia said, a spurt of fear spiking at the thought of having any contact with the Fox brothers.

'I understand your hesitance, Little Bird, but I insist. A parcel will arrive today. After you have viewed the contents, I would appreciate it if you would destroy them. It is, of course, a matter of trust. You could turn them over to your police friend. Or to the other Families.'

Lydia wanted to tell him not to send anything, that apologies and reassurance were not necessary, but she could feel a wild beating of wings and the urge to fly was strong and they told her that would be a lie. 'Don't call me that,' she said, instead.

WHEN THE PARCEL ARRIVED, Lydia wasn't surprised to see it was the same delivery guy Paul had used before. The one with the interesting magical signature. 'Interesting' in this case meaning 'terrifying' as she had no idea what it meant. The first time Lydia encountered him was when he had showed up at her gym and she had almost passed out from the strangeness of his power. It didn't seem quite as overwhelming today, but that might be because she was distracted by her physical pain.

He flashed a bright white smile as she took the padded envelope. 'You want help with that?' His hand stayed outstretched, as if he was reaching for her.

'What?' Lydia took an instinctive step back.

'You've been injured,' he said. 'Let me.' With that, he touched her face with his fingertips. Lydia felt an instant warmth, far greater than ought to be possible from skin-to-skin contact. In that split second, the ache of her facial bones, the tenderness in her bruised skin disappeared.

He trailed fingertips down over her shoulders and torso, lightly caressing her chest in a way that ought to have meant an instant knee to the goolies and a restraining order, but the warm goodness of it pushed every thought of retaliation straight out of Lydia's mind. Her ribs stopped hurting. Abruptly and completely.

When he dropped his hand, Lydia shifted her body, testing the absence of pain. 'How did you do that?'

He smiled again, more gently this time. There was a tiredness around his eyes. 'Until next time, Lydia Crow.'

Lydia carried the envelope into her office, dropping it onto the desk and heading instead for the bathroom. She lifted her top in front of the mirror and confirmed what she expected to see. The livid black and purple bruising which had bloomed over her ribs and stomach had completely gone. She twisted, enjoying the fact that the movement didn't cause any discomfort whatsoever. And checked her sides. Nothing. She dropped her T-shirt and headed back to the office.

There had never been anything remotely close to healing magic in any of the Families, as far as Lydia knew. Certainly nothing on that scale. Paul was using the man as a courier, did that mean he knew about the healing magic? Was it something he had sent deliberately? If she asked him and he didn't know, she might be revealing a powerful magic about which the Fox Family were currently unaware. The Fox Family who were, right at this moment, not high up Lydia's buddy-list.

Making a mental note to speak to Charlie and maybe her dad, instead, Lydia ripped open the padded envelope. It contained a large photograph and a smaller envelope. The photograph had been printed A4 size, full-colour with a glossy finish. It showed the Foxes she had met the day before standing in a formal line. Lydia felt bile rush to her mouth as she saw the familiar faces. The people who had so recently hurt her. There was something else, though. They were covered in bruises and cuts. Ones which would, if Lydia wasn't mistaken, match the ones she had been given pretty closely. It wasn't exact, but it looked very much as though somebody had systematically meted out the same beating as they had given her.

The smaller envelope was fat and Lydia guessed the contents before she opened it. A stack of twenties. Counting quickly, Lydia found the exorbitant fee she had quoted had been doubled and paid in full.

Her phone rang and she picked it up. 'You got your payment? And my gift?'

'Looking at it right now,' Lydia told Paul. 'This is hush money I assume? To stop me pressing charges?'

'It's your fee, plus a little danger money. If you stay on the case and find who killed Marty, you will get a bonus, but it's your choice.'

'Danger money,' Lydia said. 'More bribery. I can't believe I thought...' She stopped speaking, not wanting to sound pathetic. This whole situation was embarrassing enough already.

'They did it for the look of the thing,' Paul said. 'They fronted up to Maria and her hired help, but didn't want it to signal a pact between us and the Crows. They didn't want to broadcast that you're working for us.'

'Have they heard of using their words?'

'You think Maria and Alejandro would believe them?'

'You told them to do this?' Lydia felt a cold stone in her stomach. 'You told them to make it look like your Family still hates my guts.'

'No. I did not.'

There was something about Paul's voice which made Lydia believe him. But wasn't sure if she was being an idiot to do so. Paul was the strongest of the Fox siblings. They all looked to him for direction, as far as she could tell. No matter how much he protested otherwise.

'I would have found another way. A way that didn't involve your physical harm.'

'Then who?' Lydia said. 'Who hates me that much?'

'That's what I'm going to find out,' Paul said, grim determination in his voice.

Lydia knew that she should leave Alejandro to Charlie, but she couldn't. And having been healed from her injuries, it seemed a shame not to demonstrate her health and happiness to Maria's father. It would get back to her and maybe instil a dose of respect or, at least, wariness on Maria's part. Of course, Fleet would say that she was courting trouble, inviting Maria to make bigger, more violent or heavily-muscled plans for the next attempt, which was exactly why she wasn't going to tell him. Her whole Family legacy was built on being smart and fearless and never, ever giving in, even in the face of overwhelming odds. It had made the Crows the biggest, baddest and most powerful of the Families for hundreds of years so Lydia was going to put her faith in it as a strategy.

She called Silver & Silver and asked to be put through to Alejandro. The secretary didn't hesitate when he heard Lydia's name.

'I've got information for you,' Lydia said. 'Can I visit?'

'You are welcome any time, you know that.'

'I mean, without being bundled into a white van.'

There was a pause on the line. 'I have no idea what you're referring to. Have you had an unfortunate experience of late? I must admit, I did worry when I heard that you were taking up private investigation. It sounds like a dangerous occupation.'

'Not really,' Lydia said. 'I have so many checks and balances, so many nuggets of information sequestered around the place. Everybody knows that they can't hurt me. Who knows what little details might be released to the police or the press or another Family? No one is stupid enough to try anything. And that's putting aside my position as Henry Crow's daughter.'

There was a long pause. Then Alejandro said: 'I hear everything you're saying, but I have no idea why you feel it necessary to say it.'

He was smooth, she had to give him that.

'I'll meet you at Grey's Inn garden. Nice and public.'

LYDIA DUCKED through the passageway which led to the hidden garden square of Grey's Inn. It was still in the heart of the legal world, but she felt safer out in the open than in the Silver & Silver offices, or one of their preferred pubs. It was a chilly day and the leaves were dropping from the ornamental trees. Some clever gardener had planted seasonal shrubs and flowers in the beds, though, and they were an attractive mix of orange, red and burnished yellow.

Alejandro was bundled up in a black wool coat and fedora hat. His silver-tinged beard was immaculately trimmed and his tanned complexion glowed in sharp contrast to the pasty office workers who sat on the benches with takeaway sandwiches and coffee cups.

'It's good to get fresh air,' Alejandro said, by way of greeting. As if Lydia had been purely thinking of his health and wellbeing.

She thought she caught his gaze lingering a little longer than usual on her face and neck and it made her happy to think that he was looking for bruises that weren't there and would be studying her posture for pain he simply wouldn't find.

'I need you to rein in Maria. It's not acceptable.'

'Some might say you ought to have thought of that before you went after my family.'

'Some might,' Lydia tilted her head. 'But you are a more practical man, I believe. A realist. And Maria has been acting of her own volition for a while, now. At least, I assume that's the case.'

Alejandro took a cigar from inside his coat and put it between his teeth.

'I'd rather you didn't smoke,' Lydia said.

'You sound like my doctor.' He produced a silver lighter and flicked it open, releasing a tall flame.

'What are you going to do?' Lydia said, ignoring the fact that Alejandro had lit the end of his cigar and was puffing enthusiastically on it. 'She is your daughter, but if this escalates it will be bad for everyone.'

'You mustn't throw around threats,' Alejandro said. His eyes were narrowed, either from the smoke or anger.

'I didn't start this,' Lydia said. She barrelled on as he opened his mouth to argue. 'Maria started it when she murdered Yas Bishop.'

'Yas is not one of us.'

'Silver?'

'Silver,' Alexandro waved a hand. 'Crow. Us.'

'She was a human being,' Lydia said. 'Not being Family doesn't change that, doesn't make her expendable.'

'I can't reprimand my daughter based on something she has done in retribution. You must see that.'

236

'I see that you have a problem,' Lydia said. 'How you solve it is up to you. And there's something else.'

Alejandro inclined his head. 'Please elucidate.'

'You have the Silver Family Cup in your office. It's supposed to be in the British Museum. That was part of the treaty agreement.'

'I don't require a history lesson from a child.'

Lydia didn't say anything.

'It's not as if the Crows honoured that part of the deal,' Alejandro continued, defensively. 'Don't think we don't know that the coin you put in was a fake.'

'Before my time,' Lydia said. 'I'm curious, though, as to who might have suggested such a thing to you. When did you decide to retrieve the cup?'

'What do you mean?'

'It's just something I've been thinking about. Who would prefer us to be fighting, to see our old alliances break down? Seems to me, whoever told you it was time to take the Silver Cup from the museum, will have motives of their own.'

Alejandro's face closed down. 'I don't act on orders from anybody else.'

'Not even suggestions? Tip-offs? Information is power, after all.' Lydia knew that she was sailing into dangerous territory. Suggesting that the head of the Silver Family had been played was hitting him where it hurt, right in his sense of his own intellectual superiority.

'Now, I know I'm not your favourite person right now,' Lydia continued. 'I know that there are retributions and tit-for-tat and all that respect bollocks, but I also know that I hate being manipulated. And if someone is trying to make our Families fall out, that's a good enough reason for me to want to bury any bad feelings and make nice. What do you say?'

Alejandro tilted his head. 'You might be trying to play me right now.'

'I might,' Lydia said. 'But I'm not my father or my uncle. I don't run the Crow Family. I'm out.'

'And you expect me to believe that?'

Lydia hesitated. 'You're right. That's too simplistic. I'm not out but I'm not in charge, either. I would really like us not to be walked into a war, though. To that end, I strongly advise you get your house in order.'

CHAPTER TWENTY-FOUR

Lydia had been in touch with Faisal. He said that the phenomenon of the mysterious empty train carriage hadn't been repeated and that he would really rather not take Lydia back down to the disused tunnels. Lydia knew the door code, of course, and could access the tunnels without him, but she would prefer the company of a guide who knew his way around. The idea of walking that dim subterranean maze unguided made her whole body go cold. Unfortunately, no amount of coin-spinning or bribery was enough to convince Faisal. Not helped by the fact that Lydia wasn't putting her back into it, power-wise. She was holding back, stung by the recent delving into her Family's criminal past. She was a Crow, but she wasn't a bad one. She wasn't organised crime. She was her own person and she was going to do things her own way. And that meant that she would avoid using magic to coerce an innocent person, if it was at all possible.

It was tiring having a moral code and Lydia longed to open the fresh bottle of whisky she had picked up, but she was trying to ease off the booze, too. All of which meant she was in a foul mood by the time she was trying to coax Jason out of the building.

'I've told you, I can't do it. It hurts. It feels weird. I don't like it.'

'Stop whining,' Lydia said. 'Come on. You'll never get anywhere with that attitude.' She sounded like the worst kind of teacher and that made her even grumpier. Lydia took a deep breath and tried to modulate her voice to something a little softer, more encouraging. 'Please, Jason. Just try.'

He looked like he wanted to cry and Lydia felt like hell.

'It hurts,' he said, again. They had made it to the pavement outside The Fork and Jason's form was getting thinner by the second. Lydia could see the brickwork of the building through his torso.

'Okay, back inside.' If she kept pushing he was likely to just disappear and that would be it for tonight's attempt. Just inside the door of The Fork and Jason solidified in front of Lydia, the relief clear across his face.

'I need a drink,' Lydia said. She made do with a coffee, but made it a double-shot from the cafe's machine, needing every burst of energy she could get.

Jason was hovering uncertainly by the window.

'Come and sit down,' Lydia said. 'It's okay. We'll figure something else out.' She had had a thought, but had been ignoring it, hoping that her other plans worked.

'What?' Jason said. He crossed the room and perched on the chair opposite Lydia. 'You look weird.'

'Charming,' Lydia said. 'I've got an idea but I kind of don't want to say it. I don't know if I can face doing it. Or whether you'll want to do it.'

Jason's lips twitched. 'Well that's nice and clear. You have to tell me now or I'll be imagining all sorts of depraved activity.'

'You know Marty's ghost stepped into me? What if you did that and then I carried you outside the cafe. I'd be like a protective, I don't know, vehicle...' Lydia trailed off.

'Like a tank.'

'Please don't call me a tank,' Lydia said. 'More like a vessel.'

'A vessel?' Jason was outright smirking now. 'You don't strike me as the religious purity type.'

'Rude.'

'It's a good idea, though.'

'Is it?' Now that the words were out of her head she had hoped the concept would seem less creepy. It really didn't, though.

'No idea if I could do it. I'm a bit more solid than poor Marty.' With a touch of pride, Jason said. 'I'm really strong.'

'Not out there,' Lydia said bluntly. 'We could go outside and try it. When you're all wispy and vibrating like one of those weird exercise machines.'

'Exercise machines?' Jason looked mystified.

'You know, they advertise them on the shopping

channels. They jiggle you to fitness or something.' Lydia shook her head. 'I'm getting off track. It doesn't matter.'

'I jiggle?' Jason was saying slowly. He looked kind of horrified.

'Wrong word,' Lydia said. 'You vibrate. It's hard to look at. Hurts my brain.'

'It doesn't feel great, either,' Jason said. 'I have to concentrate really hard to keep myself here. Keep myself present and me. Like I'm exhausted and I'm trying not to fall asleep. But much worse.'

'And you still don't know where you go?'

He shook his head. 'I told you, I don't remember anything. It's just lost time. Just a blank and then I'm back.' He stood up. 'I'm game.'

Lydia didn't stand up and his face fell. 'It's okay if you don't want to.'

That did it. This was Jason. The man had saved her life and he was desperate to meet another spirit. She had failed to solve the mystery of his death and that of his wife, she had to at least try this. And there was every chance it wouldn't work, anyway. She was probably getting worked up over nothing. 'I don't know if it will work,' she said. 'I do power you up, make you more solid. And that seems stronger when we're touching. That's going to actively work against us here.'

'I think you need to relax,' Jason was saying. 'You look all tense, I don't think that will help.'

Lydia pressed her lips together to stop herself from snapping at him. She was reliving the freezing sensation of Marty's ghost entering her body. The terror. His and hers, mingled and amplified and the awful cold that seemed as if it might freeze her blood and veins, every muscle so that her lungs could no longer contract, her heart could no longer beat. That had only been for a couple of seconds. What would it be like for a longer period? What if she died?

'I know,' Jason turned on his heel and headed for the stairs. A few moments later he returned with the unopened whisky bottle. 'Get some of this down you.'

Lydia untwisted the cap. So much for cutting back. Still, needs must. She tilted the bottle, not bothering to find a glass. The whisky burned going down her throat and it was delicious. Within moments the familiar warmth spread through Lydia's body and she felt the panic turn down a notch. She could do this. It was Jason. He wouldn't hurt her.

'We need a signal,' Jason said. 'You can say 'get out' if you need me to, but we should have a back-up in case that doesn't work.'

He meant, 'in case she couldn't speak' which brought a fresh spurt of terror. But he was right. 'If I clap my hands, you need to leave.'

'If you even look like you're trying to clap, I'll get out,' Jason said, very seriously. Lydia felt the knot in her stomach loosen. 'Give me a back-up signal, too.'

'A back-up for our back-up? I love the way you think.' Lydia touched his arm in gratitude. 'Okay. If I stamp my right foot like this-' she stood up and demonstrated. 'That also means skedaddle.'

He nodded. A flash of excitement crossed his face. 'Are you ready?'

Lydia took another deep swig from the whisky

bottle. Things already seemed more manageable, but she noticed that her hand was gripping the bottle so tightly that her knuckles were white.

Outside a drizzle had started and the late afternoon had turned to twilight. Headlamps on the cars passing glowed with watery light and several windows in the surrounding buildings were lit from inside. Lydia went back inside and put on her leather jacket and sneaked a last pull on the whisky. She wasn't stalling for time. It was just good sense.

'Right,' Lydia faced Jason. 'I'm ready.'

He was visibly vibrating with the effort of being outside The Fork, his teeth clenched and a muscle jumping one cheek. 'What do I do?' he managed.

'No idea,' Lydia said. She reached out and touched his chest with the flat of her hand. It was predictably cold. 'Hug me, I guess, but a bit... More?'

Jason stepped forward and put his arms around Lydia. He was chilly, but he felt more insubstantial than usual, which was good. She opened her mouth to say 'can you...' when she felt a familiar freezing sensation which stopped the words in her throat.

She closed her eyes and concentrated on breathing, not panicking.

The freezing sensation filled every millimetre of her body. She could tell that her body wanted to shiver but that it was frozen solid, no movement was possible. Which was going to make it difficult to use the special 'exit' signal. Don't panic, Lydia. She sucked air in through her nose and forced herself to stay calm. 'Jason?' She thought the word, rather than speaking out loud, just in case he was somehow sharing her thoughts. Her eyes flew open, that was a terrible thought. Why hadn't she considered the possibility that she might be inviting Jason to root around in her psyche.

She couldn't see Jason and, perhaps it was her imagination, but maybe she felt slightly less frozen. She tried to speak. 'Jason?' The word came out in a croaky whisper, but there was an immediate reduction in the cold that filled her body. With that, she was able to flex her fingertips and open her mouth a little more easily.

'Are you there?'

Immediately, her head nodded. Without her intending to do so.

'Argh!' Lydia didn't mean to shout, but the sensation of being controlled by another being was bloody awful, worse than anything she could have imagined. It was downright eerie.

'Don't do that!'

Lydia experimented with moving her legs and found that she could walk. There was no way she was going to make it all the way to the tunnels in this state, though. Not under her own steam. She ordered an Uber and practised walking up and down the pavement while she waited.

When the driver arrived, Lydia was feeling a great deal warmer. This either meant she was adjusting to having Jason on-board or that he had disappeared and had gone to the place he had no control over. He could be floating away in the netherworld between the world of the living and the dead and she was about to visit the tunnels for no reason.

She called Faisal and to say he wasn't thrilled to hear from her would be an understatement. 'I can't,' he said, more than once. Lydia told him she would make it worth his while. She had sixty quid on her already, and figured she could promise him another fifty. Her determination not to override people's free will with her Crow magic was going to be a costly way to do business.

Eventually Faisal caved and agreed to meet her at the entrance to the disused tunnels at Euston; the place she had first encountered Marty's ghost. It was quiet on the platform and Faisal was easy to spot in his hi-vis jacket. He scowled as he pocketed the cash. 'I can't keep doing this. I'm going to get fired.'

'You won't get fired,' Lydia said with total confidence. If she had to break her new rule and put the whammy on someone, she would make sure Faisal didn't lose his livelihood for helping her. 'And you're doing a favour that will help a man in distress. This is a good thing.'

'Who is in distress?' Faisal wrinkled his nose. 'Hang on, scrap that. I don't want to know. Don't tell me.'

Lydia realised that she felt entirely normal, maybe a little bit colder than usual, but it was hard to judge. She had the disappointing sensation that Jason had, indeed, disappeared. She pretended she didn't remember the door code, letting Faisal key it in and then walked in ahead of him. Lydia figured that the more Faisal felt in control, the better.

'I really shouldn't be letting you down here. It's not open to the public. We're not insured for it. And you could get lost.'

Lydia shivered. 'That's why you're looking after me. To make sure I don't.'

They walked down the tunnels in awkward silence. Lydia couldn't muster the energy to make conversation, as she was looking inward to see if she could sense Jason, while also sending out her awareness, on high alert for the whiff of Fox.

The dark and dusty tunnels were eerily familiar on this third visit and Lydia thought about saying to Faisal that she could make her own way to the crime scene. Then she imagined the metres of rock and rubble and buildings above, and felt them pressing down with a tangible, oppressive force, and she compressed her lips and forged on.

The emergency lighting cast a sickly glow and the air was stale. Passing a branching tunnel with a low ceiling and an ominous dripping sound, Lydia thought that it wasn't the ideal place to get to know intimately, but investigators didn't get to choose. She should have become a hotel reviewer or a chocolate taster.

Just at that moment, she felt the brush of fur along her cheek and the scent of rich earth after a summer rain filled her nose. She stopped walking. 'We're nearly there.'

Faisal gave her an impressed look. 'You have a good memory.'

'You need to wait here for me,' Lydia said. Her fingers itched to produce her coin, but instead she added. 'I'll give you another twenty.'

'Fine,' Faisal said. He pulled out an old iPod and began playing a gem-matching game.

Lydia walked a few feet, the Fox scent getting stronger with every step. An archway led to the old ventilation tunnel, the place where Lydia had found Marty's body. There wasn't any police tape and the only sign that it had been a crime scene was a discarded pair of over-shoe booties in blue plastic. There was no sign of Marty's ghost, except for the strong Fox scent. He had to be close and Lydia tried not to imagine him watching her from the shadows.

'Jason?' She whispered his name. 'Are you here?' She had been going to say 'there' or 'still inside', but they both felt impossibly creepy.

A chill appeared in her stomach, in an extremely small and concentrated area. It was as if she had swallowed a pebble of ice, which was growing with every passing second. Now, her entire abdomen was burning with the cold. 'Jason?' Lydia said, a little louder, trying all the while not to allow the panic to grow along with the sensation of being flash frozen from the inside out.

A ghostly shape was emerging from the curved side of the tunnel. It was almost entirely translucent and extremely difficult to see in the dim light. Lydia recognised Marty's stringy long hair, though.

'Jason! Now, would be excellent.' She closed her eyes for a couple of seconds as the tingling and burning of cold morphed into acute pain. Any second now she would go numb, surely. She squeezed her eyes and curled her fists, willing the pain to pass.

And then, abruptly it did.

'Bloody hell.'

Jason's voice, carrying through the air, was as miraculous as the sight of his thin form, wavering inches from her. He moved back and smiled. 'It worked!'

Through Jason, Lydia could see Marty's form and, through that, the tunnel stretching away into the distance. Two sets of vibrating images had given her an instant headache but she couldn't look away.

'Marty,' she said, keeping her voice as gentle as possible. 'Don't be afraid. We're here to help.'

Jason turned to look and Marty's ghost drifted to the other side of the tunnel. It didn't move naturally the way that Jason did. Marty's ghost moved like a thing that could fly, a thing that was not of this world.

'Jesus,' Jason breathed the word, like a true invocation rather than a curse. 'Is that what I look like?'

'Not usually,' Lydia said, keeping her eyes fixed on Marty. 'Don't be scared,' she said, again. 'Can you see my friend Jason? He wanted to meet you. We're just here to talk.'

Marty's mouth opened, but no sound came out. He didn't look like he was trying to scream or shout, though, unlike last time they met. His previous expression of agonised fury had been replaced with something approaching relaxation. It showed how handsome he had been in life and let Lydia see the Fox Family resemblance.

'I'm Jason,' Jason was saying. 'I'm like you. You're not alone.'

Lydia felt her throat close up as she heard the emotion in Jason's voice.

'It's all right, mate,' Jason was saying, now. 'I just wanted to meet you. I just want to talk.'

Lydia kept her mouth shut. It seemed as if Marty's form was shaking a little bit less, perhaps even seeming more solid than it had done. It was hard to say in the dim light and with the Fox scent thick in her mouth and nose and the weakness she felt after carrying Jason.

Jason took a step toward Marty and then froze. Marty's mouth was opening wider than before there was a dry rasping sound, just on the edges of hearing.

'I know it's hard,' Jason said. 'I was bloody terrified. But it gets better. I promise.'

Marty was still staring in Jason's direction, his mouth gaping, but something seemed to shift behind his eyes. A flicker of life. Of understanding. His mouth closed, transforming his face into something more recognisably human. He took a shimmering step forward, floating still, but looking like he was trying to walk.

Jason hadn't stopped speaking, he was keeping up the stream of comforting phrases, so gentle and kind and patient that it made Lydia want to hug him.

Marty raised his arms, as if reaching for something. He made the strange rasping sound again, and it eventually morphed into a recognisable word. 'Katy.' The word was drawn out, spoken like a caress. It was quiet, whispered really, but so filled with longing that it raised every hair on Lydia's body.

'It's all right,' Jason said. 'You're all right. We just want to know what happened to you.'

Marty shook his head very slowly and deliberately. He rasped 'Katy' again, more clearly this time, and then floated into the side of the tunnel and disappeared.

'Bugger,' Jason said, turning around in a circle. 'Has

he gone? I think he's gone. Should I follow him?' He moved toward the place Marty had gone.

Lydia felt a spurt of panic. 'Don't!'

'What?' Jason stopped and looked at her, still translucent like something superimposed on the scene.

'You might get lost. You might not be able to get back. What if you just disappear?'

Jason's expression softened. 'You really do care, don't you?' His form appeared instantly more solid. Although that might have been the effect his satisfaction had on his features. Annoying.

'Shut up,' Lydia said.

They agreed to wait for a few minutes, calling for Marty in quiet, non-threatening tones, to see if he would come back.

'I'm going to find him,' Jason said.

'No,' Lydia said. 'It's too risky.'

'We've come this far,' Jason was already moving away from her, in the direction Marty had disappeared. 'It's our best chance to find out how he died. And I want him to know he's not alone.'

'Don't,' Lydia said, panicking now. But Jason had reached the side of the tunnel and then moved into it. His solid form dissolving into the shadowy space between the curved girders.

'Jason!' Lydia's voice was thin and frightened in the dead air.

She waited, the minutes crawling by, but Jason didn't return.

251

CHAPTER TWENTY-FIVE

Lydia had her phone out, staring at the clock until her vision went blurry. She set the timer for five minutes and told herself that if Jason didn't come back in that time she would do something. She didn't know what that 'something' was going to be and couldn't follow the train of thought without feeling sick, but the small decision made her feel a little better. Come on, Jason, she willed. Come back. Please come back.

As the digital clock counted down the final minute, Lydia felt a wave of 'Fox'. Out of the shadows, Marty appeared, his shape coalescing against the curved metal girders which formed the sides of the ventilation tunnel. It took Lydia a moment to realise what was wrong with his face. It was something she hadn't seen before and Lydia didn't recognise it at first. Marty was smiling. His mouth was open wide and, somehow, the dark holes of his eyes seemed slightly less sad than usual. It was creepy as hell.

'Jason,' Lydia said, keeping her voice calm and low. As if she could will him to appear with the strength of her conviction.

For a moment she thought she had succeeded, as behind Marty, confusingly visible through his translucent form was another figure. Then Lydia realised it wasn't Jason. The figure was smaller and female, with a long dress and apron and large dark eyes which held an intelligence and comprehension which was at odds with her ethereal appearance.

'It's all right,' Jason said quietly, right next to Lydia's ear, making her jump. He must have come through the tunnel behind her. Lydia was overwhelmed with relief but didn't have time to process it properly, as two ghosts were hovering in front of them.

'He's not alone after all,' Jason's voice was barely above a whisper and Lydia found she was shivering. She clenched her jaw to stop her teeth from clattering together.

The female figure inclined her head to Marty who turned and smiled beatifically. 'Katy,' he said, his voice rasping, but unmistakably joyful. The female ghost took Marty's hand and the two figures drifted away down the tunnel.

Lydia turned to Jason. 'Did that look like Katy to you?'

'Nope,' Jason said. 'As far as I could gather, Marty spent weeks looking for her after he died. And now he's found her, he's much happier.'

'But it's not Katy?' Lydia whispered, keeping her eyes on the figures, which were turned away from them. 'Who is it?'

'No clue, but her clothes suggest she died a long time ago.'

'Should we do something?' Lydia spoke without thinking. She had absolutely no idea what she would be able to do. Marty and what looked like a ghost from Victorian-era London were drifting off into the sunset together. Abandoned ventilation shaft. Whatever.

'I think that might be our lot,' Jason said, as the figures disappeared.

'Where did you go?' Lydia's fear at losing Jason was coming back.

'There are loads of spirits down here and they were all talking. We were in the wall, I think, or the ground. It was very dark and I didn't like it. Couldn't really concentrate. Pretty sure she's the one who frightened him to death, though. Don't suppose she meant to.'

Jason sounded strained.

'How do you feel?'

'Happy I tried,' Jason's voice was even quieter than before. 'Nice to be out of The Fork, even if we are underground.'

'But?' Lydia could sense something else.

'Bloody knackered,' Jason said. 'And kind of in pain. Which is weird, when you think about it. I guess I must just really remember what pain feels like and be able to recreate it, even though my body is like this.' He swept a hand down, indicating himself. Which made Lydia notice something - he was almost entirely translucent,

255

now. She had to really concentrate to pick him out against the darkness of the tunnel.

'I think we should get you home,' Lydia said. 'Hop on board.' She tried to keep her eyes open this time, so that she could see what happened, but it was the same as earlier. The moment Jason touched her, the cold forced the breath from her body and she closed her eyes reflexively.

GETTING home was harder than the journey out. Lydia took a cab, again, but it felt like it took longer. There was a creeping feeling of despair alongside the coldness. She felt sick and exhausted and wanted to close her eyes, but also had the fear that if she fell asleep she might not be able to wake up. She put her headphones in and blasted loud rock music as a distraction and gripped her coin.

As soon as she walked through the door to the café, she felt Jason leave. It was unmistakable as the sensation came alongside a wave of sickness which had her doubled over and retching. Lydia ran, hunched, to the kitchen, holding a hand over her mouth and just made it to the sink before throwing up the contents of her stomach.

She rinsed her mouth with water from the tap and then slid down the cabinets to sit on the floor, sweaty and shaking. Once the nausea had passed and her fingers were no longer trembling, Lydia called Paul. Whatever else she might think about him, Marty was his blood, his kin, he deserved to know the truth.

Too tired to be cautious, she told Paul that she had

reason to believe that Marty had been frightened to death by what he believed to be the ghost of his ex-girlfriend.

'Katy?'

'The very same,' Lydia said. 'The guilt he was carrying, combined with the depression and paranoia, plus his heart condition. Poor guy thought he saw Katy and it was all over for him.'

There was a short pause as Paul digested this. 'You think he was hallucinating?'

'Or he saw something.' Lydia just wanted the conversation over with. 'He could have seen a ghost. A load of graves were dug up when that part of the tunnel was built. Perfect conditions for an unquiet spirit, if you believe in that kind thing.'

'Makes sense,' Paul said. 'Luke got drunk and was talking about seeing a girl down there. Said she was dressed funny. I was concerned about his mental faculties, so this is better. Thank you.'

Lydia was surprised at how quickly he accepted her outlandish explanation, but she wasn't about to kick a gift horse in the mouth. 'So, we're done?'

'I'm not done,' Paul said. 'I have made progress on the other matter and will let you know when I've got more.'

It took Lydia a moment to realise that he was talking about the attack. 'It's over,' Lydia said. 'I just don't want any more trouble from your family.'

'It was Tristan.'

'What?' Lydia was stunned. Paul was turning on his own father in public. To a Crow, no less.

'It seems that the boys hadn't just been urban exploring in the tunnels. They had been meeting up with some Russian and needed somewhere they wouldn't be observed or disturbed.'

Lydia immediately thought about Dmitry, the courier she had tailed from Maria's to JRB's office. 'A courier?'

'An employee of some kind, I would guess,' Paul said. 'He claimed to have information on some secret Crow plan to attack our family. I don't know who he was working for, but Tristan lapped it up, apparently. He wasn't too pleased that we had started up our old acquaintance.'

Lydia didn't know what to say. There was a block of ice in her stomach, fear at the thought of Tristan Fox gunning for her.

'You've got nothing to worry about,' Paul said, reading her mind. 'I'm sorting it.'

Lydia found her voice. 'Let's just stay out of each other's way. Deal?'

'If that's what you want,' Paul said. 'I thought we made a good team, though.'

'I work alone,' Lydia said. 'You know that.'

'So you keep saying, Little Bird.'

LYDIA SLEPT HEAVILY THAT NIGHT, no whisky required. Acting as transport for a ghost turned out to be really tiring. When she woke up, late the next day, she felt vaguely sick and her head was pounding. There was nothing to eat in the kitchen so once she had showered and the paracetamol had taken the edge off her headache, she went downstairs to sweet talk Angel.

Angel was behind the counter ringing up a takeaway order for a customer. Lydia waited until they had walked away, before saying. 'Anything going spare?'

'Menu is on the board,' Angel said.

'I was thinking more along the freebie line,' Lydia said. She wasn't entirely serious, but it was fun to annoy Angel. Angel narrowed her eyes and put her hands on her hips. 'Glass of water? Smack in the mouth?'

Lydia held up her hands. 'Kidding. I'll take a croissant. And a bacon roll. And one of those custard tart things.'

Angel raised an eyebrow. 'Anything else?'

'Coffee.' Lydia had brought her own mug and she held it out. Angel gestured to the machine, so Lydia ducked behind the counter and helped herself.

'You keeping busy?' Angel said, as she placed the tart onto a plate with a pair of tongs.

'Moderately,' Lydia said. She wanted to say 'I just solved my first 'ghost murderer' case' but wasn't sure whether that would even be accurate. The unknown female ghost might not have intended to kill Marty. So it would be manslaughter at most. Unless you could prove malice aforethought. Lydia's mind was wandering. She needed to eat.

Angel had already left, heading out to the kitchen.

Lydia hoped Marty's ghost and the woman would be happy. He thought she was Katy and maybe that was enough to release his spirit to wherever they went.

Angel returned with a bacon roll.

'You got cash? Charlie says your line of credit has been revoked. Something about you not doing your part?' She raised a perfectly defined eyebrow.

'Yeah,' Lydia muttered. 'I'm not flavour of the month. How much?'

Lydia already had her credit card ready to pay for breakfast when Angel shoved the roll at her and inclined her head. 'Take it. I'm feeling generous.'

AFTER EATING, Lydia intended to find Jason and see how he was doing after their adventure. Instead, she fell asleep and woke up with her head on her desk, a damp patch under her cheek where she had dribbled. Sitting up and wiping her mouth, Lydia felt the bones in her spine and neck crack. There was a noise and it took Lydia a moment to realise that it was her phone.

'There's been a development,' Fleet said. 'Can you meet me?'

Lydia splashed water on her face and headed to Burgess Park and the Bridge To Nowhere. It was their old meeting spot, back when they were still very unsure of each other and it made Lydia feel both nostalgic and vulnerable.

Fleet was in his suit and there were shadows under his eyes. 'I spoke to the lead detective and she said they're treating Marty Benson's death as suspicious. It's been moved from the Transport Police to the Met.'

'It was a heart attack,' Lydia said. 'Pre-existing condition.' Lydia thought about explaining to Fleet that she had met the murderer the day before and she wasn't going to be easy to cross-examine, but there was no point. It wasn't information he could take back to his colleagues.

'A witness came forward and said that you were seen in the tunnels around the time of death.'

'Well that's not a surprise, I found him.'

'No, earlier than your statement. And alone. No Faisal.'

'And what am I supposed to have done? Shouted 'boo'?'

'I know it sounds ridiculous, but there's another statement. A Mr Jack Fox has come forward and given a witness statement. He spoke to the flo and said that he saw you and Marty Benson arguing.'

'Flow?'

'F.L.O.' Fleet said. 'Family Liaison Officer. Once they had an identification for Marty, it's standard practice to check in with his next of kin. By all accounts, they weren't easy to track down, but Deshan is very thorough. Very diligent.'

'Great,' Lydia said flatly, unable in the moment to appreciate the work ethic of one of Fleet's colleagues.

'Anyway, he said that you seemed very angry. He says he heard you shout 'you're dead'. Jack is Paul Fox's brother, one of them. You probably know him?'

Lydia ignored the dig. 'I never met Marty Benson,' she said instead. *Just his ghost.* And that had been brief. 'You know that.'

'It's his word against yours, and the lead thinks it's enough circumstantial to open it as a suspicious death.'

'It's being passed to MIT?'

Fleet nodded and Lydia's heart sank. The Murder Investigation Team would swing into action, now, going back over the existing evidence and making their assessment.

Fleet's next words came wrapped in an apologetic tone. 'There are staff shortages so they're cobbling together a team from wherever possible.'

'What are you saying?'

'I've been seconded to it.'

'Well that's just perfect,' Lydia said. Uncle Charlie was going to have a coronary from shouting 'I told you so'.

'Won't it be considered a conflict of interest. With our relationship?'

'I love it when you say "relationship",' Fleet said, the ghost of a smile on his lips. 'But, no. They can't afford to be precious. Average number of open murder cases for each SIO is sitting at twenty. Besides, it's not like I've been broadcasting our personal connection. I thought you would prefer it was kept private.'

'Hell Hawk,' Lydia said.

Fleet reached for her. 'It'll be okay,' he said, dipping his head to kiss her mouth.

Lydia's body responded, as always, but it didn't quiet the clamour in her mind.

ONCE FLEET HAD LEFT, heading back to the office and the team of people intent on proving she was involved in the death of Marty Benson, Lydia walked back to The Fork. She still felt zombie-like and unable to process things properly. If this was what carrying a ghost around did, she wasn't keen to repeat the experience. In her office, she ate some toast at her desk and looked for a distraction. She was trying, very hard, not to take Fleet's actions as a personal betrayal. It was his job, after all, and he could hardly refuse to join the MIT on her case when Lydia had told him not to advertise their connection. She couldn't have it both ways. Which was annoying.

Still, as far as she was concerned, the case for Paul Fox was over and that meant she could turn her attention back to the rest of her business. Her sadly-neglected business. She opened her desk drawer which held the photograph of the bruised and beaten Fox family. A group, which now she looked at it again, clearly included Jack Fox, Paul's brother. No wonder he was pissed off.

There was also the money Paul had sent, still bundled neatly. Lydia might not like where the cash had come from and why, but she was a realist. She always had a list of equipment she needed for Crow Investigations, not to mention the need for a new car. She had reported the Volvo as stolen and would have to wait for the insurance money to come through. When it did, it would need supplementing in order to get anything halfway serviceable, so she peeled off a few large notes and put them back in the drawer for that purpose. Then she took herself to her favourite security shop and bought a replacement for the binoculars she had lost along with her car, and some surveillance items like a nifty audio-recorder which was hidden inside a plug socket, and an expensive car tracking device which promised to magnetically adhere to the underside of a vehicle and provide real-time tracking.

While in the shop, she chatted with the guy who ran the place and he mentioned that he had a deal on encrypted hard drives. He started talking about data protection for her clients' private information and Lydia stopped listening. Not so much because she didn't care about privacy and the laws of the land which governed it, but because she had been taken by another idea. The sight of the external hard drive made her think about her old laptop and backing it up, which made her think of a faster machine with larger storage, which made her think about Jason. If she blew the rest of the money from Paul on a shiny new laptop for herself, she could pass her old one onto Jason. He had the motor control necessary now, and the internet would be a way for him to leave the building in a way that didn't involve hitching a ride inside her body. Perhaps he could do his maths stuff on there, too, or find some other mathematics enthusiasts to correspond with? Yes, there was a chance he'd stumble into pornland, but the guy was facing an eternity alone. Access to rude videos might be just the thing to cheer him up. And who was she to judge?

Once she had everything up and running on her new laptop, she wiped her old one and carried it through to Jason's bedroom. He was standing in the corner, looking forlornly at the blank wall, arms dangling at his sides.

'I brought you a gift,' Lydia said, putting the computer onto the bed.

The transformation was instant and gratifying. Jason

went from hangdog to excited puppy and she had to ask him to stop hugging her as she was going to get hypothermia.

'Sorry. Yes. Right.'

'Shout if you need a hand,' Lydia said. 'I'll leave you two to get acquainted.'

CHAPTER TWENTY-SIX

The next day, Lydia slept in. She had no urgent case to work and she didn't expect to hear from Fleet. He had explained that he would have to step away in a 'purely practical sense'. Another phrase which ran around Lydia's mind, inspiring dread, was 'we should cool off on physical contact and stop communicating in traceable ways'.

Lydia checked on Jason and found him hunched over his new laptop, his curtains drawn. He looked up, the glow from the screen illuminating his face in the otherwise dark room and smiled beatifically. At least somebody was happy. And it had taken his mind off Amy.

She had showered and was making a mug of lack-lustre coffee in the kitchenette when she heard somebody knocking urgently on the flat door.

It was Fleet and she knew something was wrong

instantly. He was wearing a suit, but hadn't shaved and his eyes were wild.

'We have a problem,' he said, walking in.

'Don't we always?'

'I'm serious,' Fleet said. 'MIT are getting ready to bring you in. They like you for Marty's death and everyone has been running around getting very excited. They're waiting on hearing from the CPS but it won't be long.'

'That makes no sense,' Lydia said, anger flowing through her, fast and pure. 'If I killed him, why would I take an employee of the London transport system to visit the corpse? What kind of idiot murderer would do that?'

'Killers do sometimes like to visit the scene of the crime. It's a glory thing.'

'Do they take a witness along for the ride?'

Fleet shrugged. 'Not as a rule. But some do wait around for the police, stand behind the line gawping like any other member of the public.'

The thought cut through Lydia's fury, distracting her. 'Really? Why?'

'Enjoying the spectacle. Relishing the aftermath. Standing in plain sight of the people who are going to try and catch them. It makes them feel powerful, I believe.'

'Bloody stupid behaviour.'

'Killers aren't usually known for their smarts, no matter what TV dramas would like you to believe. Most people kill on impulse and poor impulse control is corre- lated with low intelligence.'

'But there are always exceptions.'

'Of course. Sociopaths are more likely to have above-average intelligence. But, again, not as often as you might think. They're not all Sherlock.'

'I'm not a sociopath,' Lydia said. She held out her little finger. 'I pinkie swear.'

'This isn't a joke, Lyds. They are getting ready to arrest you. It might even be today.'

'I don't think you're supposed to tell me that.' The anger had drained away and was being replaced by something else. Denial. This simply could not be happening.

'I'm definitely not supposed to tell you that. Don't make me regret it'

'By running? Crows don't run.'

Fleet closed his eyes briefly. 'Please. Just get out.'

'I can't,' Lydia said. 'It would reflect poorly on you. They know you know me. No matter how careful we've been, somebody knows. They would assume you tipped me off.'

'I don't care about that.'

'I do,' Lydia said. 'And I didn't do this. I'm not running away.'

'This is serious,' Fleet said. 'I can't stop it.'

'That's okay,' Lydia said. She was numb and her mind seemed to be working more slowly than usual. A moment later she realised what was happening. She was drowning in shame. She was the Crow who had been stupid enough to trust the Fox. All that time, Paul had been playing her, playing with her. All the time he had been laying his trap and she had walked right into it. In the Aesop tale, the Fox flatters the crow into opening her beak to sing, which means she loses the tasty piece of cheese she was carrying. Lydia had been flattered into working a case for Paul, imagining that he asked for her help because she was good at her job and he genuinely respected her investigative skills. Put like that, it was embarrassingly naive. 'And you can say it.'

'Say what?' Fleet was at the front window, peering out at the street with a tense look on his face.

'I told you so,' Lydia poured a glass of whisky and knocked it back. 'You were right. I was an idiot to trust Paul Fox.'

'This isn't the time,' Fleet said. 'None of that matters. You need to go somewhere safe. Once the team get here, I have to do my job.'

Lydia felt cold and sick and very, very small. How had she been so blind? How had she fallen for Paul's act?

Fleet was pacing, one hand on his forehead. His phone buzzed and the expression on his face when he read the message was enough to jerk Lydia from her pity party. 'What?'

'They're here,' Fleet said, his voice urgent. 'It's happening.'

'Fine,' Lydia shut down her computer, tidied the piles of paperwork on her desk. 'Should I pack a toothbrush?'

'This is serious,' Fleet said. 'I can't stop it.'

'I'm well aware,' Lydia replied. 'Why don't you get on with it? Or do you need to wait for back up?'

'Please don't make this any harder than it already is.' Fleet's eyes were impossibly sad, but he was still going to stand to one side while his colleagues put her in a marked car.

There were feet on the stairs outside and Lydia's proximity alarm alerted her to what she already knew. She switched it off and picked her jacket up from over the back of her chair.

Shapes behind the ribbed glass and then hammering on the wood of the door frame.

Fleet opened the door. 'No need for all that,' he said. His body was blocking Lydia's view, although she imagined some disappointed junior with a brand new battering ram and some training he was eager to put into practice.

A couple of uniforms wearing stab vests came into the flat, spreading out as if preparing to search. Another copper in plain clothes introduced herself, although Lydia didn't seem to be taking things in properly as she promptly forgot her name, and then explained that there was a warrant for her arrest and that they would like her permission to search the property.

'No thanks,' Lydia said. 'I think I'll wait for the paperwork on that.'

'Your cooperation would be both appreciated and noted,' the officer began, but Fleet cut across, reciting the standard police caution Lydia knew well from television, film and books. It was surreal. Her lover was saying 'you do not have to say anything, but it may harm your defence...' and she couldn't take it in.

'Are you going to cuff me?' Lydia said, feeling a spurt of panic. The image of the dead crow's wings zip-tied to the balcony railings jumped into her mind.

'Not if I don't have to,' Fleet said.

The uniforms swivelled their heads to look at him. It happened in unison like a weird dance and Lydia had the sudden urge to laugh.

'There's no need,' he said to the room at large. 'You're happy to come along and get this sorted, aren't you?'

Lydia nodded. She didn't trust herself to speak.

As they left the flat, she caught sight of Jason standing in the bathroom doorway, mostly hidden by the half-open door. One of the uniforms gave it a curious look and Lydia realised it must have been shut when she had walked past on her way in. She wanted to wave or to say something, but she just met his gaze and tried to convey 'everything's fine' with her eyes.

Walking through The Fork was excruciating. Lydia kept her eyes focused forward, but still caught the avid expressions of the punters enjoying a side show with their food. It would be a story for them to dine out on later. 'I was in this cafe and suddenly a whole group of police were marching this woman out'. She saw Angel looking shocked, her mobile in her hand. She would call Charlie, no doubt. That was probably good.

It was cold outside and Lydia was glad she had put her jacket on. She was put into a car with the two uniforms. Fleet said 'I'm following in my car.' Lydia couldn't bear to look at him.

THE CUSTODY SERGEANT booked her in, taking details and chatting to the arresting officers as if she was deaf in between asking questions about drug use and suicidal tendencies. The holding cell. Waiting room. Whatever the modern copper had been taught to call it was exactly as depressing as she expected. A single hard bed with a blanket. Blank walls. And air which seemed imbued with panic and despair, with an unhealthy dose of old vomit and industrial strength pine air freshener.

Lydia sat cross-legged on the bed and closed her eyes. She would breathe and concentrate on not panicking. She would not think about the locked door or the municipal building with its terrifying blandness, its layers of procedure and paperwork, the system into which she had been absorbed. She was powerless. There was nothing to do but wait and hope that the system spat her out again, as quickly as possible.

They had offered her a phone call and she had said 'not yet, thanks,' thinking that Angel would tell Charlie and the only other person she would have called was Fleet. And he was in an office somewhere in this building, maybe drinking coffee and sharing banter with his fellow coppers. His colleagues.

They hadn't charged her, which meant there were twenty-four hours before they had to do so or release her. Police didn't usually bring you in and search your property and take a DNA swab on a whim, though. Not with resources stretched as they were. Lydia couldn't pretend to herself that this was just a fishing expedition.

The next time an officer slid open the shutter on the door to check on her, to see if she needed the bathroom or a cup of water, she heard someone shouting and moaning in one of the adjoining cells. The trapped feeling intensified and a surge of pure adrenaline spiked through her system. 'I think I'll take my call, now, if that's all right?'

The officer said that was no problem and fetched back-up to escort her to the desk. The custody sergeant moved away to give her the privacy required by law, but it hardly felt like enough. Charlie picked up after two rings and Lydia's knees buckled at the sound of his voice. 'I'm working on it,' he said. 'Bit tricky with the way things are with the Silvers. They're the best, but they aren't too pleased with us at this moment.'

Lydia closed her eyes, blocking out the station and pretending, just for a moment, that she was back at The Fork. 'I know. Don't we have our own solicitor, though?'

'Sure,' Charlie said. 'But it's not that simple.'

'What do you mean?' Lydia opened her eyes, focusing on a tired-looking spider plant on top of a filing cabinet behind the desk. It was pale and sickly and needed dusting.

'In or out, Lyds, makes a difference.'

'You won't help me if I'm out?'

'I'm not saying that, I'm saying it makes a difference.' Charlie didn't sound happy, but there was a current of resolve. Firm, unmovable. 'Come on, Lydia, you're not a child anymore.'

'In,' Lydia said. 'Now get me the fuck out of here.'

CHAPTER TWENTY-SEVEN

They had taken her phone and she didn't wear a watch. With no window to judge the changing light, Lydia had no idea how much time had passed. She kept thinking she could hear the caw of a corvid, and assumed she was hallucinating from fear. She didn't know why she was reacting so poorly to being locked in a room. With no natural light. Like she was being buried underground. Maybe it was something in her DNA, another gift from her Crow Family heritage, but she knew she was not going to last the night in his place, let alone be able to tough out jail.

The door scraped open and Lydia was led into an interview room which was labelled 'consultation room four'. The wording reminded her of hospital. Maybe all the institutions shared signage, but whether it was to confuse or calm, she didn't know. A uniform with a crisp white shirt and a high ponytail smiled kindly at Lydia and offered her a cup of tea. The human warmth was enough to make her want to sob. She was frightened and could feel her wings desperately beating. It was an instinctual and visceral reaction that she was unable to stop. Another fragment of her precious control slipping away.

Sitting in the interview room didn't help. The grey walls seemed to press inward, while the fake beech table with two chairs opposite hers and a bulky audio recorder plugged into a wall socket had the air of a film set. It was disturbingly familiar, a sight she had seen on a hundred crime dramas, but also unique and different and unpleasantly real. A sign on the wall said something about SmartWater, a phrase she didn't recognise or understand. There was the smell of food. Maybe beef mince. It reminded her of school dinners and her stomach turned over.

'We'll start as soon as possible,' the nice-looking officer said. 'Sorry about the delay. Just waiting on your legal representative.'

Lydia had been given the option to contact a personal solicitor and had declined, so they were going to be in for a long wait. They had offered a duty solicitor, too, the desk sergeant waving vaguely at an anonymous door behind which, presumably, a keen legal mind was sitting in private communion with a wrongdoer, inno- cent or their late lunch. Who knew?

She wondered, vaguely, whether if there was a long enough delay, waiting for the non-existent solicitor, that they would run down the clock on their twenty-four hour window. After that time, if they hadn't charged her, they would have to let her go. Free on a technicality. An administrative cock-up. Like Maria Silver, only she, Lydia Crow, was innocent. Of this particular crime, at any rate. Her mind was still spinning, her thoughts coming fast and staccato. Beating a panicked rhythm.

Five minutes passed, in which the nice officer tried to make small talk and Lydia managed one-word answers. Not because she was trying to be awkward but because she felt as if something heavy was sitting on her chest and she could hardly breathe. There was a knock on the door and a uniform called the officer out. 'Excuse me,' she said, apologetically to Lydia. 'Shouldn't be much longer. You want a biscuit or something?'

Nice cop, Lydia thought. Was she leaving so that Nasty Cop could take her place? Or would they send in Fleet? Sexually Talented Cop. Romantically Involved Cop. Ethically Compromised Cop. She was losing it.

The room emptied and Lydia leaned back in her chair a little, determined to get a hold of her cognitive powers. She had to stop spiralling and start working through the problem. Paul Fox had been setting her up all along, but why? And how could he have done it? She began to run over every conversation, every move she had made since opening that stupid padded envelope.

The door opened and Lydia took her time in looking up. She had just been recreating the moment she searched Marty's sleeping quarters, trying to work out if there was anything incriminating in her actions, or anything which could be construed as such.

'Lydia Crow, always a pleasure.'

Her head snapped up as her senses bombarded her

with the strange power that always accompanied the courier.

'You?'

He smiled and Lydia felt the warm glow which had spread through her body when he had healed her. In that second, she could feel his touch again and had to glance down to confirm that his hand hadn't appeared on her chest.

His teeth and the whites of his eyes gleamed and even the fluorescent lighting couldn't dim the healthy glow of his skin. The power which rolled from him seemed stronger than before, or Lydia was in a weakened state, either way she felt like she was going to be sick.

'Sorry,' he said, as if aware of the effect he was having. 'It's a small space. And you're tired, I bet.' He pulled a chair out and sat down, looking completely at home.

'You're police?' Lydia managed to say.

'They've got a solid case against you, witness statements which suggest a sustained campaign against the deceased, plus a motive for wishing him harm. Furthermore, they have found evidence at your flat which hasn't been disclosed yet.'

Which wasn't an answer. 'What evidence?'

'Mobile phone. It's a burner which was used to communicate with Marty Benson on a number of occasions in the lead up to his death. They will be building a case around this to suggest that you harassed the deceased, who was in a fragile state of mind, and that you lured him to the tunnel with intent to harm.'

'What phone? I have never spoken to Marty Benson.' Lydia was speaking in between steady shallow breaths, trying to regulate the nausea. She needed to keep a level head until Charlie did whatever he was going to do. She saw him flying in on the back of a raven, tattoos writhing and the fire of retribution lighting his cold eyes. It was a pleasant thought. Equally good would be a confident solicitor in a sharp suit. Probably not a Silver, not given recent events, but the Crows had to have other contacts.

'The evidence shows a large number of phone calls from the Nokia found in your flat to Marty's phone, varying in duration, but concurrent with a pattern of harassment.' Lydia tried to think it through. Marty hadn't had a mobile phone on him when he died. At least not one she had found in his pockets or one which Fleet had mentioned. It was paranoia to think he would have held something back, not told her about a bit of evidence like that, especially considering all the chats they had had while trying to identify Marty. Lydia knew it was panic leading to paranoia, but the doubt was there. She had been wrong about Paul Fox, maybe she was wrong about Fleet, too?

'Where was Marty's phone?' Lydia said. 'The phone I am supposed to have called from the burner which has been planted at my flat?' She didn't know if it was stupid to admit that she had been to the music hall on Cable Street, looking for Marty or his drug-purchasing clientele, but sod it. Besides which, she had been with Fleet. And Alex had already shown how eager she was to drop Lydia in the Thames. With her hands tied together and a weight on her legs. 'I visited his current place of residence and didn't find a phone.'

'Or you did find a phone and you got rid of it, knowing it would incriminate you? You see how this goes?'

The nausea was abating and Lydia could feel her brain cells starting to fire properly. 'Aren't you supposed to introduce yourself before an interview? Name, rank, badge number? That's what everyone else has done.'

He took a pen and pack of yellow sticky notes from his jeans pocket and wrote something down. 'Let me save you the trouble of saying 'this is a set up'. I know you didn't do this. I know that whatever mobile they've got in an evidence box back there is not yours.'

Lydia produced her coin, squeezing it tightly and taking little sips of air through her mouth. She no longer thought she was going to throw up whatever was left in her stomach, which was a relief. But the sickness was replaced with confusion.

'But when all is said and done, it's pretty handy. I would be lying if I didn't say there wasn't something useful about your current predicament. I'm part of a division which is very interested in the Families and their abilities. The NCA and MI5 are obsessed with the Crows and their past, all the little favours and influence and protection rackets and all that mafia stuff. My department is very small, very select, and we have a different remit. Can you guess what that remit covers?'

Lydia shook her head. 'Surprise me.'

He just smiled and Lydia had to force herself not to smile back. Her coin was having an effect and she could feel her equilibrium returning. His power made her feel sick, like she was on a rollercoaster being turned upside down, all motion sickness and blurred vision. But as she got a little more used to the feeling, anchored by the edges of her coin digging into the soft flesh of her palm, she could pick apart the impressions and begin to identify them. There was the sense of candlelight flickering and salt on her tongue. Feeling the intensity of her frown as she concentrated, Lydia saw flashes of burnished gold, silky material unfurling, rippling and writhing, and heard a roaring sound which might have been the ocean. She tried to focus on the sound, but he was speaking and that made it even more difficult.

'There are stories,' he was saying. 'Myths. Folk tales. Historical fact blurred with half-remembered truths and events twisted in the telling.'

'Are you telling me there's a police department for fairy tales?'

'My job has been to look into things that aren't covered by the other government, regulatory or enforcement bodies.'

'Have you told your colleagues that you can heal people with your hands? They might put you on the same list.'

He smiled widely. 'That's a funny accusation to make. It makes you sound deluded. Of course,' he paused, 'that's the issue, isn't it? The stuff you grew up with, the things you know and can do, they sound quite mad in this context.' He indicated the grey room. 'I imagine your game plan has always relied on avoiding places like this.'

Lydia shrugged. 'That's the same for everyone, I would have thought. Who plans on getting arrested?'

'Question is, what are you going to do now? I'm giving you lemons, are you going to make lemonade?'

'I've never understood that expression,' Lydia said 'I like lemons. Not bothered on lemonade.'

'I like you,' he said. 'And we have much in common, I think. I'm not your enemy, here.'

So many people had said that to Lydia recently, she felt she ought to have made a bingo card. 'You're my friend, is that it?'

'I'd like to be.'

The penny dropped and with it, Lydia's stomach. 'You're offering me a deal.'

He nodded. 'One time offer. When I walk out that door, it's no longer an option. I'll leave you in the capable hands of the law. You can take your chances, of course, but CPA is very happy with the case and are going to agree your charges. You won't make bail, a man is dead after all, and whatever happens, you'll be caged for a good few months.'

Lydia could feel the panic lapping at the edges of her mind, but she refused to look at it. She stared into his eyes. 'I'm innocent. I'll be out in a few hours, anyway.'

'Maybe.'

His tone was gentle and not openly derisive. It implied that he doubted it, but didn't want to upset her. Which was somehow more devastating than open hostility. 'What do you want?'

'I told you. Just friendship.'

'And what does that mean? Exactly?'

'Friends share,' he said.

'I don't,' Lydia said. 'Ask anyone.'

He smiled. 'Special friends, then. Someone you can confide in, chat about your cases, your conversations, your Family.'

'No,' Lydia said.

'What about the others? Paul Fox, the Silvers, the Pearls?'

He was right, hearing the names in this little grey room felt wrong. Scary. Paul Fox had shafted her, she felt no loyalty to him or his brothers.

'I won't betray my family,' Lydia said.

'The Crows are on the straight and narrow these days, isn't that right? If so, you don't have anything to worry about.'

Lydia wasn't dignifying that with an answer.

'I know you're hoping that your uncle is going to show up any moment and spring you, but the truth is he can't. At least, I don't believe he can. I might be wrong and you can take that chance, but I honestly think this is your best option.' He stood up. 'What do you say?'

Lydia shook her head.

He looked disappointed, but not surprised.

She had expected him to try a bit more convincing, and was still mulling over the strange honesty of his words as he moved toward the door. It was the phrase 'I might be wrong'. She knew that he was probably trained in persuasion and this modest style was undoubtedly a technique, but she could feel herself falling for it. 'You expect me to trust you and I don't even know your name,' she said, playing for time.

Pausing at the door, he turned around. 'The only name I could give you would be a lie and I don't want to do that. I think you would be able to tell, and I'm trying to get you to trust me.'

'You think this over-sharing is going to make me believe you?' Lydia was struggling. She had trusted Paul Fox and he had been setting her up. She couldn't even think about Fleet, it was too painful and too complicated. This man-boy had healed her physical injuries, appeared to give her information about a set-up, and not asked her outright for anything compromising. Yet.

'Last chance,' he said, hand on the door handle.

'Fine,' Lydia said. 'I will share information. Some information,' she amended. 'But I will never betray my family. Never. If that's a deal-breaker then so be it.'

He smiled. 'Good enough. Shake on it?'

Lydia stood and held her hand out, the one with the coin stuck to her palm.

When he grasped her hand she felt the clink of metal against metal and she felt her eyes widen in surprise. He was also holding something metal hidden in his palm. She felt with her senses to try to get a good impression, but all she knew was that it wasn't a Crow coin and it wasn't silver. At least, not silver with a capital 's'. Their eyes met through her confusion. His were serious and it made him look ten years older.

Lydia had the unshakeable feeling that she had just made a huge mistake but he was already moving away and opening the door. He left it ajar and the sound of somebody in one of the adjoining 'consultation' rooms drifted in, loud and clear. It was a woman swearing at high volume, a string of expletives which ended with a wail of 'I don't want to be here.'.

You and me both, sister, Lydia thought. Mistake or not, she knew she would make it again.

LYDIA ENDURED the reverse procedure of being booked in, her jacket and Dr Martens returned, and more signatures given. Fleet was nowhere to be seen and she didn't know whether she was relieved or not. She was surprised to see from the clock behind the desk that she had spent most of the night in the station. It felt like a week.

Outside and away from the CCTV, Lydia let herself stop moving and take several deep breaths. It was early, not yet seven and the sun had just risen. A jogger on his way to lap Camberwell Green pounded past, headphones stuck into his ears, and the sky above the blocky edifice of the magistrates' court was streaked lavender, lemon and rose gold. Lydia walked onto the scrubby grass of the green and slipped off her boots. She hadn't bothered tying the laces, being so desperate to get out of the building and into the light and air. She pulled off her socks and felt the ground with her bare feet, scrunching her toes like John McClane in Die Hard.

It was better to think about films and the tang of exhaust fumes in her nostrils and cool earth on the soles of her feet than the last twenty four hours. After a minute, she put her socks back on and laced up her boots. It was time to go home.

LYDIA SAW the light spilling onto the street from inside the cafe from several metres away. The Fork was packed. She had a good view through the big windows fronting onto the street and saw her Aunt Daisy and Uncle John, several cousins she hadn't seen in years, her parents sitting at a table at the front, and Uncle Charlie pacing up and down between the tables and chairs. Angel opened the door for her and gave her a sympathetic half-smile. 'Coffee?'

'Please,' Lydia said, surprised by the welcome.

The moment she got into the room properly, conversation kicked up a notch, a clamour of questions and exclamations. She went straight to her parents and gave them both quick hugs. Jason was by the door which led to the toilets and then up the stairs to their flat. He looked a little less solid than usual, but he was there and capable of raising a single eyebrow in greeting. A rush of relief flowed through Lydia and she let herself acknowledge how worried she had been at the prospect of leaving him. They had no idea how long he would survive without her powering-up presence and she had no wish to test it. She smiled at him and he nodded before disappearing. Presumably back to his beloved computer.

She had called Charlie on her way back to the cafe and had no idea how he had assembled everybody so quickly. She said as much and he frowned. 'We've been here all night. Trying to work out a plan of action and waiting for the solicitor. John knew someone good, but he couldn't get here until,' Charlie broke off and looked at his watch. 'Nine. I'd better call him off.' He turned to John. 'Can you?'

Uncle John nodded and moved to a quiet spot near the door to the kitchen, mobile in hand.

Charlie hugged her, then, his massive bulk a comfort. Until he whispered into her ear. 'How did you do it?'

She pulled away from him and turned to address the room at large. 'Thank you for being here and for being willing to help. I really appreciate it. They let me go without charging me, probably because the evidence they had was non-existent and the witness testimony was recanted. Or they heard it was about to be recanted. Either way, it's over.'

'For now,' Charlie said. 'They arrested a Crow. There will be repercussions.'

'No,' Lydia said. The chatter stopped and Lydia looked around at the faces, some familiar, some less so, and felt the wave of 'Crow' that came from being with so many family members at one time. It was something she remembered from gatherings and family events throughout childhood, but it felt stronger than before. Her senses were in overdrive and her blood fizzed in her veins. Every detail was hyperreal and distinct, from Daisy's Mulberry handbag to the bottles of ketchup and brown sauce on the tables and the tattoos on Charlie's forearms.

Lydia chose a table in the middle of the cafe and sat on the top, her feet resting on a chair. She knew that if she didn't phrase things just right, Charlie would use this for his own agenda. She also knew that her mum had been right. If she didn't step up and take control, the Family would control her instead. 'Right,' she said. 'The police are the least of our worries.'

Charlie opened his mouth to speak and Lydia raised a hand to silence him. Waves were coming from her, she could feel them vibrating through the air, sending energy or something into the room, twirling and coiling around the Crows present and weaving them in a kind of spell. Charlie closed his mouth and Lydia didn't think he had ever looked so surprised.

She looked around, catching every eye, and then smiling to reassure them. Then she began: 'Let me tell you a story...'

THE END

THANK YOU FOR READING!

I hope you enjoyed reading about Lydia Crow and her family as much as I enjoyed writing about them!

I am busy working on the fourth book in the Crow Investigations series. If you would like to be notified when it's published, you can sign up for my FREE readers' club:

geni.us/Club

If you could spare the time, I would really appreciate a review on the retailer of your choice.

Reviews make a huge difference to the visibility of the book, which make it more likely that I will reach more readers and be able to keep on writing. Thank you!

ACKNOWLEDGMENTS

I am exceedingly lucky to have many supportive and loving people in my life, all of whom put up with my obsession with writing. They even manage to remain encouraging and excited (or, at least, do an excellent job of pretending to be interested!) and help me through the inevitable tricky patches during the creative process.

I am also deeply grateful to my lovely readers for enabling me to keep on writing and publishing as my job. I love what I do and am grateful every single day - thank you!

Thank you to my wonderful author pals; Clodagh Murphy, Hannah Ellis, Keris Stainton, Nadine Kirtzinger, and Sally Calder. Your support, good company and friendship is one of the best parts of my writing life.

As always, my 'muggle' friends deserve some kind of medal. I disappear for months when I'm deep in a draft and, when I surface, I blether on about story craft and the arcana of publishing... You're all very patient and lovely and I appreciate it. Much love and thanks to Catherine Shellard, Lucy Golden-Taylor, and Emma Ward.

I also want to express my gratitude to my whole family for their ongoing support and encouragement. Thank you to my dad, Michael, my parents in-law, Christine and Chris, and to Matthew, Fay, Bea, Alex, Angela and Simon.

This book would not exist without the vital work of my editor, cover designer, early readers, and wonderful ARC team. Thank you, all.

In particular, thanks to Beth Farrar, Karen Heenan, Melanie Leavey, Jenni Gudgeon, Paula Searle, Ann Martin, Judy Grivas, Deborah Forrester, and David Wood.

Finally, thank you to Holly and James for their excellent advice and cheerleading, and for being the Absolute Best.

And to my Dave; I love you more.

ABOUT THE AUTHOR

Before writing books, Sarah Painter worked as a free-lance magazine journalist, blogger and editor, combining this 'career' with amateur child-wrangling (AKA motherhood).

Sarah lives in rural Scotland with her children and husband. She drinks too much tea, loves the work of Joss Whedon, and is the proud owner of a writing shed.

Click below to sign-up to the Sarah Painter readers' club. It's absolutely free and you'll get book release news, giveaways and exclusive FREE stuff!

geni.us/Club

Made in the USA
Las Vegas, NV
29 December 2021

39711869R00177